ORACLE

THE BOOKS OF SAM

JP FRANKHAM

First published in 2011
by Hirst Books

This edition
Published in 2025 by
Matthew James Publishing

matthewjamespublishing.com

an imprint of
Andrews UK Limited
West Wing Studios
Unit 166, The Mall
Luton, LU1 2TL

andrewsuk.com

'Do you see, nothing went the way "prophecy" ordained?'

Melkira nodded, but his sword did not come down. He said nothing. Sam tilted his head and moved towards the open window which looked out over the London Domain.

'Are you not going to tell the rest of the story?' Melkira asked.

'Do you need to hear it?'

Melkira thought a moment. 'I still have many questions. About the events I did not witness.'

'That is the start of freedom,' Sam grinned. 'Very well. Where was I?'

'Will had become upiór, although he went through the pontus faster than any before him. His hunger overtaking his reason.'

'Yes, and Frederick could not comprehend what he had unleashed.' Another smile. 'But he would learn; they all would.'

Melkira's face set in a frown of anger. 'Yes, we did. The things—'

'And in London, Jake fretted. Confused by his reaction to Will's disappearance, and worse, the complete lack of response from Will.'

Melkira shook his head, his brown locks dropping over half his face. 'He did not understand. You cannot blame him for that.'

Sam laughed. 'Of course not. He had no idea. But was he so innocent?'

Melkira considered, and for the first time lowered his sword. 'No. Not innocent, far from it, but he was blinded. By his emotions.'

'Ever was it so. Very well. You want answers, then let us continue... Nineteen years past, March 2011...'

1. The Day After

It was the next morning, and Jake had slept a restless sleep, irritated in no small part by an itch on his left shoulder that he could not seem to get rid of.

He had slept on the couch, reasoning that whatever time Will pitched up, he'd disturb Jake intentionally or otherwise. But when his alarm had gone off, and after a quick check of the house, it became quickly apparent that Will hadn't returned.

It was so unlike Will. To not be in touch for a whole weekend was bad enough, but to not return in time for the work week...? That was unheard of. Jake tried to keep his mind on other things as he himself got ready for work; seeing Amy later, Curtis' safety... He wanted to call in sick, but he couldn't afford to do that, and besides, sitting around Will's house was not going to make things any better. He'd have to tell people, Will's family for one... Lunchtime. He'd go over to see Will's parents on his break.

So much for not thinking about it. Will was still in his thoughts when he glanced out of the window upon hearing the beep of a horn. Mike was out there in his little white van. Jake held up his hand and mouthed 'Give me five minutes'. Mike gave him a thumbs-up.

He picked up the landline and quickly dialled the High Street Ken store, hoping that Steve would be there already.

'Jake...? Still no sign of Will?'

'Nothing,' Jake said, scratching his shoulder slightly, the itch having returned.

'Shit. Wish I could say I've heard from him, but last I heard he was heading to a night club with that Charlie guy.'

Jake bit his tongue. *And you encouraged him to go*, he wanted to say, but right now wasn't the time for blame. He just wanted to find out why Will hadn't returned, then he'd do the blaming.

'Guess he's having a good time, then,' Steve continued. 'No drama. I mean, I can cope, I can put off Kurt for a little while longer.'

Jake had forgotten about the whole Kurt situation. One of Will's managers caught fiddling the books. Will had been worried about how to handle that.

'Listen,' Steve continued, 'if you hear from him before I do, let him know he needs to be here by Thursday, cause then we'll have no choice but to sort out the shit with Kurt.'

'Right.' Jake didn't even say goodbye, annoyed by Steve's lack of concern, and put the phone down.

As he threw his jacket on and stood at the open front door, Jake looked back inside one last time. Never mind lunch break, he knew he'd never be able to focus at work. He had things that needed to be done. One way or another, he'd be leaving work early.

Will was out there, and he needed help.

*

Something was wrong with Frederick.

Celeste had known this since visiting him yesterday. He'd been distracted. She had scraped the edge of his mind, not enough for him to feel, but enough for her to realise that he was hiding something. Celeste didn't dig any deeper, such an intrusive act was not her way.

They had been together for the best part of three centuries and, other than when she had first encountered him in Posen, she had never needed to enter his mind to get information from him. She would not start now.

She had to confess, though, at least to herself, she was sorely tempted. Even more so when the waves of confusion and hurt had struck her in her private chamber at the Residence that night.

Frederick was not particularly adept at mind trawling, but the blood bond between them only increased in strength over the years, and sometimes the intensity of Frederick's emotions transmitted themselves over great distances. This was one such case; miles separated the Residence on Canvey Island from Frederick's apartment in Chalkwell, but she could feel his confusion as if he were standing right next to her. She had tried to contact him, but he had not responded. Troubled as she was, Celeste decided to leave it until the next day, when hopefully Frederick had slept on whatever was ailing him.

She was not one for sleep; after living for over 780 years, she'd had more than enough sleep and chose to spend most of her time awake. Nights were traditionally the time for bogeymen and monsters, after all. She remembered a time when her people were considered such, a time when the night was their domain. Those times were long gone now.

With the forming of the Three in 1788, she had made a conscious effort to put aside the darkness of tradition and set about civilizing the vampire world, a development that had already begun with the natural evolution from savage blood drinkers to upiór. Decade by decade their old weaknesses faded, as more and more the human blood on which they lived turned them into almost perfect copies of the humans they once hid from, at least on an external level. Except for their eyes, which seemed to get more otherworldly as their bodies became worldlier.

Sophistication was no stranger to Celeste. She had been raised into a noble family as a human, and that nobility was something she had clung to fiercely after she had been violated and turned into a vampire by that bastard Pierre. She had refused to become a monster like the rest of them, and in the twelfth century vampires were still every bit the monster myth insisted on. After the revolution of '88, she claimed the vampires as her own (although, the lay-upiór did not realise this, believing they were being ruled by the Three as a body), and being able to bring a level of civility to her people was something she had longed to do. With her new position of power, she had finally been able to do just that.

With no interest in sleep, she wandered the streets of Essex, wrapped up against the storm, secretly enjoying the wet and cold railing against her, free from her entourage of bodyguards, observing the sleeping world that was barely worthy of her people. There may have been Sekhites abroad in Essex, but Celeste had not survived for 755 years as an upiór without learning how to handle herself. Theodor and Frederick worried for her safety, but their feelings for her clouded their reasoning; both tended to forget that she had lived a long life before she had found either of them. Only Eryn seemed not to care.

Eryn. How she liked to keep the table uneven. Still, Celeste was glad that the normal animosity between Eryn and Frederick seemed to be subsiding a little. Things were drawing to a point, with great changes around the corner, and the Three and their most trusted advisor could not be seen to be in dispute.

Already Julius was beginning to show his hand, as she had always known he was bound to do eventually. Willem's role in the prophecy was still uncertain, and his emergence as an upiór was untypical, add to that the involvement of Sekhites...

Celeste sighed. They all needed to be unified against the potential threat of the Brotherhood of Sekhmet. Denouncing the Brotherhood in 1788 had been hard enough, the revolution had cost many lives on both sides, but the cost now would be much higher.

Rumours of discontent had already reached the ears of the Three; stories of upiór beginning to question their rulings, delving into the teachings of the Brotherhood, and it was only a matter of time before their world would be in turmoil once again.

The Book of Sekhmet was clear; the Seeker would arrive and find that which he sought. What it did not say, however, was that as a result, loyalties would be secured. Prophecy said their world would be united, but Celeste felt certain that her people would be torn apart by the fulfilment of the Seeker's role. And if Willem was not the Seeker...? Then who was? And what role did Willem serve? Frederick, who knew more about the Book than almost anybody, insisted Willem was a part of it.

Still, she wasn't sure what to do. She had always revered the Ancient and it went against every ounce of her being to consider he was wrong. So, she did not. Prophecy could not be denied, but it could surely be controlled.

*

'What'd I tell you? One day he'd be trouble.'

The look Sandra Adomako gave her husband wasn't hard to read, and Jake took a little pleasure in the affront written on his face as a result. It wasn't often that Will's mother got the upper hand with Eon, but once in a while that old Chiswick fire came out and the Guyana man knew better than to push it. So, he just sat back in the chair and returned to his paper.

Jake was sure Eon was glued to the chair, since whenever he visited, the old man was always sitting there, either watching the TV (which explained a lot about Lawrencia) or reading his newspapers, a pile of which were sitting on the little metal table by the side of his chair.

At least Sandra wasn't rooted to one spot; already she'd pottered about her kitchen to prepare Jake a snack and some tea, glad to see him again. It wasn't often that Jake came to see her, which he always felt a little bad about, after all, following his mum's death in '89 Sandra had become something of a foster mum to him.

'How's the tea?' she asked, settling back into the sofa.

'It's good, thanks,' Jake replied, glad that Eon was no longer involved in the conversation. Eon never seemed to get on with anybody, except for Sandra, and even then, Jake had his doubts about that these days.

Jake had already explained about Will, although he played up the internet romance angle as Will simply meeting up with a pen pal. Neither Sandra nor Eon understood the internet, so it was easier to simplify things for them. Sandra had agreed it was unusual for her son to disappear like this; he'd never been in trouble before, even as a kid he was always well-behaved.

'What can we do?' she asked.

'Well,' Jake said, 'I think we need to go to the police and report him as a missing person.'

'Isn't that a bit drastic? He's not even a day late yet.'

Jake shrugged his shoulders. 'Yeah, but nobody has heard from him since Friday. I'm probably overreacting here, but dare we risk it? Anything could have happened, and if something bad has happened then it's best the police have a head start in their investigation.'

Jake watched her as she took it in, and he could see she was more worried than she liked to admit. He didn't blame her, but he needed her support in this.

'This is definitely out of character, especially considering the stuff he's got going on at work,' he added, just to make sure she got the point.

Sandra sat forward; decision made. 'Okay, when do you want to go?'

At this, Eon put his newspaper down roughly. 'We're not going to no police station.'

'We stood by when Lawrencia took off,' Sandra reminded him. 'And look what happened there.' She turned away and sniffed back a sob.

'First, I'm going to talk to Mr Townsend,' Jake explained. 'Way I figure it, if both of Will's parents are there, showing a united front, the police will have to listen.'

At least, he hoped that was true.

*

Celeste returned to the Residence several hours later, still troubled despite her meander through the Canvey marshland.

The weather was beginning to settle, and with the sun came light grey clouds that pushed aside their darker friends, signalling the start of what could be a glorious day. Celeste wished her mood was as glorious, but much was troubling her. However, she had determined that upon returning to the Residence she would resume work on the official wedding portrait of Prince William and Kate Middleton. Not her most prestigious work; royalty really wasn't what it had been back in her day, but nonetheless she loved capturing these moments of history. She had done countless official portraits over the centuries, under various *allonyms*, and she always considered it a shame that she had missed out on doing the official portrait of Charles and Diana back in '81. Thus, there was no way she would miss out on doing one for Diana's firstborn.

The audiences were few and far between today, which was just as well since she was in no mind to offer pearls of wisdom to her people, and was quite content to slip away into her painting.

Upon seeing Eryn at the door of the Residence, though, and the serious look on her face, Celeste just knew that the day was not going to improve her mood one bit.

'Eryn, a delight as ever,' she said. 'To what do I owe the welcoming committee?'

'I've found out a few things about our little slain boy. Things I think both you and Theodor will need to hear.'

Celeste walked past her, and Eryn followed her into the Residence. Normally news of a murder would not interest the Three, but when the murder was being labelled a 'vampire killing' by the local news, and the boy had been found with a wooden stake through his heart, they could not simply ignore it.

6

'Such things as?' she asked Eryn.

'His name, and more importantly his sister's name. Or rather his half-sister; one Maia Ash.'

At this, Celeste stopped. She turned to look at Eryn, the cloud over her face now echoing the dense clouds being swept away by the sun.

'Frederick's daughter,' she said softly.

*

Amy had agreed to meet Jake at Centre Point, since she was already in the West End meeting clients. He had arranged to meet Mr Townsend in a few hours, so a break for lunch suited him just fine.

The weather had kicked into high gear again, and, not one to be fooled and caught out by any sudden storm like the previous night, Jake kept his jeans on this time, with his jumper tied about his waist so that his arms at least gained a little benefit from the sun. He also carried his light jacket, since his usual heavy-duty coat was just too much to lug around London on the off chance of bad weather.

No sooner had he got off the 88 than he got a message from Amy saying how she fancied some McDonald's for a change. This worked well for Jake since he rather fancied a Big Mac himself, and so he popped into the restaurant at the top end of Oxford Street.

They now sat on the wall edging the water fountains, adjacent to the Centre Point Tower, which stood like claws reaching to the sky behind them. As was the norm, it was a case of hit or miss as to whether the fountain would be on, but they were lucky to have chosen a day when the fountains were deactivated, which saved them, as well as passers-by, the inconvenience of being randomly sprayed by misty water.

They were not the only people availing themselves of the non-active fountains, and so were sitting a lot closer to each other than was comfortable given the heat of the sun blaring down on them. But they both decided to forebear in light of enjoying each other's company.

Amy was dressed in her usual smart-skirted suit, although she had taken the blazer off, which contrasted sharply with Jake's own 'whatever he could find' mismatch of clothes.

She popped the lid of her cappuccino and sipped the hot liquid. 'Ergh, Micky Dee's don't really make the best coffee, do they?'

'A common consensus there. This is why I'll stick with one of their vanilla thick shakes.' To prove his point, Jake sucked at the straw around which he'd spoken, and let out a satisfied *ahh*.

'Hmm, but vanilla? It's so...'

'Vanilla?'

'Boring.'

'Yet still lovely.'

They both laughed, and Jake had to admit it felt good. Laughs had not been plentiful in the last few days for him. Amy watched him, as he scratched at the itch on his shoulder.

'What is it?' she asked.

'Not sure. Been bothering me since last night.'

'Let's see.'

He turned and let her push down the collar of his t-shirt.

'Oooh, hello. Did you scrape against something...?'

'Not that I remember. Why?'

'You seem to have a scar there.'

'What?' He reached out to try and run his fingers across it. He could feel something. 'I've never had a scar there... Anyway, if I scraped against something it'd just be a scratch?'

'True. But no, it's definitely a scar. Weird shape, too. Almost like a... symbol of some kind?'

Jake grinned. 'Not 666 I hope...? My middle name is Damien after all.'

'Damien? Oh. *The Omen*. No, you're not the Antichrist, not that there is such a definite article in the Bible, of course.'

'Isn't there...? Since when...?'

'Since before it was mis-translated, deliberately as well.' Amy grinned. She loved to impart archaic knowledge. '666 is a transliteration of Nero Caesar's name, if you use the original Greek spelling, then the Hebrew numerical equivalent is 666, and that's who the Book of Revelation was referring to.'

'Oh. Okay, didn't know that.' He turned and looked at her. 'Didn't know you were a Biblical scholar among other things.'

'I'm not, just like to read is all.'

'Maybe you should talk to Will's dad. He's into all that Bible stuff.'

'Well, maybe one day. Which reminds me, how'd things go with Will's mother?'

'Well. She's onboard, so now it's just a case of getting his dad to agree.'

'Potential problem?'

'Not so much, no. There's no issue between Will and his dad really, but Mr Townsend went a bit odd after the divorce, turned to God, all the usual shit.'

'Nothing wrong with a belief in something bigger.'

'Suppose not, but there's a difference between turning to religion and becoming obsessed with it.' Jake shrugged. 'Whatever, it's his thing and it did him well, I guess. Maybe my own dad would have dealt with my mum's death better if he'd found some religion? Don't know.'

Amy nodded, her eyes searching. 'You'll have to tell me about this sometime. We can compare childhood trauma stories,' she added with a wink.

Jake smiled softly, still amazed at how easily she calmed him. Even when talking about deeply painful stuff, just looking into her eyes made everything seem okay. Not for the first time he thought she'd missed her calling. Counselling would have suited her so well.

'Deal. Speaking of childhood trauma, I had this wild idea, and not too sure how you'll feel about it, since you clearly don't think much of Lawrencia...'

'Girl's got problems,' Amy said, nodding.

'Tell me about it. But problems you'll possibly relate to? Having gone through something similar... Well, vicariously through your mum?'

'I suppose we did at that.' Amy pondered this, clearly not overly impressed by the idea.

'With your ability to soothe and relate, you're so qualified. Don't do it for Lawrencia, if that's sticking in your craw, but for Curtis. Shit's coming on, and the kid is caught up in it.'

Amy stared daggers at him but folded. 'Oh, okay, for Curtis' sake. But like I told you last night, coming out of an abusive relationship is not easy, and don't think for a second the intervention of someone who's basically a stranger will do the job.'

Jake put his milkshake on the wall beside him and took her hands in his. 'But it means a lot to me that you'll try. It'll be a weight off my mind while I try and sort this crap with Will out.'

Amy leaned forward and kissed him on the forehead. 'You're a rogue at times, Jacob, but you're also very generous of heart.'

Jake grinned, and put a finger to his lips. 'Shh, don't tell anyone, I have a rep to maintain.'

Amy laughed. 'Your secret is safe with me. Promise.'

*

Celeste was not happy by the big reveal, and the Three all agreed that such an incident was problematic at best, especially given the closeness of prophecy. Celeste wanted to know more, so Eryn furnished her with everything she had found out from Rochelle.

The dead boy was Darrell Jenkins, son of Brian and Julie Jenkins. According to reports from Social Services both Darrell and his half-sister, the daughter of Julie from a previous relationship, were made Wards of Court twelve years ago after concerns were raised about their abusive home life. Brian Jenkins was remanded in custody after allegations of child and spousal abuse, and was now serving a thirty-year sentence. Maia Ash, still using her mother's maiden name, left home three years ago after her eighteenth birthday and the annulment of her status as a Ward of Court. Darrell still remained a Ward, though, and after his mother's suicide last year was sent to a children's home, with a view of potentially fostering out. This never happened, and in December he went missing. Despite minor reports since, he hadn't been seen until his body was discovered in Southchurch Hall Gardens on Sunday morning.

Theodor made the obvious leap at this point of the story. Clearly Darrell had hooked up with his sister who, already a renowned hunter thanks to the inherited genes from her father, had taken it upon herself to teach her younger brother some survival skills. It seemed likely Darrell fancied himself as some kind of hunter, which was the only scenario Celeste would accept. She could not believe Frederick would kill an innocent boy. Eryn wasn't sure she agreed with that conclusion; she was never convinced by Frederick's purity of heart.

'Is it conceivable that this was an accidental meeting?' Celeste asked over the lip of her wine glass.

Eryn knew she slept little, if at all, and wasn't surprised to see her drinking wine so early in the day. Eryn sniffed, fancying the soft aroma of raspberries with just a hint of cinnamon, the unmistakable scent of a ten-year-old Grenache Rouge.

For her own part, drinking during the day was a big no-no, unless it was blood. That was a drink Eryn liked to start the day with. She turned to the cabinet to pour herself a glass, now that her stomach was rumbling at the thought. As she did, she caught Theodor's response.

As ever with Theodor there were no words, just a general sense of what he meant. Being Theodor's fledgling, Eryn could pick up Theodor's thoughts with ease, although they never consisted of actual words. Real thoughts rarely did; words were merely sounds and reverberations exhaled from the voice box, and due to their everyday usage, humans tended to think in words. Theodor had not uttered a single word since 1708 after his tongue had been severed in a brutal act of vengeance, and even though he had occupied several vessels since then, he still refused to speak; penance for some perceived sin he had committed long before he had met Eryn.

There was much mystery surrounding Theodor's past, and even now after almost three centuries together, Eryn knew so little. Theodor's life before meeting Celeste was a closed book, one that only Celeste had read. All Eryn knew was something bad had taken place, and after losing his tongue Theodor had chosen to never use words again. As such, Theodor's thoughts were no longer expressed with words, but rather images and feelings, so much more complex than any words could describe. But still amazingly easy to understand for people like Eryn and Celeste, who had been privy to Theodor's thoughts for three hundred years.

'I agree,' Eryn said, turning back to Celeste and Theodor, her glass now full of A-Positive. 'It doesn't seem too likely, does it? I reckon Maia sent him here, maybe as some kind of test.' She shrugged. 'Maybe she's in the area, too.'

'Hmm.' Celeste sipped her wine, her thoughts her own.

Eryn watched for any sign that would give away what Celeste was thinking. She looked at Theodor, but he shook his head. Even Celeste's own fledgling was closed off to her. A rare thing, although Eryn wasn't entirely surprised. She never understood how both Theodor and Frederick could occupy the same place in Celeste's soul, but she did understand that at times there was conflict over this. Now was one such time.

Finally, Celeste spoke. 'We need to bring Frederick in. Theodor, I want you to go and get him.'

This surprised Eryn. She would have expected Celeste to simply call him herself, after all, Frederick would never ignore a summons from his eternal consort. Eryn narrowed her eyes; things were not so green in paradise after all. Theodor nodded his agreement, and briefly Eryn got a sense that he was not only agreeing to Celeste's command but also with Eryn's summation of the current state of play between Celeste and Frederick.

'Eryn, do whatever needs to be done to find out if Maia is anywhere near Essex.' Celeste closed her eyes for a moment and frowned. 'I cannot sense a hunter's presence nearby, so she's not local.' She opened her eyes again. 'We cannot afford to have a hunter running free at this time.' Celeste stood and went to walk out of the room. She stopped at the door. 'If she is in the area, put our people on the alert. She needs to be removed.'

'Frederick will not be happy,' Eryn pointed out.

'No. But that is much of a muchness right now. Things are fragile, and quite frankly we cannot afford to humour Frederick much more. His daughter's continued existence is now a real problem. For all of us.'

Eryn watched the door close behind Celeste. Up until now, they had allowed Maia to go unchecked (well, Celeste had at least), despite the potential danger she represented. Clearly, the rules had changed.

Eryn looked to Theodor, who sent her a thought.

Her eyebrows went up. So, Frederick was hiding something from Celeste. Although she didn't say anything to Theodor, Eryn was sure it had something to do with that Willem. If so, Eryn knew she would take great pleasure in exposing Frederick before Celeste.

Even paradise could not last forever.

2. MAKING CONTACT

'Jacob, it's been a while, sir, please come in.'

Mr Townsend ushered Jake into his little flat, glancing along the balcony left and right before closing the door.

Jake remained standing in the hallway, feeling like an intruder. He had only visited the flat a couple of times over the years, never really feeling comfortable with the spiritually-minded for some reason, and each time Will had been with him. When it came to visiting what used to be the old Townsend family home, now the Adomako home, Jake felt perfectly at ease and happy to wander freely, regardless of the steely gaze of Eon. But here, in this flat, he was little more than a visitor and, despite the path Mr Townsend had taken in his life, Jake still respected him far too much to just assume he had the run of the flat.

'Now, let me take a look at you,' Mr Townsend said, doing exactly that.

Jake felt uncomfortable being appraised like some child, but he allowed Mr Townsend his moment and took the opportunity to do the same with Will's dad. He could still see a lot of Will in the old Welshman, both were thin but not especially tall, but whereas Will still had a thick head of dark hair, Mr Townsend's was now grey and thin. Jake felt sad looking at him, remembering the strong man that had often taken him and Will on outings. Now Mr Townsend just looked old, carrying himself like a typical granddad, dressed in clothes of a bygone era, topped off by a threadbare cardigan. Times had not been easy on him, and Jake wondered if living in Hackney had really helped.

'You're looking healthy, eating well, I hope?' Mr Townsend asked.

'Well enough, but not too much. Can't ever say no to a good meat pie,' Jake said with a grin, knowing full well what was coming.

'Excellent. I got some nice steak and kidney pies from the bakery the other day. Care to join me?'

'Would love to.'

Jake wasn't just saying that to please the old man, he really did like Mr Townsend's pies. He wasn't sure where they were bought, but they were possibly the best pies in London. He'd tried asking the last time he visited, but Mr Townsend wouldn't divulge his secret.

He followed the old man into the kitchen, which had definitely seen better days, and waited by the door as Mr Townsend fished two pies out of the fridge.

'Now, what did you want to speak to me about?'

'Well, Mr Townsend, it's about Will.'

Mr Townsend turned around and wagged a finger at Jake. 'I tell you this every time, Jacob. Call me Francis, if the Lord wanted me to be called Mr Townsend I wouldn't be blessed with a Christian name.'

Jake didn't know about that. He'd known the man most of his life, and he'd always been Will's dad, not some mate who he could joke around with. Using the first name was a breach of some unspoken rule. Granted, he called Will's mum by her first name, but that felt different somehow.

'Francis,' he tried out, the name feeling wrong on his tongue. 'Will's gone missing, and we need your help.'

Francis stopped what he was doing, and placed the pies on the sideboard. For a moment he stood there, using the sideboard to balance himself, and Jake feared he might go into shock. Instead, as if galvanized by the news, Francis stood up straight and Jake saw some of the old strength return to his grey eyes.

'Whatever it is, son, you've got it. What must I do?'

*

Whatever needs to be done.

Those were the words Celeste had used, and Eryn intended to follow them to the letter. It had been hours since and still there was no sign of Frederick. Theodor had gone to find him, but he was not home and, since then, following repeated attempts by Celeste to contact him telepathically, there had been nothing. There was no doubt that Frederick had picked up Celeste's calls, but he was evidently ignoring them. Never before had Eryn known anything like it; even when he'd been mysteriously called off to Moldavia, Frederick had still kept in contact with Celeste, and that was a mission of the utmost secrecy.

Eryn smiled at the thought of Frederick going against Celeste. It was an angle she could surely use later, with a careful bit of prodding.

For her own part, Eryn had exhausted almost all official avenues and had learned that Maia was no longer in Essex. She had been spotted in Southend on Saturday, but the upiór who claimed to have seen her couldn't swear to that. And if it was her, she'd been with two others. An old man and a younger boy – the latter certainly suggested some accuracy to the sighting. Either way, nothing since. Which, Eryn decided, meant she was not an immediate problem. When Eryn reported this to Celeste, she would be content, and probably draw the same conclusion as Eryn.

Maia had used her brother, given him a head full of twisted ideas about upiór and told him the biased story of Frederick's liaison with her mother twenty-one years ago. Thus, turning Darrell into a weapon of vengeance, unleashing him on her unsuspecting father. It was a foolish thing to do, to send a human hunter after someone of Frederick's ability, and Maia must have known that.

There was clearly more to it, like the identity of the old man, and Eryn wanted to know what.

She was wandering Benfleet, having dumped her bodyguards, making a private call on her mobile. It was taking a while for the call to connect, but then she was calling Rome and there were various switchboards and cross-network connections to make to ensure that the call could not be traced. Eryn had spent many long years guarding her back, and did not intend to slip up now. If this call proved successful, then she knew she'd have the perfect method for widening the growing chasm between Celeste and Frederick.

'Eryn!' She was almost caught off guard by the effusive response, as sudden as it was. 'It has been too long, my dear girl. Gianni tells me you've been making waves about our followers.'

Eryn smiled at the Western colloquialisms amid the Italian accent. Like all long-lived upiór, Julius' accent only contained a trace of his native tongue, having assimilated various regional accents and phrases from his many visits to other countries, yet somehow after 427 years of life, still Julius was able to maintain the infamous enthusiasm expected of those of Italian descent. Not that his pride in his history had prevented Julius from exploring the world. That was the thing with being alive for so long, as much as you loved your home country you just had to get out there and see the world.

Eryn wasn't at all surprised to find out that Julius was aware of her earlier investigation. Still...

'How is Gia?'

'Still on the fence, as you say.'

'Yeah, but not enough to ignore news that travels so fast, right?'

'Well, of course.' Julius laughed, but Eryn did not join him.

Even now, after all these years, Julius underestimated the reach of the Three, despite repeated attempts by Eryn to tell him otherwise.

'We are very well connected,' Julius said.

Eryn knew this. She had been one of them since the beginning.

'Good, I'm always glad to hear that. That's exactly why I'm calling.'

'Yes, I didn't think it was a social call. You know, Eryn, we really ought to meet up soon, like we did in the old days. Sociality seems to be lacking a great deal in my life,' Julius sighed. 'The price I pay, I suppose, for my position.'

'Can't fault it. And it's not going to ease up any time soon, is it? We're nearing the time for the Brotherhood to claim its rightful place again.'

'That we are, my dear, that we are. So, what can I do for you?'

'I need you to find the hunter Maia Ash.'

'Ah, Frederick's daughter. Are we planning on getting rid of her at last?'

'Not this time, although that is what Celeste wishes. No, I want her prepared to remove Celeste. Things are not looking good here for our erstwhile leader.' Eryn could almost hear Julius' smile and went on to briefly outline the complications rising in Essex, in particular detailing the slow parting of the ways between Frederick and Celeste. When she finished, she added, 'We need to make sure that the chasm is one neither can jump again.'

Julius was silent for a moment. 'Well, I have heard rumours. If true, tracking down Maia should prove to be simplicity itself, after all, she has shacked up with one of our own people.'

A hunter and an upiór working together...? That was alarming in any circumstances.

'Possibly not the best upiór to work with, after all, Edward Lomax's own mental state is a little... erm, uncertain. I'll be in touch.'

The line went dead before Eryn could question what Julius had said. She knew the name Edward Lomax, and was well aware of the nefarious methods he used. Eryn smiled. If he was already working with Maia, then that explained much. And made her the perfect wedge to place between Celeste and Frederick.

*

Frederick had felt Celeste's call from the moment Will had vanished, but he'd been in no state to respond, and so had not.

Mental discipline wasn't his strong suit, but he knew enough to keep Celeste out. Often he could feel her probing the periphery of his thoughts, but she rarely intruded. Her concern for him was making her clumsy, and keeping her out was proving easier than usual.

Frederick hated going against Celeste, but he could not allow her to get even a hint of what happened to Will, not until he had found Will and got him ready.

Frederick was worried about him, out in a strange world that was not designed for him. He'd be out there, confused and scared by what he'd become, with no knowledge or understanding. A lost child in a world of strangers. Frederick had to find him, keep him safe, and teach him.

Frederick had not gone against Celeste just to lose Will now. He *had* to find him.

Most of the night he had tried to reach out with his mind, get a sense of his fledgling, but each time proved as fruitless as the last. Several times he fell asleep, exhausted by the mental workout and still weak from being almost drained by Will. He had woken and feasted, not on blood as was to be expected, but on food and drink. Upiór could survive quite well on normal sustenance, much as a human could, but blood was that extra pick-me-up, the little something that kept their preternatural abilities sharp. Blood would come later, first he needed to get out there and start looking for Will.

All day he had been searching. First of all, he intended to try every haunt that might attract the attention of a new upiór, and once he'd exhausted all those avenues then he'd look at the mundane places a human might seek solace. Including family and friends. He had already tried blood banks, the hospital, even got his own police contacts involved, but no one had any information for him. So now he was checking the more obscure sources of information and was nearing a pub down the backstreets of Westcliff.

He looked back as a train rumbled past, heading into Southend Central train station, and was reminded of how the weekend had begun. It seemed so long ago now, but it was only four days.

*

Lizette couldn't wait to get home, to see how her houseguest was getting on. If she'd had a landline at home, she would have called a few times during the day to check up on him, because she couldn't deny, as Jordan had reminded her, she was fucking nuts for letting a stranger stay in her house. A *male* stranger at that... But, on the other hand, and she couldn't explain why, she felt perfectly fine with him being in her—

She noticed a man passing the pedestrian crossing she was waiting at. She recognised him, but it took her a moment to recall his name. She unwound the door window and poked her head out.

'Hey, Fred,' she said. 'World of your own?'

'I was a bit.'

Lizette didn't really know him, but he was a local, lived not far from her in Chalkwell. They often bumped into each other in the local Spar, passed pleasantries. And, she had to admit, it *might* have had something to do with his deep brown eyes and thick head of hair.

So shallow.

Not that anybody could blame her. Living home alone, no boyfriend, barely a social life. A woman had needs, and there was nothing wrong with a little window shopping from time to time.

'Bit out of the way for you, isn't it?' she asked.

'Just going to see a friend. On your way home from the college?'

'Yeah.' She noticed the now green light. 'Anyway, better get going. Nice seeing you.'

'Yeah.'

She waved slightly and pressed down on the accelerator.

She glanced at the wing mirror, and saw Fred enter a pub.

She shook her head.

Honestly, getting turned around by a handsome face. What're you like!

Which took her back to her houseguest.

He still had no name. She took him in last night, wrapped him in her dressing gown (as much as she'd like to, she couldn't just have him sitting around naked) after he'd agreed to a warm shower. They'd spent a short while talking, him enjoying the Ceylon tea she'd made for him. It became clear he could recall general things, the standard everyday kind of information; who's the current PM, the President of the United States, what objects were. But nothing specific related to him.

Eventually, realising she was losing more and more sleep and had a long day ahead of her, she'd left him on the sofa with the spare duvet (the thinner one she used during the summer). She still could see him lying there, the duvet pressed against him by the weight of Garth, who decided he quite liked the idea of sleeping next to the houseguest (they'd need to get a name for him!). He hadn't moved by the time she got up four hours later, so she didn't disturb him. She went about her usual morning routine, which this time included sending a message to Jordan, asking him to bring in some spare clothes. (And *that* was quite a conversation over lunch!) Before she left, she fed the cats, and wrote a quick note for her houseguest, telling him to make himself at home, and she'd be back around six that evening.

As she continued along towards Chalkwell, she blinked away the tiredness she still felt. Four hours sleep wasn't enough, not to function on a Monday. First day of the week was always the busiest and most stressful for her, not only due to a full day of lectures, but because of the inevitable messages from Linden about the kids, and the usual wrangling of what's to come this weekend. (She didn't know why they had to go through it every week, after all the kids pretty much did what they wanted when they were at hers. Sometimes they stayed with friends anyway. Which was fine with Lizette; at thirteen and fourteen, they should be with their friends, not stuck indoors all the time with their parents.) All she wanted to do was get home...

Thankfully the traffic was quite light, so getting through Southend Central and onto the backstreets proved easy enough, and the roads of Chalkwell were as empty as ever. She made good time and pulled up outside her house.

For a moment she sat there, looking at the green front door. All seemed quiet. Inside, however...

She was sure it would all be okay.

*

Such places existed all over. On the surface, they looked like any other pub, full of people supping alcohol, reading newspapers, playing the gaming machines. But behind the façade was the truth, hidden away in a back room, a place so exclusive that most people wouldn't have a chance of gaining access. Frederick was not one of those people. As far as the owner of the pub knew he was also one of the Black Veil, a 'real' vampire trapped in a human world.

With a nod from the landlord, a young man who was barely legal removed himself from the bar and came over to Frederick. He eyed the young man, who offered his hand with a smile, just two friends meeting for a quiet drink. Although considering the seedy look of some of the older patrons, it must have looked like he was picking up a bit of trade. Frederick smiled, tempted to take the young man in front of them all. Show the landlord what a *real* vampire was like. It wasn't like he was full up on blood.

Instead, he embraced the young man in a hug and was delighted by the catch of surprised breath. Frederick released him and held him at arm's length.

'You're looking rather tasty,' Frederick said, beaming.

The young man's smile didn't falter, although the confusion in his eyes was clear, which only made Frederick smile more. 'Yeah, cheers, mate. Shall we, erm, go somewhere a little more private?'

'Capital idea,' Frederick said, linking arms with the young man and allowing himself to be led away. He glanced back at the old men watching him, lustful eyes gleaming, and winked at them. One of them gave him a thumbs up. Frederick suppressed a laugh. Humans were quite twisted.

They reached a door with the words 'Function Room' engraved below the blackened-out window, and the young man pressed a few buttons into the entry coder. With a click the door was released and he led the way in. Frederick followed him.

It had been a while since he'd been in a Blood Bar, but he had been to many over the years, and no two were ever quite the same. But of them all this was his favourite.

Unlike so many others, those of the Black Veil didn't succumb to the usual vampire trappings, and weren't taken in by the clichés of TV and film. No dark shadows, no black walls, and certainly no cobwebs or bat motifs. Instead, this Blood Bar was decked out in lush splendour. A celebration of their lives as vampires. Satin and silk drapes in deep reds lined the walls, hanging in the booths, with mauve walls and a mahogany finish to the actual bar and seats.

It was only early in the evening and most of the 'real' vampires were either still at work or more likely at the gym, engaged in the expected social activities, blending in with their mortal friends, and so the bar wasn't busy, with only a few patrons. A young couple sat in a booth, sipping blood laced with cinnamon, while they necked each other for more immediate pleasure. A few others were in heated debate at the bar, while a single figure sat in her own booth, reading a book while taking the occasional sip of blood from the goblet sitting on the table.

Frederick smiled and walked over to the bar. He ordered a flagon of blood for himself, O-Negative. Once the bartender had given him the flagon, Frederick quaffed it all down, enjoying the thick substance running down his throat, immediately feeling his preternatural senses sharpening. For a brief second, he reached out his mind, hoping the fresh blood would give him the edge needed to touch Will's mind.

Still nothing.

Sighing, he walked over to the booth and slid onto the seat opposite the solitary woman.

At first she didn't look up, although he knew she'd noticed him. Only when she had finished the paragraph she was reading did she finally grace him with a look. She offered a smile, showing him the fangs that had cost her several hundred to install. They were quite small, but big enough to notice if you knew what you were looking for. Frederick suspected she didn't smile a whole lot. Fangs on a midwife couldn't have been that much of a soothing thing for pregnant women about to give birth.

As usual, when he saw her, she was dressed in blacks and purples, wearing her top low to show off her ample cleavage. Her jet-black hair, with its single line of purple running down the right side, was worn long and straight.

'Lord Otto,' she said, by way of greeting, using Frederick's Black Veil name; Lord Otto von Hohenzollern. 'How is the Kingdom of Prussia?'

'Long gone,' Frederick replied with a smile of indulgence.

'You're looking well. Still moisturizing?' There was a twinkle in her eyes. She was teasing him.

He had told her many tales of his homeland, but she still wasn't sure whether to believe he was as old as he claimed. Unlike others in the Black Veil, Frederick had the distinction of never having lied about his past (other than a few embellishments, like the station of his family seat), although almost all of those he'd told the story to were convinced he made it up. Much like their own 'pasts'. Lady Reisha, to use her chosen Veil name, wasn't sure if he was telling the truth or not. This made her, from Frederick's point of view, plenty more interesting than any other in the Black Veil.

'You'd be surprised what a bit of moisturizer can do.' He indicated the goblet. 'Can I get you another?' She nodded with a raised eyebrow, and Frederick motioned to the bartender for two more. He reached out to the still-open book and flipped it over to see the cover. 'What are you reading?' He frowned. '*Seeking the Seeker*?'

'Yes, an interesting read. Talks about a vampiric prophecy of a chosen one who will lead us to the Progenitor; the Vampire Queen who created us.'

Frederick didn't answer at first, but he took note of the author of the book. Barratt Kemp. He would have to look into it later, although he suspected it was written by a 'scholar' from the Brotherhood, getting their good news out.

Frederick forced a laugh. 'Prophecy, eh? Sounds like the scope for a good film. Even if it's a bit of a worn idea.'

Lady Reisha shrugged. 'Probably right, but without you here to regale me with stories of historical vampires, I have to look elsewhere.' The drinks arrived, and she thanked the bartender. 'Where have you been anyway? Not seen you in these parts for, what, a year?'

'I've been travelling. Recently returned from France.'

'Ah, visiting your sire?'

Frederick answered with a smile. 'How goes your own little enterprise? Still keeping you busy?'

'Same old, supply and demand.' Her eyes still held the same twinkle, and Frederick couldn't help but smile at her audacity.

Her 'little enterprise' was so wonderfully macabre that Frederick just had to put her in touch with Rhys at the blood bank once he had learned what it was. But for Rhys and Lady Reisha to do business, however, Frederick needed to check her credentials, and in his investigation, he discovered that she was indeed a midwife at Southend Hospital, and further, her real name was Robi Aston.

While working with expectant mothers she would supply them with extra iron supplements; the pretext being to keep them healthy and strong while they carried their child to term, since their bodies had a higher blood volume than usual, and the iron was important for the health of the foetus. Of course, they didn't need as much iron as she administered, but the extra iron helped her end product. Once they had given birth, Lady Reisha would take the afterbirth, now rich in iron, to be used for *research*. More often than not, mothers in labour would agree to anything to be rid of the afterbirth, and so she rarely ever met resistance.

This afterbirth she would sell on the black market to those with questionable tastes, in particular 'real' vampires who found the iron-rich afterbirth something of a delicacy. Since putting her in touch with Rhys, who had access to *real* vampires, her little business had increased nicely with many upiór now benefiting from Lady Reisha's reprehensible scheme.

Frederick couldn't see himself enjoying afterbirth, but he had learned not to judge his people, and tried to live by the motto of the Order of the Black Eagle; to each his own. At the end of the day, it fed the desires of blood junkies, and no one got harmed in the process. Ultimately a win-win for the Three.

'Actually, Rhys mentioned you were back in town,' Lady Reisha said. 'So, I wondered how long before I'd see you again.'

'And here I am.' Frederick reached out and took her hands in his. 'I have been busy, which is actually what I need to talk to you about.'

Lady Reisha leaned in closer. 'Oh, do tell me more.'

*

She climbed out of her car, picked up her work and the bag of clothes, and pushed the door closed with her foot. Luckily, she didn't need to worry too much about locking the doors, as they locked automatically once she (or rather the key fob) was far enough away. Nonetheless, she glanced back when she reached the front door, just to make sure, and was rewarded by the flashing of the car lights as the doors locked. She juggled her work and the bag and fumbled for her keys.

She entered her home and was pleasantly surprised.

From the hallway it was immediately clear that her houseguest had been cleaning; not to say her home was usually messy, but living alone did tend to produce a certain lackadaisical attitude. And her busy work schedule didn't really help. Her papers were neatly stacked on the small desk in the hallway, the pens in the tidy. Even the tiled floor had been moped. She glanced into the kitchen and wasn't surprised to see all the washing done, the sideboards clean and organised.

Someone has a wee touch of OCD, she thought. Not that she minded, since she did too, if she had the time.

She placed her work on the table and entered the living room.

And stopped, a smile on her face.

Now only in a towel, the houseguest was flat out on the sofa. For a moment her eyes lingered on his back, then she cast them around the room. The TV was on, showing yet another news report about the charity dinner that Baroness Meredydd was holding at Caerfyrddin House later in the week, and the rest of the place was sparkling. Lizette couldn't get over how much housework had been done, not only a general tidy, but her houseguest appeared to have polished every single surface and ornament in the room. She looked back at his sleeping form.

'Bless you,' she said, and placed the bag of clothes on the coffee table. She didn't really want to wake him – he looked so peaceful – but she couldn't spend the rest of the evening with him half naked on the sofa. Not least because Jordan had insisted on popping over later, to make sure she was safe.

Reluctantly, therefore, she leaned down and gently nudged him, and was surprised by the smoothness of his skin beneath her hand. It was so soft, reminding her of her neighbour's new-born grandchild.

He stirred immediately. One eye, then both. He squinted, looked up at her, and for a moment seemed confused.

'Good morning,' she said to him.

'Huh? What?' He moved quickly, almost dislodging the towel, and manoeuvred himself into a sitting position, one fist grasping the edge of the towel tightly. 'Did I fall asleep?'

'You've had a busy day,' Lizette said, stepping away, doing her best not to look at his perfect chest. The skin was so smooth, no hair, no blemishes... She looked him in the eyes, and was startled by them once again. She had almost forgotten about the strange redness to them... They reminded her of an albino, and she wondered if such a thing was possible. Usually, as far as she knew, albinism affected the skin and hair, as well as the eyes, but, looking at her houseguest, she figured that clearly there were exceptions.

He smiled. 'Yeah, sorry. Only so much you can do with a whole day to yourself. And I couldn't really go out and enjoy the lovely sun,' he added, glancing down at his near-naked self.

'Aye, well lucky for you I can help with that.' She reached for the bag and handed it to him. 'I think they should fit. You're about the same build as my TA...'

He accepted the bag gratefully and rummaged in it. 'This is brilliant, thank you,' he said, and went to stand.

'Whoa there, Nelly,' Lizette said, raising her hands to stop him before he dropped the towel there and then.

He looked up from the towel which he *had* begun to open, frowned, and then laughed. 'Oh, yeah. Sorry.' He sat down again.

'It's no bother,' Lizette said, feeling the colour rising in her cheeks.

'Don't know why I did that.' The man smiled. 'Used to being on me own, maybe?'

'Maybe. You can get dressed in... Well, not the spare room; that's my kids' room and I don't like other people using it. Bathroom is best. I need to get out of these clothes myself, but first maybe a brew?'

'Sounds great.' He stood, and once again Lizette found her eyes drawn to him. She looked away quickly. Yep, having a half-naked man around the house was definitely no good for her. *You barely know him!*

He clearly noticed, and laughed, embarrassed a little. 'Yeah, maybe I should try these on first...?'

'Sorry, I shouldn't...' Lizette really didn't know what to say.

'It's fine. I mean, I'd probably be the same if the positions were reversed...' He frowned. 'Well, I guess I would be... Hard to be sure.'

'Still nothing then?'

He shook his head.

'Okay,' Lizette said, 'go get dressed, and I'll put the kettle on. We can talk properly when...' She shrugged. 'You know.'

'When I'm decent?'

'Aye, that.'

With another smile, flashing those brilliant perfect teeth, her houseguest left the living room.

For a moment Lizette remained where she stood. She wafted herself with a hand, and let out a breath of air. She couldn't remember ever being like that with Linden...

She turned to the TV and listened to the news report. Even though she'd heard more than enough about the charity dinner in the last few days, she was glad of the distraction. Anything to clear her mind of her houseguest for a moment.

3. Blank Slate

'I need your help,' Frederick told Lady Reisha. 'I've lost someone very dear to me, and you have contacts in the Veil that I do not, and I'm hoping that news of a newly turned vampire might have reached someone.'

Frederick knew he was playing a dangerous game. As a result of working alongside Rhys, many of her contacts were now upiór, not that she knew this, but if a new upiór was roaming Southend then it seemed reasonable that at least one of them would have picked up the scent of this new blood. Frederick couldn't ask them directly, as it would attract far too many unwanted questions, but such an enquiry from Lady Reisha would raise no warning bells.

'And what do I get in return? Other than the company of our most reclusive member? More stories?'

'No,' Frederick said, very aware of the path he was about to step on. 'I will prove to you that every word I have told you is one hundred percent true.'

Lady Reisha couldn't resist. 'Then I will find out what I can.'

*

The clothes did fit, which was a relief.

He didn't much like sitting around the house half naked, at least not the house of a stranger. But, then, he supposed he shouldn't forget, everybody was a stranger to him. *Including* him.

He stood in the bathroom a moment longer, looking at himself in the mirror. He was a stranger to himself. The face looking back at him didn't seem familiar at all, and as for the eyes... Like so many other things, he knew they were wrong, that the strange pinkish-red look of them wasn't right,

27

wasn't normal. He peered closer. His vision was perfect, possibly even better than perfect, and as he focused in on his reflected eyes, he was sure he could see through them... Literally *through* them, right to the optic nerve. The red wasn't some weird pigment of the iris, it was the blood.

His eyes were transparent.

He pulled back, feeling his heart beating faster at the shock of the realisation.

That wasn't normal.

What happened to me?

He didn't know. Didn't know anything; not a single thing about his past, about his family, his friends... not even something so simple as a name.

He sat on the closed toilet seat and reached for the shoes Lizette had provided. They were a little tighter than he'd have liked, but serviceable. He should probably keep them on, with enough wearing he might stretch them a little. And if he hoped to be outside at some point, he'd need to be able to walk comfortably in them. So, he kept them on and stood, shifting his weight from foot to foot, wiggling his toes as much as he was able.

'They'll do, Sa—'

There! On the tip of his tongue. A name.

He closed his eyes. Thought. Searched.

It had come from somewhere. Sa... something or other.

Sampson... Saul... Sandy... Sacha... Sacheverell? No, none of those names sounded right.

Generics, too much general knowledge, not enough specifics. But deep down, the details had to be there. He must have known his name at some point, surely. Somewhere, entrenched in his memory, were the details he needed, the...

'*You will always find me, Samay—*'

There. A voice from the past. A woman's voice. Of course, he didn't have a name to go with it, or a face, but whoever it was had started saying his name. Started, because he heard the cut off, an even vaguer voice talking over hers, but he couldn't hear the other voice.

It didn't matter. He had a *name*.

Sam.

*

Frederick and Lady Reisha spent a couple of hours discussing things, him telling her what it meant to be an upiór in the world of the twenty-first century, how she'd be entering a whole different universe, a way of life that had been born of centuries of bloodshed and carnage. Most important of all, Lady Reisha had to forget all the lore she'd ever learned. She seemed thrilled at the prospect, and Frederick left her with much to do and think about. He also left her with a vial of Red Source, just to give her a hint of the world she was going to enter.

He took with him the book she had been reading. Lady Reisha didn't need to read such nonsense now, since she would soon learn the truth about the Seeker, like all upiór free of the Brotherhood's propaganda. He intended to spend the evening looking into the book and, using his official contacts this time, he would track down the author. A confrontation was needed; either Barratt would be re-educated or dead. Either way, his position as a scholar for the Brotherhood would end abruptly.

By the time Frederick reached Chalkwell, the rain had started falling again; it was only a light drizzle so the walk from the train station to his place wasn't that much of an issue. The book was buried under one arm, protected from the elements beneath his leather jacket.

He wasn't paying that much attention as he walked up his street, since he had his phone to one ear listening to the ring.

'Robin!'

Frederick almost smiled at how pleased Stephen sounded.

'It's been all weekend. I tried calling, but... Where's Will? Jake's been onto me a few times now, and nobody has seen him... Did your plan succeed? Whatever it was?'

Frederick almost ended the call, tired of Stephen's babbling. He'd already answered the one question Frederick wanted the answer to. Will had not made it back to London. Which meant, probably, he was still in Southend somewhere.

Frederick stopped and lowered the phone, ignoring Stephen's voice on the other end. Something had caught his eye. He looked around and spotted the little blue Yaris parked just behind him. He glanced at the house opposite the car. Although he had passed the time of day with Liz, he hadn't previously known where she lived.

He shrugged it away. It wasn't that important. And, he decided, pressing the red button on his phone, neither was his call to Stephen.

*

'Sam?' Lizette said.

'Yeah, it just... came to me. Well, Sammy at any rate. I heard someone's voice, but I can't remember who it belonged to.'

Lizette was pleased for her houseguest – for Sam. She couldn't imagine what it must have been like, to go around for a whole day with no idea who you were. Without a name.

'Sam's good,' she said. 'Although I quite like Sammy too.'

'Not too sure about "e",' Sam said, smiling, 'but yeah, Sam kind of suits me.'

Lizette sat back on the sofa and sipped her hot coffee. Sam looked a little odd in Jordan's clothes; he seemed comfortable enough in them, but they just didn't sit right on him. The skinny jeans, the sweatshirt which said *Weekend forecast: Grilling with a chance of Beers!*, and the shoes. They just didn't strike her as the kind of clothes he would normally wear.

'How was work?' he asked, surprising her with the sudden change of topic.

She shrugged. 'Work was long and arduous. Don't ever go into teaching.'

He smiled slightly. 'Maybe I already am a teacher.' He quirked his lips. 'Who's to say?'

'I don't get the feeling of academia about you.'

'What sense do you get?'

'I have no idea.' Lizette laughed. 'Which isn't much help, sorry. Maybe you're a house-husband? Or work in social support?'

'Maybe.' Sam looked around the lounge. 'I'm a dab hand with polish, eh?'

'Aye. Not seen my place look so clean in... oh, ages.'

They sat in silence a moment, both enjoying their drinks.

'It's been an odd day,' Sam said. 'I mean, obviously it's been an odd day, but... But all day I keep getting a feeling I'm missing something really important.' He grinned. 'Well, obviously the lack of memory is important, but there is something else. Something I need to do.'

Lizette thought a second. 'No medical books, alas,' she said, 'so I'm no expert on amnesia, but I'd have thought something very traumatic happened to you to make you lose your memory.'

'But what? I mean, losing my memory – check, that's bad. But walking around the streets of Chalkwell naked... I mean, how does someone get into that kind of situation?'

'Prank gone wrong?'

'Maybe, but I don't think so.' He smiled slightly. 'Maybe I'm an escapee from some mental asylum?'

Lizette shook her head, glad that Sam was able to joke about the entire situation. A natural coping mechanism, which at least told her he was emotionally okay despite everything. 'If you were, I'd never have left you in my house.'

Sam continued to laugh a moment, then said, 'Thanks for that, by the way. I like the way you have your home.' He looked around the room at the paintings hanging on the walls. 'You said you teach history? Mythology a big part of that?'

'Why...? Oh, the books and paintings. It's more of a hobby, really.' Lizette pointed at the big picture above the mantelpiece. It depicted a voluptuous woman in a flowing white dress, combing her thick mane of red hair while looking into a hand-held mirror. 'That one's Dante Gabriel Rossetti's *Lady Lilith*. It's of little interest beyond the fact that my real parents loved...' She stared at the painting, and said softly, 'My parents died when I was very young and...'

'I'm sorry. Losing something of great value is hard.'

'Aye, obviously you understand that. Anyway, it was a long time ago. And I was raised by a very loving set of foster parents.'

'That's good. Good to have people who can anchor you.'

Lizette turned her head to him, and placed a hand gently on his knee. She looked him in the eyes, and once again found herself falling into them. She forced herself to look away.

'Something tells me you and I are going to get along fine, Sam.'

'My anchor.'

'Yes,' Lizette said softly. 'Until you're able to set sail on your own.' She stood suddenly. 'Look, let me get my laptop so we can do a little research. Maybe find a possible cause of your amnesia?'

For a moment there was fear in Sam's unusual eyes; eyes that just seemed to want to swallow Lizette whole. She shivered, but continued looking in them from the doorway.

He shook his head and offered a smile. 'Sorry, yes, that would be great.'
An obvious lie.

What have you got yourself into, Lizzie?

'We'll get you all restored somehow,' she told him.

*

He dropped the book onto the seat of the lounger and placed his jacket over the back of it, before walking straight into the kitchen, which could only be reached via the living room. With the clouds gathering outside, the room was darker than usual, so he flicked on the light switch located just outside the kitchen. The room was bathed in light and Frederick almost jumped in shock.

He hadn't sensed her at all, which said a lot for his own preoccupation with the mobile in his hand, as well as the book. Celeste sat there, in the corner chair, looking directly at him, her face a mixture of concern and disappointment.

'Hi,' Frederick said, feeling a bit daft, but unsure what else to say. 'Would you care for a drink?' He continued on into the kitchen, not waiting for an answer.

He put Will's mobile on the side and flipped on the kettle, suddenly in dire need of caffeine, and walked over to the window. From there he saw the black car that was used to ferry the Three around Essex. It was parked outside his house, directly opposite the path leading to the front door. No doubt the chauffeur was still sitting inside, waiting patiently for Celeste. Frederick shook his head and turned back to the cupboards, surprised at himself for not even noticing the car parked there.

As he prepared a coffee for himself, he nattered on, talking nonsense, anything to fill the silence. Celeste didn't respond once, which was not a good sign. Once the coffee was done, he pulled out a wine glass and poured Celeste something red. He didn't know what it was; wine wasn't his thing at all, but Will had insisted on buying a bottle for when they returned from the nightclub. The bottle was unopened.

He emerged from the kitchen and handed the glass to Celeste. She took it gracefully and sipped it, her eyes never leaving Frederick. Feeling the weight of her stare, he turned and crossed to the lounger. He picked up the book.

'*Seeking the Seeker*,' he said, brandishing it as he sat down. 'Seems the Brotherhood is getting bold again. Which is to be expected, right? After all, now that the time of prophecy is nearing, Julius is going to have to make his move.'

'Which does lead to the question, how does Julius know that the time of prophecy is drawing near?'

Frederick let out a breath of air, glad that Celeste was speaking. Anything but the silent treatment. She looked down at the wine.

'We've been very careful about what we revealed of the prophecy once the Book was in our hands. Only the Three, and you, know the full details.'

'True, but the Book went missing for a long time before the Ancient gave it to me.'

Celeste nodded. 'At which time it was barely a collection of notes, half transcribed visions and memories. Even when you got it the Book was incomplete, and the passages pertaining to the prophecy were mostly new. No one read of the prophecy until you and Melinda.'

'A version of it was out there, badly translated and missing key passages.' Frederick blinked. 'You think she gave information to the Brotherhood before she... died?'

If Celeste noted the accusatory tone, she chose to ignore it. As far as Celeste was concerned, she did what was needed and there ended the discussion.

'I very much doubt that, Frederick. But someone has.'

'An inside job, then?'

Celeste nodded. 'How is Willem?' she asked abruptly, throwing Frederick off. He blinked. 'Don't insult me, Frederick, not after all this time. You forget that I know you, probably better than you know yourself. I made you.' She raised the wine glass. 'Plus, you don't drink wine, and I've never known you to own a single bottle before, and then, of course, there is this.' With dramatic effect she raised her free hand and slowly pointed to the backpack that sat on the floor next to the chair.

Frederick swallowed. He was so intent on the conversation, glad that he had Celeste's interest, that he had totally failed to notice Will's backpack. He took a deep breath; time for truth.

'He's out there, but I can't find any trace of him.'

'It would seem Eryn was right about you and Willem.' Celeste sighed. 'It was bound to happen to you one day, I suppose. Took me five centuries to find a consort...'

'Or two,' Frederick interjected, unable to keep the bitterness in check.

'Or two,' Celeste conceded, with a small smile. 'So, I'm not surprised it's happened for you, too. But,' she added, shaking her head sadly, 'you should have come to me, Frederick.'

'I know, but for almost three hundred years I've been yours and yours alone. Now, though...' Frederick shrugged.

'*Mon toujours*, tell me everything.'

So, he did. Everything that had happened since Friday night, including his concerns about Will's Rebirth. Celeste listened intently, and when he had finished, she sat in silence, digesting what had been said.

'Very well, a difficult situation,' she said. 'Worse than we thought last night. I have yet to speak to Eryn and Theodor, so we haven't even breached the idea of going to Ai Ling about it all... Perhaps now is the time.'

It was the last thing Frederick wanted, but what else could the Three do? In the past, vampires had been born of lust and criminal violation, more often than not new vampires didn't want to be immortal. They were victims, and thus ill equipped for the new life that had been forced upon them. Even now new upiór were made in such ways, but these were few and far between. The Rebirth Council had been assembled by the Three to govern such things, to ensure that those who were to become upiór were fully aware of the path they were about to walk on. Like Reisha. Will, however...

'We will need to find him, Frederick. He may not be the Seeker, but he is now our responsibility, plus, as you've mentioned, there are aspects of his Rebirth that are troubling.' Celeste stood and walked over to him. He went to rise, but she motioned him to remain as he was. 'I shall return to the Residence to inform Theodor and Eryn. Best that it be I and not you. Eryn doesn't need further ammunition against you. You look into this Brotherhood book; see if you can find the author.'

'And Will?'

'We shall discuss that more fully tomorrow. We must proceed carefully from herein.' She turned to leave, but stopped once she got to the living room door. 'Oh yes,' she said, looking back, 'you'll be interested to know that the hunter you killed was the half-brother of Maia.'

Frederick opened his mouth to speak, but Celeste shushed him with a look.

'I see you knew this.' She shook her head, troubled. 'Another thing to be discussed tomorrow.'

*

'Dissociative Fugue,' Lizette said, leaning forward to turn the laptop to face Sam.

She had ordered in some Chinese food, and began researching his amnesia as they enjoyed it. While he sat on the sofa, Garth snuggled up beside him, Lizette sat on the opposite chair, the coffee table between them.

'*A type of amnesia that is caused by an extreme psychological trauma instead of physical trauma, illness, or another medical condition,*' Sam read. He scanned the text. 'Autobiographical memories... Yeah, that sounds about right.'

He reached into the Egg Foo Yung with his chopsticks, his movements tentative. Lizette usually ordered Chinese in, but Sam had insisted they collect it themselves.

He really wanted to go outside. So, they did.

Unfortunately, Sam didn't recognise anything on the short trip in the car. Lizette took a more circuitous route back, in the hope that something would nudge a memory of how he got to her garden, never mind where he actually came from. But, nothing.

When they returned and laid the food out, spreading out the foil containers into plate mode, she was quite prepared to offer him a fork, but he wanted to try the chopsticks. Lizette was fascinated by this willingness to try everything. Much like he was now, slowly placing a piece of the Foo Yung into his mouth, he was a little timorous about it all, but more than willing to try. In some ways there was a childlike innocence about him, but that illusion was shattered when she looked into his eyes.

They held a fierce intelligence, and something else. She wanted to say 'haunted', but she wasn't sure. Whenever she looked too closely, the redness of his eyes put her off; it was almost as if his eyes were transparent, and she could see the blood flowing behind them. This was, of course, patently ludicrous.

'What do you think?' she enquired.

Sam glanced up from his chewing. 'Nice. If it wasn't for the obvious physical differences, I'd swear I was Chinese. This stuff is incredible.'

'Hmm.' Lizette steepled her fingers, in what her students called her contemplative pose. The one she used when she was about to impart some insightful comment on their assignments. 'Can't say I remember the first time I tasted Chinese. Problem with being raised in Motherwell, Chinese became a staple diet.'

Sam smiled at this. 'You'd think that would be more of a China thing than a Motherwell thing, really. Mind you, this stuff is not very close to real Chinese food. I have a Chinese friend who used to...' His voice trailed off, and his face lowered. 'Who used to... do something.'

Lizette waited in silence, carefully watching the ticks of his facial muscles as he tried to recall the specifics. General stuff he was good with; the everyday things of life were no problem for him, but when it came down to anything remotely personal it was like he hit a wall. And judging by the look on his face it was a very large and painful wall.

He shook his head. 'No, it's gone.' Sam looked back up, and swallowed hard. 'What's happened to me, Liz?'

'I really wish I knew.' She reached out for the laptop. 'But, according to my research, this fugal state can last for days or weeks, sometimes even months. But it's rarely permanent.'

'Rarely?'

'Well, I'm no doctor. My expertise is history, not medicine. That's why I think we need to visit my doctor tomorrow; perhaps she can recommend a good psychologist. Get an expert to look at you.'

Sam physically pulled back at the idea. He shook his head and stood. 'No,' he said, turning to the window, looking out towards the Thames Estuary. 'I can't place anyone else in danger.'

Lizette frowned. 'Danger?'

Sam didn't answer, so Lizette walked over to him. She gently placed a hand on his shoulder. 'Sam? What kind of danger?'

'I don't know,' he said, slowly turning until he was facing her. 'But I just get a feeling that the more people know, the more dangerous it will be. Whatever happened to me... It can't happen to anyone else.'

4. Sinking In

Another rainy evening.

Jake stood under cover from the worst of it, watching as the traffic moved up Fulham Road in the direction of the Broadway and down towards Putney.

The clouds had started to gather as he stepped off the bus at the Broadway about half six, and with only a five-minute walk to Will's house he knew he'd been saved a soaking this time. By the time he'd finished checking, and discovering no change in the house at all, the rain had begun, but he had already called Amy and she was on the way to pick him up.

They spent a few hours together at his flat, watching *Thor* – not Amy's ideal choice of movie; she only watched it with Jake out of sympathy – and then some mindless TV. He wasn't feeling all that chatty, his mind on what he had to do that evening. For her part, Amy attempted to take his mind off the dread he was feeling about making the report to the police, and she outlined her plan on how to proceed with Lawrencia. Jake was glad that she had totally come on board with that since it freed his mind up to worry about other important things.

Now he waited outside the 'pig farm': Fulham Police Station. Looking like the proverbial drowned rat, he espied Mr Townsend (*Francis* he reminded himself, still unsure if he'd ever get used to that) walking down the Fulham Road. Although his head was lowered, no doubt to protect his face from the oncoming wind, Francis walked with a strength that belied his years. Jake smiled, glad of the old man's support.

As he neared, Jake stepped out into the rain, immediately wishing he'd brought a hat with him, not quite enjoying the coldness of the water crashing down on his stubbly head.

Perhaps it was the honing of some sixth sense over the decades, or more likely coincidence, but just as Jake came into his line of sight, Francis lifted his head. They shook hands and walked towards the steps leading into the station house.

Francis looked around. 'No sign of Sandra?'

'No,' Jake said, with a sigh. 'I had hoped she'd turn up. She seemed all for it when I spoke to her earlier, but... I don't know. Eon is one funky son of...'

Francis held up a hand. 'Yes, he is, but let's not dip to his level, son. Sandra chose her own path many years ago. If she can't be here, for whatever reason, that's not our problem.'

Jake felt a depth of sadness at these words, but he couldn't argue the point. Francis had been married to Sandra for a very long time and Jake had no place to comment on their opinions of each other. It was sad that they'd split in the first place, but Jake kind of hoped that Francis' faith would have given him cause to forgive her. It was probably stupid of him, but he had been holding onto a little hope for them. Will's disappearance should have been the thing that brought them some form of reconciliation.

Francis opened the door. 'Come on, then, let's do this, let's bring my boy home.'

Jake nodded. One parent would have to be enough.

As he set to step inside, a voice he recognised came from behind. 'Hold the door for me.'

Jake grinned and turned. Sandra was walking up the path to the station. She looked grim, as if she'd just had to endure the worst moment of her life. Behind her, pulling away, Jake spotted Eon's beaten-up car. The Guyana man was behind the wheel, his face matching the storm outside. Jake turned to hide his smile.

'Sandra,' Francis said, still holding the door open. 'It's been quite a while.'

Sandra only stopped once she was in the foyer of the police station. She removed the plastic rain hat she wore and looked her ex-husband up and down, then turned to Jake. 'They'll let anyone in these days, won't they?'

Francis laughed. 'It's good to see you, too,' he said, allowing the door to close.

'Of course it is,' Sandra said. 'I'm the best thing that ever happened to you.' She removed her raincoat and handed it to Francis; he graciously took it and hung it over his arm.

Jake was quite taken aback. Almost sixty and she still scrubbed up well. And it was pretty clear that she'd made extra effort to dress for the occasion. Francis raised an eyebrow, and Jake saw so much of his son in him. He felt a sharp sting in his heart, his breath caught in his chest for a moment, and turned away from the awkward reunion.

*

Once they'd explained to the officer at the desk that they were there to make a report about a missing person, they were seen to pretty quickly. If you called waiting half an hour before being called into a private room quickly. Jake wasn't so sure he did, but both Francis and Sandra seemed quite content with the time factor. In part Jake suspected it was because, at their age, they were very glad to be out of the rain and the chance for them to catch up after a few years seemed to appeal to them, too. Jake didn't have the heart to explain to them this was not a social occasion, but he consoled himself with the knowledge that at least they were talking again. He guessed, when he reached his sixties, he'd probably take every moment to chat to old friends too. After all, in six decades of life, you'd probably have seen so much that you were no longer in a rush for anything.

The officer that ushered them into the private room was a short woman of Portuguese ancestry who introduced herself as PC Becky Medeiros. She explained she would be the initial investigating officer; it would be her job to take down all the information she deemed relevant to the case.

Once they were all seated and Medeiros had arranged her papers, she began. 'Obviously, we will do everything we can to help you find your...?'

'Son,' Francis offered.

'Son,' Medeiros continued, barely missing a beat. 'But we'll need to make a risk assessment to find out what level the danger is to him, or possibly others. This will help us decide what measure will need to be taken in our efforts to find him.' She picked up a pen and placed it ready to write on the form before her. 'We'll start by taking a few important details which I will later circulate to every station in the UK. First of all, what is your son's name?'

Jake was silent through most of the initial questions – name, age, home address, description – but had to butt in when it came time to answer a few more personal questions. The answers to which neither of Will's parents had.

Jake gave the officer a description of the clothes Will was wearing, and where he was last seen. But when it came to asking if there had been any recent out-of-character behaviour, Jake had to pause.

There were some things that Will didn't want his folks knowing, and normally Jake would be the first to protect Will's privacy. However, this situation was anything but normal.

Medeiros sensed his hesitation, and sat forward, speaking gently.

'I understand that some of this information may be delicate, and quite likely personal, but in order to help us with our investigation we will need *all* relevant information. However minor it may appear; it could be the linchpin of our initial enquiries.'

'I...' Jake stopped, casting furtive glances at Francis and Sandra.

Medeiros nodded. 'I see. I'm sure Will's parents won't mind if we...'

'Mind?' Sandra said. 'Of course we mind. If this involves our son, then we want to know. Isn't that right, Francis?'

Francis didn't seem as sure as his ex-wife. He placed a hand on her knee. 'Sandra, Will's private life is none of our business, and if Jacob is protecting that, then we ought to...'

Jake interceded, his mind made up. 'No, it's fine. If it helps, I'll tell you, and when Will returns he can bitch me out all he likes.' He offered a weak smile, imagining how Will would react once he learned that his parents knew all about his secret internet romance. He would be freaked, but at least he would be home. Jake could deal with that.

So, he explained all he knew about the events leading up to Will's walk towards Fulham Broadway station. He mentioned how he found a lot of Will's behaviour a little out of character, but in Will's defence, Jake made a point of explaining that the unusual behaviour was intentional on Will's part. He was, at the behest of Steve, pushing himself beyond his usual boundaries. Jake was careful to include Will's desire to help his sister when he returned, and the business at work that Will had also planned on his return home. But when Jake came to explain about the developing romance between Will and Charlie, Medeiros stopped him.

'An internet romance? And it was this Charlie that Will was going to meet?'

Jake nodded, aware that both Francis and Sandra were exchanging worried looks. They were of a different generation, but they had heard about the dangers of the internet as reported by the naysayers in the press. And it was clear that to their minds Will was going to be a casualty of such dangers.

'Well, yeah,' he said to PC Medeiros. 'But it's a common enough thing,' he added, realising how much doubt was in his voice. He snatched another glance at Will's parents, and it was clear they also noted his tone.

'That is certainly true, Mr Caulfield, but...' She stood up and gathered her notes together. 'I will be back in a few moments, once I've consulted my supervising officer. If you'll excuse me?'

No one spoke as she left the interview room. Sandra merely kept her eyes on Jake, as if blaming him for Will's disappearance. Francis, on the other hand, watched Medeiros walk out and only when she had closed the door did he turn to Jake.

'Why didn't you tell me this before?' He glanced at Sandra, and offered a smile. 'Sorry, Sandra. I meant us.'

Jake let out a breath of air and looked to the floor. He was going to kill Will for putting him in this situation.

*

They were taking a walk along the Estuary esplanade near Chalkwell. Clouds were moving in the darkness about them.

Sam wore a coat that Jordan had left at Lizette's a few weeks back, after a planning meeting, and much like the rest of Jordan's stuff it fit Sam quite snugly, making him look like some kind of British Eskimo.

'I only moved to Southend in 2003,' Lizette told him, thinking that if she shared more about her own past, it might shake something in Sam. 'After spending most of my life in Motherwell. But I was born in Northumberland, not that I spent long there, since my parents were killed in a car accident. I don't remember much about them, except they were very loving.'

'Did your great aunt take you in?'

'No. I was fostered out; none of my family were in the position to raise a child at the time. I lost touch with most of them over the years, but me and my great aunt keep in touch now and then. It's no big deal, just the way my life has gone.'

Sam nodded. 'Must be great to know where you come from. Anybody special in your life?'

Lizette was caught off guard by the sudden question, and took a moment to gather her thoughts. 'Well, there was once... My ex. Linden. I had two children with him, both teens now. They live with him most of the time.'

'See them often?'

'As much as possible. We don't like to disrupt their lives too much.'

Sam smiled. 'Yeah, nobody wants that. And I suppose it's quite a distance for them to travel.'

'Not too bad. I mean, Basildon is only fifteen minutes away on the train.'

'Oh, I assumed they'd be up in...' Sam shook his head. 'Doesn't matter, I guess.'

They stopped to look out at the estuary. Far away, on the opposite side, they could just about make out the lights of Kent.

Lizette placed a comforting hand on Sam's shoulder. 'Maybe we can work out a little something of your past? Like your accent; it's a bit refined, but I detect a definite hint of London in there.'

Sam frowned. 'You think?'

'I do.' Lizette smiled at him. 'That's a start, right? I'm pretty good at placing accents. West London maybe.'

Sam was silent for a few moments, while he thought about that. He nodded slowly. 'Yes, London sounds right somehow. And...' He shook his head, his eyes roaming the distance. 'I get the sense of... I don't know. Flight? As if I were fleeing something.'

'The same something that made you lose your memory?'

'Could be.' Sam blinked, and turned to Lizette, tears slowly falling from his eyes. 'It's so damned frustrating.'

'Yes,' she said, reaching out and hugging his shoulders with one arm, and was pleasantly surprised when he moved in closer, leaning his head against her shoulder. 'But we're making progress. We now know you're from London, that you fled for some reason, and it was something pretty bad. More than we knew last night, when I found you *naked* in my garden.'

She was pleased to hear Sam laugh, and enjoyed the slight vibration as his body shook with the laughter.

'Yes, sorry about that.'

'Hey, don't be. I'm not.'

Sam turned his head, bringing his nose barely an inch from Lizette's. 'You're quite sweet, really.'

This pleased Lizette even more. 'Just don't go telling anyone else that. I have a reputation as a hardnosed bitch to maintain,' she said, laughing too.

Heedless of their laughter, the clouds grew darker, and the first drops of rain fell, signalling the imminent arrival of the forthcoming storm.

*

They emerged to be assaulted by the full force of the storm. Lightning flashed in the sky, illuminating the worry on their faces. Jake was quiet, lost in his own world, and stopped at the top of the steps while Francis and Sandra descended.

'Searching his house?' Sandra was saying. 'Will's lost to us, isn't he, Francis?'

'Come on, you daft woman,' Francis said and pulled his ex-wife closer to him. Even after all these years he felt responsible for her, and the pain written over her face was echoed in his own heart. But he had faith, and he was sure they would find their son somehow. 'It's just routine,' he pointed out, 'you heard the lady. They need to search his house for any kind of clues that will point to why he'd go missing.'

'It was that man. That Charlie person Billy went to see.'

'We don't know that. And perhaps they will find something in Will's house that will tell him where this Charlie lives.' Francis looked back up at the steps. 'Did you ever speak to Charlie, Jacob?'

Jake shook his head. 'No, but I want to. I warned Will something would go wrong,' he said, the anger suddenly bubbling over, 'but he wouldn't listen. He's so fucking stubborn sometimes.' He stopped abruptly and blinked away the rain from his eyes. 'Sorry, Sandra.'

Sandra looked up from where she was wrapped in Francis' arms. 'It's okay, love, you're upset.'

Upset. Francis was no mind reader, but he knew that to call Jake's state of mind 'upset' was an understatement. For a second, he saw Jake at thirteen; both he and Will running down the stairs into the lounge, their faces red. Francis smiled and released Sandra.

He walked over to Jake and reached out a hand. 'It's going to be okay, son, he'll be found.'

Jake pulled away from the touch of support, and said, 'He better be. Damn him for doing this to me.'

Francis lowered his head, no longer wanting to intrude on Jake's pain. He'd known all those years ago, but Jake was oblivious to the truth. Now, though, it seemed that truth was beginning to hit home.

'Come on, Sandra, let's flag a cab. Jake needs some alone time.'

Sandra attempted to argue, but Francis shushed her and gently led her away from the police station and towards Fulham Road where they'd have more chance of hailing a taxi.

As they walked away, he glanced back at Jake. The man stood like some stocky statue, unaware of the ferocity of the rain as it washed over him.

Francis really hoped Jake would find some comfort soon, it broke his old heart to see one of his boys in so much hurt.

Without looking up Jake turned and walked away, heading toward Clem Atlee Estate. Francis smiled sadly.

Roaming in the rain. He remembered such painful days of his own, just after he'd been thrown out of his home, and couldn't blame Jake for feeling as he did.

*

Amy stood at the end of Jake's bed, watching him sleep. It was just after five thirty in the morning, and she was about to head to work, having to leave even earlier to navigate the traffic between Fulham and the Docklands. It was going to be a long trip, but she had needed to stay at Jake's last night.

When he'd returned from the police station he was a wreck – and soaked through, to boot. Over a cup of Oxo, he told her everything the police had said, and she tried to get him to see that it was good. The police dealt with missing persons a lot more often than people probably realised, and they knew what they were doing. But Jake wouldn't be comforted, recalling stories of the missing that were never found.

It was what he never said, however, that troubled Amy the most.

She wasn't stupid, and she could read people pretty well. It didn't matter how close friends he was with Will, to be this despondent spoke of only one thing.

She left the bedroom, her mind rushing through various scenarios of how to deal with this latest development. Just before she left the flat, though, she placed a post-it note on the TV, telling Jake to meet her for lunch.

They definitely had to talk about this, but when it came to what she would say, Amy had no idea. Hopefully by the time lunch arrived she would have been hit by some inspiration.

*

Lizette poked her head through the crack in the living room door and looked in on Sam who was still fast asleep on the sofa.

It was half six and time for her to head to work; more lectures to prepare for. Normally she would have prepared the night before, but her time with Sam superseded her usual routine. Strangely she didn't mind as much as she thought she would.

She wanted to believe she was reading into things, her rational mind telling her that the feelings weren't real, just the side-effect of this unusual situation. No more real than the sense of closeness you could get by talking to people on social media, like so many of her students did, falling for people that they didn't really know. But another part of her mind was telling her to give in, to let the feelings become what they wanted to *be*.

The downside of letting herself be taken away with such feelings was what might happen when he rediscovered his memories. He might already be in a relationship with someone, maybe even married... And that would surely throw a large spanner at things.

She checked her watch. She really had to be off.

For a moment she remained where she was, though, contemplating going into the room and kissing Sam gently on the forehead. But she decided against it; if he woke up as she kissed him it could confuse matters, and he had enough going on at the moment.

Things would progress as they progressed.

*

It was a violation that Jake felt acutely. Will's home was abuzz with activity, seeing more people wandering around in it than ever before, and Jake didn't like it.

He was restless, constantly moving from kitchen to lounge, upstairs, and then back down, checking to see what the police were doing. He *knew* what they were doing, of course, but he needed to see with his own eyes, driven by some sense of unwanted invasion of privacy. And with each circuit of the house, the fact that Will could be in serious danger struck him deeper and deeper.

His mobile had been left as a point of contact for the police since Francis did not own a phone, landline or mobile, and Sandra didn't wish to be contacted at home, feeling the atmosphere there was already getting a little too untenable. And so, as the first port of call, it was Jake who was awoken by a call from PC Medeiros at eight o'clock. Once he was fully cognizant, she outlined how their investigation would progress today.

They would be pulling Will's phone records, a task made easy by him being on contract, to see what calls and texts had been sent and received prior to his disappearance, and if any had been made since the night of Friday 25th March. They would also be checking all CCTV on his most likely route to Southend Central; London Underground stations covering the entire journey from Fulham Broadway through to Tower Hill, and street CCTV between Tower Hill and Fenchurch Street. Although Jake had received a text saying Will was in Southend on the night of the twenty-fifth, there was no guarantee that it was sent from Southend or indeed sent by Will; it could be that Will never even made it out of London. But on the assumption he did, they would also be checking CCTV between Fenchurch Street and Southend Central, as well as talking to London Underground and Network Rail staff who would have been on duty during the given time window.

Back at home, though, officers would be visiting Will's house on Barclay Road at nine o'clock to do an onsite search to see if there was any further evidence that might indicate if he had other plans that he had not chosen to share with Jake.

Medeiros had suggested that perhaps Jake would like to be present at the search, to give him peace of mind that steps were being taken to locate his friend. Jake absolutely agreed with that, and it had seemed like a great idea at the time. But now, as he stood leaning against the stair wall, looking from kitchen to lounge, he wasn't so sure he liked the idea after all. The more he saw them search, the more he became anxious.

'Looks like you need a coffee, son.'

Jake turned his head towards the kitchen and saw Francis emerge, carrying one mug and a glass of milk. Francis had promised he'd come over, but Jake hadn't seen him arrive.

'When did you get here?' he asked, accepting the coffee gratefully.

'About ten minutes ago. Back door was open.' Jake nodded at this, never having realised how easily he had slipped into Will's habits.

Francis continued, glancing in at the lounge. 'They're really going for it, aren't they? I noticed you were distracted and in serious need of a coffee, so I busied myself in the kitchen.'

Jake looked up from the cup. 'It's much appreciated,' he said, forcing himself to take a sip of the hot liquid. The caffeine felt good on his taste buds.

'I bet you haven't had a spot of food since leaving the station last night, have you?'

Jake had to admit Francis was right. Despite Amy's best efforts, he simply hadn't been hungry. No food or drink had passed his lips since leaving the police station. Not even a bottle of beer.

'I'll grab something at lunch time. Be meeting Amy, then.'

'That's good.' Francis placed a gentle hand on Jake's arm. 'You need to look after yourself, you can't let all this get to you. You'll work it out.'

Jake nodded, not really listening. 'I suppose they know what they're doing, right?'

'Yes, I should think so. Don't worry, they'll bring my boy back.'

'Will they, though? Look at all this effort they're going to. They've even got officers going door-to-door, asking questions of the neighbours to see if anyone saw anything untoward, and someone is popping over to have words with Steve and that Kurt guy. Anyone who might have something to gain by Will being out of the picture.'

'Including that fella... oh, what's his name? Lawrencia's fella?'

Jake scowled. 'Jimmy. Yeah, I'm sure the police will have a field day with him. Asshole.'

'Well, that's good, then. The police know what they're doing, and we'll have Will home in no time.'

'But that's just it, Francis,' Jake said, hating the tone of desperation in his voice. 'Up until this morning... Well, last night really, I'd convinced myself that sooner or later I'd pop over here and find Will home, acting as if nothing had happened. But now? With all this?' He indicated the police officers, two more of whom were heading upstairs. 'It's all too real.'

Francis didn't respond, and Jake looked closely at the old man. He expected to see his own doubts mirrored in the grey eyes, but all he saw was a sense of assurance. Francis smiled and patted Jake's arm again.

'Don't worry, son, have faith. *There is an appointed time for everything.* Remember that, everything works out as it's meant to.' He glanced upstairs. 'I'm going to have a nose up there, see what the lads are up to.'

Jake watched Francis mount the stairs and shook his head. He was glad Francis had his faith and could turn to quoting the Bible for comfort, but all Jake had was the cold hard facts. The evidence of his eyes was enough, and it weighed heavy on his heart. Even if Will did return, what would be left of the man he—

Jake stopped himself and swallowed hard, unable to even complete that thought. Instead, he walked into the lounge to see how PC Wardlaw was doing.

Wardlaw still had his own cup of tea sitting beside Will's laptop, which the police constable was looking through trying to access Will's email account. Wardlaw was the only officer that Jake had made a cuppa for, mostly because the young man had been so friendly when he arrived; so chatty, in fact, that Jake felt he couldn't really refuse the request for a decent cup of tea. Apparently, the tea at the station wasn't much 'cop'. Wardlaw thought the joke was hysterical, but Jake wasn't sure he agreed, but he'd still laughed along with the officer.

He seemed very good at his job, since from the moment he had stepped into the house his eyes had wandered everywhere, taking in the smallest details, including running his eyes over Jake a few times.

A cable ran from the laptop's USB port to a small mobile hard drive, no doubt to back up all the relevant information Wardlaw was able to pull up, which he would later analyse at the station.

Wardlaw looked up, and offered Jake a large smile, his blue eyes sparkling with his perfect white teeth.

'Hi, Jake, hope this intrusion isn't too overwhelming for you.'

Jake shook his head, quite glad that someone was calling him by his first name. Mr Caulfield was a little tiresome after a while. 'No it's...' He stopped and offered a weak smile. 'Well, yeah, just a bit I guess.'

'We'll be out of your hair soon.' Wardlaw budged over so Jake could also sit on the sofa. Jake gratefully took the seat and looked at the laptop.

The screen was full of code that meant absolutely nothing to him. Although, from his small understanding of computer systems he knew that Wardlaw was now running the laptop in MS-DOS mode. Full of command prompts that were gibberish to Jake.

'How's it going?' he asked, hoping Wardlaw would dumb it down for him.

'Well,' Wardlaw began, 'I've pulled up Will's email account, and found a few emails from and to a Charlie Connolly, which is presumably the same Charlie that your mate went to see. At least one of those emails was sent a few days ago.'

'A few days ago?' Jake blinked, moving in closer to the laptop as if he could somehow mysteriously see the email through the MS-DOS coding. 'What did it say?'

'I never really read it, better software at the station, but I caught a little bit of it. Something about why did Will do something or other to Charlie. It'll be read properly later. I've pulled quite a lot of useful information from this baby, and I'm sure it'll be a big help.'

'Why would Will do what?' Jake shook his head. 'So, Will isn't with Charlie now?'

'I honestly have no idea,' Wardlaw said, patting Jake's knee. 'Could be Charlie knew we'd look at the emails and sent this to put us off the scent.'

'Thanks, that does wonders for my mind,' Jake said, with a wry smile.

Wardlaw smiled back, and patted Jake's knee again. 'I wouldn't worry too much about it right now. We'll know more later, and you'll be informed.'

Wardlaw shut the laptop down and stood up, leaning over the table to unhook his mobile hard drive and place it in his bag. Jake watched him, his eyes drawn to the way Wardlaw's trousers tightly clung to his ass. With a flush of embarrassment, Jake looked away quickly and stood.

'Um,' he began, not sure what to say.

If Wardlaw noticed Jake's awkwardness he didn't mention it. Instead, he removed his pad from his pocket and jotted something down.

'Right, that's me done here. I'll get onto this,' Wardlaw said patting his bag, 'as soon as I get to the station. This is my number,' he added, tearing a piece of paper off the pad and handing it to Jake. 'Call me.'

Jake took the paper and offered his thanks. He watched Wardlaw leave the lounge, his eyes once again lingering.

Jake took a deep breath and looked at the paper, expecting an extension number at Fulham Police Station.

Instead, what he found himself looking at was a mobile number, and a scribbled message; 'call me if you want to meet up, Toby. xx'.

5. What We Choose to Remember

Their discussions last night haunted her throughout the next day. Jordan had popped over, catching the end of their little Chinese splurge, and he seemed to get on well with Sam. Which is why Lizette was now cornering him during their lunch break.

'Well...?'

They were outside, in the secret spot teachers used to smoke, away from the students. The sound of Southend life filled the air; vehicles moving, people chattering, but Lizette blocked it out. She was focused only on what Jordan had to say.

He took a drag of his cigarette. 'I still think you're stupid. Yeah, he seems like a nice fella, but I don't know... I wouldn't take in someone I don't know like that. No matter how good-looking he is.'

'You think he's good-looking?' Lizette asked, trying to keep her tone as innocent as possible.

'I mean, I'm not blind, am I?' Jordan grinned. 'I mean, if I met him in a nightclub, then yeah, I would.'

'Hang on... Are you coming out to me?'

'Didn't think I needed to. Does it matter if I like men or women? Or both?'

'Well, no, I suppose not. I just assumed...'

Jordan ran a hand through his perfectly sculpted brown hair. 'You think it's fair to only share this with one gender?'

'I...' Lizette looked away, leaning against the wall. 'I just didn't think...' She shook her head. 'Look, we're going off on a tangent now.'

Jordan shrugged. 'Are we? You obviously like him. Saw the way you looked at him.'

'Like you said, he's good looking, I'd be stupid to deny that. But he needs help, not some sex-starved woman hitting on him.'

'Sex-starved...?'

Lizette clamped her mouth shut. She had worked with Jordan for a while now, but they'd never really talked about their sex lives before. Usually just small talk, politics, sharing the latest memes... all the usual shit people passed time with.

'I mean, if you like him, and he likes you...' Jordan shrugged again. He did that a lot, Lizette realised for the first time. 'Conventional is boring, isn't it? A man entering your life like he has... Well, bound to be a little... intoxicating, right?'

'I suppose,' Lizette said quietly. She couldn't argue with Jordan, but she didn't want to admit to any of it either. She wanted to help Sam, not seduce him. 'Not the first stray I've taken in.'

'He's no cat.'

'No.'

'Do what you feel is right, Lizzie, or, I don't know, do what is wrong? Sometimes it's good to live a bit dangerously.'

She took the cigarette off Jordan and took a long drag. She didn't smoke, but suddenly she needed to.

She coughed, and smoke spewed out from her mouth.

Horrible.

'I'm suddenly realising there's a side to you that you keep well hidden,' she told him.

Jordan shrugged. 'Sure. I mean, isn't that true for all of us?'

*

Normally a feeling of déjà vu would have been no big deal, just an odd quirk of perception, but for Sam it was so strong that he felt a wave of nausea with it. Southend Central was only two stops from Chalkwell so he elected to stand, hoping for a bit more air than he'd get if he remained sitting down.

As he stood, steadying himself with the handrail, a few people looked up. One old dear even reached out a hand to help steady him, not that her frail arm would have been much use if he had keeled over. But the thought was appreciated.

'You okay, love?' she asked.

Sam offered her a smile and said, 'Yeah, I'm good,' lying through his teeth. He felt anything but good. 'Had a bit too much last night, I reckon.'

The woman nodded knowingly. 'Enjoy it while you're young, darling.'

'I am,' he said and looked out of the window.

He actually had no idea how old he was, but judging by his looks he assumed he was either in his late twenties or early thirties. He and Lizette had discussed such a topic last night, and she erred on nearer her age, but Sam said he didn't feel that old. Which led to him getting a playful slap.

The train stopped briefly at Westcliff, and although no one got on, he was thankful for the gust of air that wafted in as soon as the doors opened. Once the train was underway again, he remained as he was, leaning against the closed door, looking out through the window, watching the backs of houses as they passed by.

He inhaled deeply, glad that the wave of nausea had passed. Although the intense déjà vu looked set to stay.

A sense that he'd taken this trip before, and for all he knew he probably had. If they had been correct about London, then it seemed likely that he could have taken this journey into Southend. The map above the door said this train serviced Fenchurch Street, and that was in London. He wasn't sure how he knew it; he just did.

He stepped off the train and headed for the ticket barrier, brandishing the return ticket he had bought with the money Lizette had loaned him, as if some force was nudging him on. With every step he took, the sense of familiarity increased.

He emerged from the station to find that the sky was still cloudy, although behind those patches of grey clouds was much blue sky; as if the heavens themselves were trying to shake off the storm of the previous night, but the clouds held on.

The storm wasn't finished yet.

There was a road verging off to the left and a path to the right. Before him was the rear of the South Essex College complex, where Lizette worked, but he ignored the building and turned right, knowing exactly where he needed to be.

He walked down a slight incline and came out into the heart of the pedestrianised Southend High Street, the main shopping thoroughfare of Southend-on-Sea. He stopped abruptly, almost forcing a group of youngsters to collide into him.

Around him were the usual group of shops, including Greggs the Bakery, Shoe Zone, a building society, and the place he knew would be there – Starbucks. He made a move towards the coffee shop. There was some presence in there, calling him.

He barely got within three feet of the shop when his legs gave way beneath him and he crumbled to the ground. He looked up, but everything was a blur, strange shapes moving around him. He closed his eyes tight, trying to block everything out and took a deep breath.

He was sitting in Starbucks, watching a man buy them a coffee. His backpack and bag were on the floor beside him. He noticed that Starbucks had Wi-Fi and he wished he'd brought his laptop with him, not that Jake was any kind of net junkie; he barely used it. But Will wanted to tell Jake about the curious turn of events the train journey to Southend had brought him. He'd certainly be interested to learn that Will was finally stepping out of the box. Will felt for his phone in his jeans pocket.

He couldn't go into much detail with text, but he could tell Jake...

He looked up as the man approached him, feeling a guilty sense of pleasure in the way the man took him into his deep eyes. Things were going in an unexpected direction, but he wasn't complaining. He removed his hand from his pocket, leaving the phone there. Telling Jake could keep.

'Hey, you okay, mate?'

Sam opened his eyes and the youth who had been reaching down pulled back in surprise. Sam didn't understand why, but the youth soon recovered and offered him a hand. Sam ignored the help, his hands automatically going to his throat, clawing for the fresh air rushing into his lungs.

Finally, his breathing slowed to a normal rate, and he allowed the youth to help him back up. He looked around, trying to focus on one thing, but his eyes continued to roam, not able to fix on anything.

'You sure you're okay, man?'

Sam looked at the youth and nodded. 'Yes,' he said.

The youth was looking at Sam oddly.

'Panic attacks,' Sam explained, wondering where he kept on getting these wild excuses from. 'They come on every now and then.'

'Right,' the youth said slowly, but before he could say anything else a female voice interrupted him.

'Sam?'

Sam blinked, and his vision came back into focus. Lizette was there, manoeuvring herself around the helpful stranger. She smiled up at the youth and reached out to take Sam's hand like an errant child.

'He's with me,' she said, and Sam allowed her to lead him away.

Sam looked back, but the youth had turned away, once again joining his mates, the story about the weirdo who'd collapsed in the middle of the high street soon to become another anecdote to share with his buddies.

Sam's eyes were drawn to Starbucks as another man emerged, and immediately a thought shot through Sam's mind; *you know who I am*. But as fast as it arrived, the thought was gone.

Once they were out of earshot, they slowed down and Lizette looked at Sam. 'What happened? I was on the way to the station when I noticed the commotion.'

Sam glanced at Lizette, then back at the way they'd come, trying his best to remember. But there was nothing. 'I have no idea. I remember getting on the train, and then I'm on the ground back there, some guy trying to help me up.'

Lizette frowned. 'That's worrying.'

'You're telling me. Try living it. It's like some fog is shrouding my mind. And,' he added, glancing back, 'that bloke kept looking at me weirdly.'

'Aye, I noticed. I think it's the eyes.'

'Oh.'

'I'm thinking a pair of sunglasses won't go amiss.'

'I wish I knew why my eyes were like this, some birth defect, or maybe...' Sam stopped suddenly and felt the colour drain out of his face. 'Oh my... Liz,' he said, grabbing both her arms and looking around the high street. 'I've been here before! I don't know how I know, but... I just *know*.'

'That's progress,' Lizette said, trying to calm him down with her arms. 'But let's take a chill pill here, people are starting to stare.'

'Sorry,' he said.

'Good,' Lizette said, smiling at him. 'Memory loss is one thing, but an insane person is something else entirely.' She placed her arm in his and together they continued up the high street. 'Time to get you some new togs.'

'Lizette, I can't keep on spending your money.'

'Why, do you have some secret stash I don't know about?'

'Maybe I do, but if I do then I don't know about it, either.'

They both laughed at this, and Sam felt all the better for it. As overwhelming as this was for him, he was glad he had someone like Lizette with him to help him find the humour in himself.

'Don't worry, once you've found your old life again you can pay me back. Which reminds me, I've got something I want you to try when you get home. All morning my mind's been running around, distracted by you,' Lizette said, pointing at him softly, 'and so I looked up a few techniques for helping to focus on the details of memory. Not sure if they'll work for you, but could be worth a try.'

Sam swallowed hard. He wanted to remember, but there was a feeling in his gut that told him not to go there. 'Okay, then,' he said, pretending he was up for the idea.

*

Frederick rushed out of Starbucks and into the gloomy weather. He skidded to a halt and looked around frantically. He was sure... But, no, there were so many people out in the town centre it was impossible to tell.

He looked up towards the Victoria; too many people heading that way to focus in. He briefly spotted Liz glancing back, but his attention was soon returned to Starbucks when the door opened and Reisha emerged, looking flustered. He threw an apologetic look her way. She shrugged it off with a laugh.

'Thought you were bailing on me, then.'

'No, sorry. I thought I sensed...' Frederick shook his head. 'Remember I told you that a fledgling upiór shares a psychic bond with their maker? Well, I could have sworn I sensed Will then.'

Reisha looked around as if she'd be able to spot him from Frederick's description. 'But no?'

'Quite.' Frederick let out a sigh of frustration. He looked back at Starbucks. 'So much for our coffee rendezvous. And besides, here comes Eryn.' He reached out and kissed the back of her hand. 'You go now; I don't want anyone meeting you just yet.'

Reisha looked disappointed, but she accepted it. 'Right, I'll call you as soon as my contact gets in touch.' She offered an encouraging smile. 'Looks promising, though. For both of us,' she added with a wink.

Frederick nodded then shooed her away. Taking the hint, she turned and lost herself in the crowd, only a second before Eryn saw Frederick standing there. Not without a little amusement, Frederick noticed that Eryn looked mightily pissed off.

'What, thought you could lose me that easy did you?' She asked, her anger making her Welsh accent more pronounced.

Frederick made a show of disappointment. 'Worth a shot.' In truth he had no intention of losing Eryn, as much as he loathed to spend a copious amount of time with her, Frederick was sure as hell going to keep tabs on her.

*

'I guess he thinks I can handle things okay without him, otherwise he'd be back already. Will's always had faith in me like that.'

Becky Medeiros eyed Stephen Krueger, not quite buying his false modesty. The young man spoke with humility, but you could see the arrogance behind his eyes. His bearing of confidence was very affected; it was the first thing she'd spotted when they had arrived at Coffee @ Town's End, that and his sweaty palms when they shook hands. It didn't mean he was hiding anything necessarily; some people just got nervous when talking to the police, putting up a false sense of bravado in case the police knew something they didn't. In her experience everybody had something to hide, alas most times that something had very little to do with the case being investigated.

'Doesn't it strike you as odd that he's not made any effort to contact you? Especially considering the disciplinary with...' She checked her notes. 'Kurtwood Kellerman.'

Mr Krueger nodded and leaned back in his chair. 'Yeah that's odd. Will was quite pissed off when he learned that Kurt might be fiddling the books. But the problem with Will is this,' he added, leaning forward again, resting his elbows on his table and linking his fingers together. 'Will's not very good with confrontations, never has been. He likes to think he is, but when it comes down to it, situations run away with themselves. He has no control of them, which is probably why he called me in to help with it.'

'And when is this confrontation due to take place?'

'Any time after Thursday, when the paperwork is returned. The evidence against Kurt is very conclusive.'

'So, the sooner he returns the better for business? You can get rid of Mr Kellerman, supposedly promote someone else to take over his position.' Medeiros looked at her notes again, pretending to read something.

Really, she just wanted to think a moment. She didn't doubt anything Mr Krueger said, but she was getting a feeling from him. That he knew more than he was saying. She passed a quick look with her colleague, who nodded slightly. He, too, had a *feeling*.

'Mr Townsend's disappearance must be putting extra strain on you? Stepping up to the plate to do his job, as well as supervise the management of the unit once run by Mr Kellerman?'

'You're telling me. But it's all good, I can deal.' Mr Krueger's laugh wasn't a natural one. The nervousness was quite blatant. 'Will be glad when he returns.'

'I don't doubt it. And when did you last see him?'

'Erm, last time I heard from him was Thursday night.'

'That'll be the twenty-fourth?'

Krueger did the mental arithmetic, and nodded. 'Yup. He was well stoked about his forthcoming trip, couldn't wait to step into a different zone and see how things went with Charlie.'

'Is that silver Volkswagen Lupo outside yours?'

Medeiros threw the question at him so abruptly that Krueger barely had time to consider any other answer than yes. She nodded at this, and scribbled something onto her pad, not taking her eyes off him, daring him to change his answer or add something.

He didn't bite, which suited Medeiros well. The neighbours on Barclay Road had already told the officers that a silver Volkswagen Lupo had been seen on the street the same time Mr Townsend had left, but none had a registration number to offer up.

She would have to check the CCTV for that street, once she had made a note of the registration of Mr Krueger's car.

She wasn't sure what Mr Krueger would benefit from Mr Townsend's disappearance, but he was certainly hiding something. And that he'd seen Mr Townsend on the morning of the twenty-fifth was almost certain. Perhaps there was something in his will; maybe the business was to be bequeathed to Mr Krueger on the event of Mr Townsend's death? She had known of worst motives.

First things first, though. She stood up and put her pad away.

'Well, thank you for your time, Mr Krueger. We'll be in touch.'

*

Once they were gone, Steve leaned his back against the door, and took a deep breath.

Allowing the officers time to get downstairs, he waited, then grabbed his jacket off the back of the chair and removed a small plastic tube from the inside pocket. He unfastened the lid and took a sip of the thick glutinous liquid.

He had to make a call, but first he wanted to relieve the anxiety he was feeling. He knew he was caught up in something big, but no one mentioned anything about police involvement.

He closed his eyes and sealed the tube, waiting for the Red Source to settle in his system.

The cop had caught him out on the thing about his car, but so what? Even if they discovered he was parked up on Will's road on Friday, what did it prove? He didn't know, but he didn't want to risk it.

Eyes still closed, he steadied himself with both hands resting on the table. It was always the same; the initial rush as the Red Source became one with him. But it soon passed, and all his concerns went with it.

He was somewhere else...

'Where shall we go next?' Anton asked, his Russian accent thick and sexy.

Steve looked up into his eyes and smiled. He put his arm in Anton's and shifted the weight of his purse under the other arm. 'You promised something special at the hotel, so...?'

Anton grinned. 'Yes. The hotel. Good choice, Grace.'

On some level, Steve knew he wasn't really there, that he was not a woman called Grace, but still, he remembered the night clearly.

Recreational drugs were designed to take you out of yourself, an escape from the real world. Red Source was the next level. It literally took you from your life and deposited you into the life of someone else. It could last minutes or hours, depending on how much Red Source you took. But eventually you would return to your own life, higher than you'd even been before. Calm, relaxed, indestructible. At least for a time.

After a few minutes, as Anton and Grace entered the hotel, Steve returned to his office.

He looked around, and smiled. He reached into his trousers' pocket and pulled out his Blackberry. No longer anxious, but still knowing he had to make a call to Southend, Steve searched in his contacts list under R and found Robin's number.

It was about time he found out how Robin's meeting with Will had gone.

*

They were just nearing the blood bank to talk to Rhys when the mobile in Frederick's jeans went off. Eryn arched an eyebrow at him, but Frederick ignored it and removed his phone anyway.

'We don't have time for social calls. More important things to do.'

Frederick looked at the caller ID. 'This might be important.' Before Eryn could ask why, Frederick flipped the phone open and placed it to his ear. 'Stephen,' he said, adding false pleasure to his voice. 'What news is there?'

'News? Mate, I was hoping you'd have some for me. Like good news from the Three.'

Frederick looked at Eryn who was showing no sign that she was paying attention, which of course meant she was listening closely. Ah well, if Stephen continued to push he could always let Eryn speak to him. That would be a conversation worth missing.

Frederick's wandering thoughts were dragged back by Stephen's voice. 'I've just had the police questioning me, ain't I? About Will. They're poking about, and I reckon they fancy I had something to do with him missing. Yeah, you heard that right, he's been reported missing. Maybe you want to tell him to phone home?'

'Yeah, I'll have a word with him,' Frederick said and closed the phone.

For a moment Eryn said nothing, just focused on the road they were crossing. Frederick appreciated the gesture, but he knew the silence wouldn't last long.

'Been planning Will's arrival for a long while then, haven't you? Secret contacts in London.'

'Well, we've all got our secrets, Eryn. Don't you think?'

As soon as he asked, Frederick wished he hadn't. Revealing that he was suspicious about Eryn would immediately put her on her guard, and would make Celeste's job a lot harder. Eryn merely looked up at the thinning clouds, chewing her lip. Frederick shrugged, realising he didn't actually care. All that mattered to him was finding Will.

Together, still in silence, they entered the blood bank.

*

Jake stood at the backdoor, smoking his third cigarette in a row. The house was empty once again, the police having all left a couple of hours ago. Once they had gone, Jake had done a circuit of the house to make sure everything was still in place and was happy to find that the police had been quite respectful, barely disturbing anything, and that which they did they returned. Francis had left only fifteen minutes ago, staying on to talk about old times.

Jake was incredibly thankful for the old man's support, and even more so for the chat. It was nice to take his mind off recent events and think back to more innocent times, times when he and Will used to just hang out without the pressures of life in the way. Jake getting into all kinds of mischief, not that his folks knew much about it as Francis often picked up the pieces before his folks returned home from work. Will never got into mischief though, he was always the straight one, the kid who behaved, merely watched, his silent disapproval only serving to egg Jake on in his latest endeavour.

Intentionally, or just coincidentally, Jake wasn't sure, but in their reminisces Francis brought up a time twenty-plus years back. He and his wife were enjoying the Saturday sports, while Jake and Will were upstairs in Will's bedroom. The way Francis told it at one point he had to turn the TV down, thinking he heard some unusual noise coming from above. He and the then-Mrs Townsend exchanged knowing glances and turned the sound back on, letting the teenage lads do their thing.

While Francis told this tale, Jake remembered his own side, although he didn't share it with Francis.

He and Will had indeed been messing around upstairs, Jake talking about the girls he fancied, and being thirteen it didn't go much beyond a quick grope here and there. While they talked, teenage Jake had found himself aroused, and before he knew it Will was reaching out and unzipping his jeans for him. Caught in the moment, at least that was how

Jake had rationalised it for the last twenty-two years, he didn't resist and quite happily laid back and allowed Will to...

Jake took a final toke on the cigarette and outed the butt against the wall.

He was reminded of his dream the other night, a dream that wasn't dissimilar to what had occurred between Will and him when they were thirteen.

'No,' he said, and turned and re-entered the house. He didn't know what he was going to do next, so he just wandered around the house, his mind constantly returning to that memory of twenty-two years ago.

For years he'd blanked a lot of it out and often tried to brazen it whenever Will thought to remind him of the moment, but now as he wandered through the house, vacant as it was of Will, he remembered more.

How he had taken great pleasure at the feel of Will's hand around him, and how he too had reached into Will's own trousers and...

He mounted the stairs.

He could continue to convince himself that it was merely an act of teenage exploration, and how he'd been lost to the moment, but the sharp sting in his heart brought on by the memory told him otherwise. And then there was the dream, and what he'd done afterwards... Although he loathed to admit it, he knew exactly what it was.

Exactly the same thing that had made his mind turn to Will yesterday morning while having sex with Amy.

He sat down on Will's bed and reached out for one of the pictures that sat on the small bedside cabinet.

It was a picture of him and Will taken a couple of years ago. They were on the grass near the Serpentine in Kensington Gardens, Jake sitting there laughing, while Will rested his head snugly in Jake's lap.

Jake took a deep breath. He remembered the day well, although as with every other moment of brief intimacy over the years, he had blocked out, or just blatantly ignored, the truth of his feelings.

Like a week ago, when he and Will had last spent some proper time together. Jake had convinced himself that the hug in the backyard was just that, a hug of support between two close friends. But the stirring in his nether regions told a different story.

But it was ridiculous. He only fancied women; he knew that as surely as he knew he could have done nothing to prevent his mother's illness claiming her. All he had to do was look to Amy to realise that truth, and yet...

A small drop of water hit the glass covering the picture, and for a moment Jake wondered if the ceiling was leaking. Then he realised.

He tried to blink away the tears, but instead they fell harder. He brought the picture to his chest and flopped back on the bed.

In deep shudders of breath, the sobs soon emerged, and with each one he felt his heart break just that bit more.

*

Sam stood before the mirror above the mantle in Lizette's living room. It was time to try the memory exercise to which Lizette had pointed him. It was all about using visual stimuli to access the memory; in this case it was the sunglasses Lizette had bought him.

The last flash of familiarity had come when he had been trying the glasses on in New Look, and she'd made a gag about how he had better not be one of those annoying pretentious people who wore sunglasses indoors. For a split second he had been somewhere else, but as with all snatches it quickly passed and he was left with no idea what his mind had been trying to tell him.

So now he stood before the mirror, the glasses in his hands. He looked down, curious to see that his hands were shaking slightly. Nerves, no doubt. If this exercise worked, then he'd remember something of his past, and he still could not escape the feeling that it was a path he did not really want to walk.

There was something dangerous in his past, an event so bad that it made him run away as naked as the day he was born. Did he really want to access such an incident? Sometimes the past was best left in the past, isn't that what he'd heard before?

Let the dead rest, and the past remain the past.

Fortune had favoured him, and he'd found Lizette. Although it had only been a couple of days since he'd become aware of himself, naked in the wet garden, he felt like he'd known Lizette a lifetime. There was something good going on between them, and he didn't want to spoil that. Somehow, he just knew that if he rediscovered his own past, everything he had with Lizette would be put in jeopardy, and did he really want that? The answer was simple; no, he did not.

Yet, at the same time, he knew he could not honestly live like this. Moments of his days missing as he blacked out, his body going on automatic, coming to and finding himself in strange situations. It all came down to need, not want, and it had to be done. Answers were needed, even if those answers were not ones he wanted.

Sam took a deep breath and placed the glasses on. He stood there, looking at his reflection, but nothing happened.

'Bugger,' he muttered, but didn't move, feeling a little foolish for expecting instant results.

Not one to give up, at least he didn't feel like he was, he refocused his attention on his reflection, blocking out everything else until all he could see was his face.

There was something wrong here; perhaps it was the way the twins were looking at him? Will wasn't entirely sure, but he'd been assured that he was okay. The male twin, in the glasses, bothered him mostly; hiding behind the shades, he appeared to be looking at Will while the second twin, the girl with the electric blue hi-lites, whispered something in her twin's ear.

The converted factory they stood in didn't have much in the way of windows, and what with the low lighting Will didn't think that the man had sensitive eyes. Will turned to Frederick, mindful that the twins continued to look at him, electric-blue still whispering while her shaded brother simply nodded in silent agreement.

Sam stood there, facing the mirror, but he was no longer seeing. Blood seeped out of his ears in a slow trickle. The memory exercise had worked, and a floodgate had been opened. Behind his sunglasses his red eyes burned with a fire and, in his mind, he was somewhere else, somewhere he just knew was Moldavia in 1790...

All around him were flames, but he stepped nimbly past them, holding the book close to his chest lest it get burned with the monastery. It was essential that he got this book into the hands of Frederick Holtzrichter, who was waiting in the vestibule as instructed.

It was a great pity that his incomplete notes had already joined the flames in the crypt, and as a result, the importance of getting the book away from Moldavia was greater still.

Plans had been set in motion so long ago, and just like him, Frederick had his own part to play. But first of all, Frederick needed the book...

6. When A Link is Forged

'So, where is it stashed to?' Eryn's voice floated in from the living room.

Frederick looked up from his laptop, which was opened on the kitchen side while he made coffee for both of them. He didn't like the idea of having Eryn at his flat, but then there was a lot going on he didn't like.

'Where's what?'

'The Book.'

Frederick poked his head through the doorway. Eryn was spread out on the lounger, leafing through *Seeking the Seeker*.

'That book not interesting enough for you?'

'Not really. Nothing new here.' She threw the book on the little coffee table in the middle of the room. 'Usual crap spouted by Julius. I'm talking about the real deal, en' I?'

'It's in a secret place,' Frederick said and went back into the kitchen.

He wasn't convinced by the 'usual crap' line. Ever since he'd made that comment about secrets, Eryn had said much about the Brotherhood that painted them in a bad light. True, she rarely had nice things to say about anything, but she was making too much of a point of badmouthing the Brotherhood. And with the likelihood of her betrayal of the Three, there was no way Frederick was going to let Eryn near the Book. Only he and Celeste knew where it was, an arrangement that had been agreed on hundreds of years ago. Curious that Eryn should be interested now.

'So, what you up to then?'

Frederick let out a sigh, annoyed by Eryn's presence. He stood up straight and allowed Eryn to see the laptop screen. She whistled.

'Don't think Celeste is going to be happy about this, do you?'

Frederick leaned over and opened the window. The place was getting stuffy. Although there was still a nice breeze coming in from the North Sea, it was incredibly humid outside, and worse inside.

'She probably won't be, but if Maia's planning something she'll let slip on her ChatBook. She usually does.'

Eryn scrolled down the page on the screen, browsing through the comments and poems. 'Emotional, en' she? This how you've been able to keep one step ahead of her then?'

'Yes. Didn't take too long to find her on ChatBook. She has no idea I'm one of her hundreds of friends.' Frederick gave a bitter laugh. 'Doubt she knows most of them, they've just been added to make her seem more popular than she is. If she isn't hunting upiór, then she's sitting at home alone emoting.'

Eryn looked up. 'Or teaching little brother how not to be a good hunter.'

Frederick didn't respond, instead he turned to look out of the window and across the Thames Estuary to Kent beyond. 'There've been no updates on her page for a day, which is unusual. Even on a hunt, she tends to update from her phone, even if she's just tweeting.'

'Tweeting?' Eryn looked genuinely puzzled.

'You really haven't moved into the twenty-first century, have you? You're becoming a relic, Eryn.'

In response, Eryn narrowed her eyes. 'Guess she wants to surprise daddy,' she said, getting back to her point.

Frederick looked back at Eryn and found himself smiling. 'Would have been more of a surprise if she hadn't...'

He blinked, looking up at Eryn who was now standing above him. Frederick looked around. He was on the floor, slumped against the wall beneath the window, his head banging.

'What happened?'

'You passed out.' Eryn reached out a hand and helped Frederick to his feet. 'I'd say it was the humidity, but since when did humidity make our people pass out?'

Frederick wasn't paying attention. For a moment he had been somewhere else. He closed his eyes, trying to remember where. He could see a woman's face, distorted as if underwater. No, not underwater. Reflected in a mirror. And not a woman, just a painting of one. Red flowing hair, white dress... And there was another face. Just for a second but...yes! It was Will.

'We need to get back to Celeste,' Frederick said, and rushed past Eryn without further explanation.

*

Jake looked down at the ringing phone in his hand. It was the third time that Amy had called in the last two hours, probably chancing her arm while having a sneaky fag break out of the office. He knew he ought to answer, but he didn't know what he could say to her. By the time he remembered he was supposed to meet her for lunch, he was well over an hour late. He sent her a text, apologising and telling her that the police invasion had lasted longer than expected. It was the first time he had felt the need to lie to Amy... but he still didn't understand why.

He had done nothing wrong, and yet his mind was awash in a tsunami of confusion. He knew he should speak to her, but there was so much going on in his head that part of him didn't want to. Something was stirring in him, and it was alarming. So much was becoming clear. All those years of close calls were starting to make a sense to him that had been missing before, but he still didn't like it.

The feelings raging in him brought with them a deep sense of duplicity, just the act of actually having such emotions was a betrayal of everything that was developing between Amy and him. He'd been a player in his time, and he'd never really cared deeply for any of the women he'd slept with. Amy was different; there was a real closeness between them that he did not want to fuck up, but how could he honestly be with her if such feelings about Will persisted?

He looked up from his position on the back doorstep. The clouds were getting denser in their greyness. It looked like London was in for another storm.

'Right, enough of this shit,' he said to the sky, and flipped open his phone.

He couldn't go on betraying Amy like this. He reached into his pocket for his phone, and a slip of paper fell out with it. He leaned down, picked the slip up and looked at it.

He felt like he was making a mistake, but sometimes the advice of someone outside the situation was necessary. Or at least that's what Jake told himself as he started tapping in the number on the paper, while his mind returned to the memory of Toby Wardlaw leaning down in front of him...

*

'Who else could I turn to? No one else has the mind-trawling skill you have, so I...'

Celeste placed a finger on Frederick's lips to quiet him. They were alone in her private chambers. To achieve what she set out to do she needed some silence and tranquillity. A mood her chambers were designed to enhance, which didn't come as a surprise to Frederick. He wasn't helping matters none, since he couldn't seem to stop nattering. He felt like a schoolboy about to meet his crush, babbling away to hide his nervousness. Celeste merely smiled at him, as if she understood.

It had been a long time since the palace in Prussia, and that night when he had emerged from the pontus, but he couldn't remember Celeste being so nervous about him. But then, he supposed, Celeste was over five hundred years old at that point already, and he was almost two hundred years less than that now. Barely a kid compared to Celeste.

She sat opposite him. 'Close your eyes and try to remember that moment you felt Willem.'

'Felt him? I saw through his eyes.'

Celeste's brow furrowed, creasing her dark skin. 'Another strange aspect of all this. Your connection, although blocked, is much deeper than is usual for a maker and the fledgling. Interesting.'

Frederick didn't say anything, but he wondered if it had something to do with the Ancient's blood. He had always felt different from other upiór, ever since he had drunk the blood of Wamukota; could it be that it enhanced his psychic connection with Will? Frederick supposed it was possible. He had never made a fledgling before, so he had not put the theory to the test. Witnessed many Rebirths, but never instigated one until Friday.

'Close your eyes, *mon toujours*.'

Frederick did as he was told and immediately he felt Celeste's mind in his. From therein words were no longer needed.

She guided his mind back. He was standing in his kitchen talking to Eryn, discussing Maia's ChatBook. He felt Celeste's disappointment, but with it came a sense of resignation, as if she had half expected him to look for his daughter himself. Then, as if a flash of lightning had struck his brain, he was standing somewhere else.

The room was reflected in the mirror, which showed him Will's face in reverse. Will was staring hard, concentrating through the sunglasses he wore, at his own reflection. While Will was focused, Frederickceleste took the chance to look around. The room was decorated in a light green, with pale red coving running along the perimeter of the ceiling. The furniture was plush; a comfortable looking sofa and chair, a coffee table set before the sofa. There was little in the room to identify the house from a thousand others in the Essex area, even the magazines on the table said little more than the owner of the house had an interest in history.

The Celeste part of the fused mind recognised the painting that took pride of place on the rear wall; Dante Gabriel Rossetti's *Lady Lilith*. And with the image came a memory, one that belonged to Celeste.

She had known Rossetti, one of many famous artists from her centuries of life, and discussed at length his techniques while on a visit to England in 1877, convincing him to paint his own sister and mother. It was an interesting memory from Frederick's point of view, since at that time he had been in France, trying to get his head around the Book still, with the help of the recently recruited Melinda, and knew very little of Celeste's solo activities. But it did not help him in learning where Will was.

They focused on sounds. The background buzz of music could be heard, but it did not come from the room in which Will stood, rather from the house next door. Muffled by brick, drywall and insulation. The house was silent, although the gentle sound of small padded feet could be heard from the hallway beyond the room; a cat going about its business.

Outside they could hear the gentle breeze, the sound of water being lapped up against the beach. Frederickceleste wasn't sure that helped much, after all there were plenty of homes along the seafront of the Southend area, including Frederick's. But it...

All around Wamukota were flames, but he stepped nimbly past them, holding the book close to his chest lest it get burned with the monastery. It was essential that he get this book into the hands of Frederick Holtzrichter, who was waiting in the vestibule as instructed. It was a great pity that his incomplete notes had already joined the flames in the crypt, and as a result, the importance of getting the book away from Moldavia was greater still.

Plans had been set in motion so long ago, and just like him, Frederick had his own part to play. But first of all, he needed the book. The blood Frederick had supped on, Wamukota's very own blood, would help him in his forthcoming task, but without the book, Frederick would not know what to do.

Wamukota had not lived over four thousand years, became the Ancient upiór (as they now called themselves), to see his mission fail along with his body. Frederick was to be the custodian of prophecy and...

Neither Celeste nor Frederick had the opportunity to ponder why they had been dragged back to 1790, to the burning monastery of Cāpriana, or just why it was that Will was reliving the events in his own mind, for the shock of being pulled back to that point in time so forcefully, had knocked them both out cold.

*

Lizette approached her house, her briefcase in one hand, coat in the other. The storm that had been threatening to start was still being pushed aside by the warmer weather.

She was looking forward to being home; couldn't wait to see how Sam looked in his new clothes. She'd seen a few of them, as he stepped out of the changing room to show her, but she had yet to see the full ensemble. Up to now, he'd been stuck in another man's style, but as of today, he'd be wearing clothes that he had chosen. Clothes maketh man, and each had their own tastes and she hoped that the clothes he'd bought indicated something of the real Sam.

Although she didn't want to admit it, she was also curious to see what he looked like in the black Ben Sherman sports briefs he'd bought from TK Maxx. Underwear hadn't occurred to her until he'd mentioned that wearing jeans without them didn't half chafe his nads. With each moment, even with his cultured accent, his words were getting more and more West London.

She passed the man-height bushes that acted like a wall around the perimeter of her house and up the path. She opened the door with a big smile and called out to Sam.

There was no answer.

She closed the door softly and listened for any sound of him, but nothing. No scuffing of feet upstairs, no background buzz of the TV, not even the sound of the shower. She glanced down as a couple of her cats wandered past.

'You kids seen Sam?' she asked, and Garth looked at the living room, then carried on his way into the kitchen, obviously expecting to be fed. 'Be with you in a minute,' she told the cats and, after dumping her briefcase and coat on the stairs, entered the living room.

'Hi,' she said as soon as she spotted him standing by the mirror, checking out his new sunglasses. 'Remember what I said about pretentious people wearing sunglasses indoors? Well, you're definitely winning no points here. And what's with the old...' Her voice trailed off as two things struck her simultaneously.

One, that he was indeed still wearing the borrowed clothes, and two, that he hadn't budged an inch since she entered the living room.

'Sam?'

Still nothing.

Suddenly full of dread, she stepped up to him and gently placed a hand on his shoulder. He didn't flinch. Lizette looked at his reflection; she on his right, Rossetti's painting on his left. She leaned in closer and whispered his name in his ear. Sam reacted with a start, his movement so sudden that Lizette almost fell over, but she regained her balance in time for Sam to rip off his glasses and point at the mirror.

'It's you!' he shouted, then staggered backwards.

Lizette moved quickly to steady him. He blinked a few times and looked around wildly.

'What...? Where...? Who...?' His eyes came to rest on Lizette. 'You. Where am I?'

'Sam, it's me, Lizette. Come back to me.'

For a moment he just looked at her, and the hatred written over his face made her heart ache. Whatever he was seeing, or *whoever*, had caused him so much pain. She placed her palm against his cheek.

'Sam,' she said, using her most calming voice, 'come back to me. Wherever you are, you don't need to be there anymore.'

Before she realised she was going to do so, Lizette tiptoed and placed her lips against his. At first there was no response, but slowly Sam's mouth opened and their tongues met. For what seemed like an eternity they remained like that, their tongues gently probing each other's mouths, but then pulled apart.

Sam smiled at her.

71

'Liz, what are you doing here? You should be at work.'

'It's almost seven,' Lizette pointed out, nodding to the carriage clock on the mantle.

'Seven?' Sam walked up to the clock, examining it closely. 'But it...' He turned back to her. 'It was four o'clock when I put those shades on. I've been out of it for almost three hours?'

Lizette's first thought was that she should be worried, but other than some dried blood on his ears, Sam seemed okay. Still, three hours...

'I take it the memory exercise worked then?'

Sam didn't answer; he just looked to the floor. When he finally lifted his head, he seemed drained of all his energy.

'No, I don't remember a thing.'

*

Amy threw her mobile onto the passenger seat and let out a hiss of frustration. She had lost count the amount of times she'd attempted to contact Jake, and now her patience was wearing a little thin.

She'd been everywhere since leaving work; first, she went home to get changed and checked her landline just in case he'd bothered to call her there, but not a dickie bird. Then she went to Jake's, used her spare key to get in, but he wasn't there, so as a last resort she tried Will's.

Now Amy sat in her car, still parked outside Will's house, having got no response. Darkness had fallen outside, and there were no lights on in the house. From that, she could only infer that Jake was not in there, either that or he'd fallen asleep. The problem with that theory was that Jake was a light sleeper and the sound of his phone would have woken him up.

'Fine,' she said, and picked her phone back up.

Do contact me when you can be bothered, she typed, then stopped herself.

She closed her eyes, her finger on the delete button. Her boyfriend had a lot going on, and it would have been wrong for her to add to it. She was worried about him, and him not contacting her was making her act out her concern with anger.

Hey, babe, not wanting to add pressure, but you probably need a chat about now. Call me. xx

She hit send and sat back in her seat. He'd call her when he was ready; in the meantime, she needed to be a little patient. Alas, patience was not always her strong suit, especially when she was worried about people.

What she needed was something to take her mind off things.

She accessed her contacts, knowing exactly the thing, and pressed call once she found the entry for Lawrencia.

*

'On the plus side, the stuff I downloaded from your mate's laptop came in very useful,' Toby said, stopping briefly to sip from the bottle he was cradling in his hands. 'And we've located a Charlie Connolly living in Leigh-on-Sea. An officer is going to be visiting him tomorrow, so hopefully he'll be able to enlighten us a little as to Willem's whereabouts.'

Jake felt a wave of relief spread over him at this news. It didn't necessarily mean Will was safe, but it did mean they were one step closer to finding him.

Of all people, Charlie was key.

'I'll tell his folks tomorrow; they'll be pretty stoked about that.'

Toby smiled. 'Not a problem.'

They were in one of those pre-club pubs in the West End, a place Toby had suggested they meet at. It was a gay pub, although from the outside Jake wouldn't have known that since it looked much like any other pub he'd been in. He wasn't sure what he was expecting exactly, probably rainbows and pink outfits, but there was nothing to indicate he'd entered a place for gay men to feel comfortable and safe. Although the guys snogging at the next table might have been a bit of a giveaway, since as a rule you didn't tend to see that in normal pubs.

Now that Jake's mind was a little more at ease about the investigation, they slipped into small talk, with a few suggestive looks from Toby. Jake took these in his stride, although in truth he felt his heart beating faster than usual. The adrenalin was kicking in, as he prepared to consciously engage in something hitherto unknown for him. But it was the only way, and as much as it disturbed him, he knew it had to be done. For both Will's and Amy's sake, as much as his.

'Sorry?' Jake had to ask, realising he had zoned out for a minute. 'Wife and kids?'

'God yeah,' Toby said, reaching into his jacket, which was lying on the seat next to him. 'We got an open relationship, you know?'

Jake didn't know, and clearly his face explained that.

'Oh, it just means we're open about having relationships with other people. Not for everybody, but it works for us.'

'How...? I mean, surely jealousy has to play a part?'

'You'd think so, but it doesn't. I think we both came to the conclusion years back that we're not meant to be monogamous. As I said, works for us.' He handed over a picture to Jake. 'Anyway, these are my daughters, Kira and Britney.'

Jake raised his eyes at the names. 'Bit gay, yeah? Britney.'

Toby laughed at this. 'Funnily enough, that was the wife's choice; she's a huge Britney fan, and since I insisted on naming one of the twins after a character from *DS9*, I kind of had to relent.' He took the picture back and returned it to his jacket. 'Surprised I have kids?'

'Well, no offence, man, but you're *very* gay.'

Toby didn't take offence at this, he had to admit that yes, he was a bit camp and was certainly a pretty boy, but gender had never been an issue for him.

'I don't much believe in gay or straight, I reckon people are just sexual. Some have fantasies about men and some women.'

'And some both?'

'Sure. Sex is sex, and I get different things from men and women, so it's not really that comparative to me. I take it you're not into the women, despite your masculine act?'

Regardless of Toby's openness about his lack of sexual preference, Jake was still a little uncertain and didn't want to commit himself to any definite answers, so he let Toby's question slide. He was only here for one thing, and although men were not something he'd really thought about before, his goal tonight was not a lot different from the amount of times he'd gone out to pull women.

Jake watched as two guys retired to the toilet, and he knew what he had to do. Small talk was fine and dandy, but he couldn't put it off any longer. He looked back at Toby and nodded towards the loo. Toby raised an eyebrow and offered a huge grin.

'Thought you'd never ask,' he said, and got to his feet.

He walked across the pub floor, nattering to people along the way, completely unbothered by what he was going to do. Jake followed him, but he held his head low. He couldn't bear to look anyone in the eye right now, receiving nods of recognition from strangers, only confirming how public a spectacle he was making of himself.

The bathroom was like any other pub toilet; smelling of piss and other funkier smells that Jake didn't want to think too much about. Two guys were in the corner, one with his back against the wall while the other was on his knees before the first.

Jake looked away, feeling something churn in his stomach. A hand grabbed his and he almost pulled it away, but realised in time that it was Toby who was leading him into a cubicle.

As soon as the door was shut, they set to it, Jake pushing himself on to Toby, his mouth immediately finding the mouth of the other man.

Toby was tense for a moment, caught off guard by the forcefulness of Jake's actions, but he soon reciprocated, and Jake felt Toby's hands unbuckling his belt. With a gasp, Jake almost pulled away from Toby, but he forced himself to remain, allowing Toby to bring him to climax with his hand. Usually, he lasted quite a while, but it was over quickly – nerves, Jake decided.

He opened his eyes to see Toby smiling in satisfaction, before glancing down at his own opened trousers. Jake followed Toby's gaze.

'Bloody hell,' was all Jake could say.

Erect dicks were not something he saw a lot of, other than maybe the odd semi in the changing rooms at swimming pools, so he was surprised by how... big... Toby's was.

'Yeah, I know,' Toby said. 'Get that reaction a lot. I'm quite the grower.'

'No shit.'

Jake swallowed, suddenly resistant to the idea, but he knew he was committed now. He closed his eyes and opened his mouth, allowing Toby to guide his head down.

*

'Are you okay?'

Sam looked up from the un-eaten food Lizette had prepared for him.

'Okay? No,' he whispered, 'far from it.' He stood up from the couch. 'Sorry, Liz, I'm sure this food is fantastic but... I'm so tired, and my appetite is shot.'

Lizette nodded, the concern in her eyes palpable. He hated lying to her, but he had to deal with this himself. He could never explain to her what he remembered, mostly because it was a jumble of disjointed images, abstract scenes that ignored the concept of cohesion. But remember he did. He needed to lie down, close his eyes, block everything else out.

While Lizette had prepared food they had talked, but Sam's mind wasn't really on the conversation. He watched her, but it wasn't just her he was seeing.

Like some double-exposed film reel, he was seeing two images at once; the scene immediately before him with Lizette pottering around the kitchen, and a secondary scene playing over that one. He tried to shift his focus from one image to the other, but it was taking too much out of him.

He said goodnight, and she said something about how a good sleep would probably serve him well. She stopped him as he reached the doorway, and he glanced back.

'Maybe you shouldn't try any more memory exercises, let your past come back in its own time?'

Sam nodded and went to the living room, wishing it were that easy.

The sluice gate was open, and the memories were already crashing through like a flood forcing its way past the Thames Barrier. All he needed now was to shut out the images of the present and process these new memories.

Before they drove him mad.

*

The door of the pub opened with a bang and Jake dashed out. It was raining but he didn't notice, he was too busy walking quickly away from the pub, still doing his belt up.

'Jake!'

He glanced back to see Toby emerging from the pub.

'Fuck off!' Jake yelled back and continued on his way.

He didn't get far before he felt the bile rise in his throat, and so he dived into a darkened alley. He crashed against the wall, no longer able to hold back. The vomit shot to the floor with a splash, and Jake leaned against the wall for support.

He had been sure he was doing the right thing. But now he just felt dirty. He didn't want to be gay, he loved his women too much, but he had reasoned he could get it out of his system by copping off with Toby. Once done he could return to Amy, cured of these crazy feelings bubbling inside. Only it had gone wrong.

How stupid was he to convince himself it would go any other way?

'Hey.'

Jake looked up and was surprised by the concern on Toby's face.

'I'm not...' Jake couldn't finish, his stomach still churning at the salty aftertaste.

'It's okay.' Toby knelt down beside him and rubbed his back soothingly. 'First time, yeah? So, the masculine thing ain't an act. It's okay. Not every man likes it.'

'I just...'

'I know.'

Jake screwed his eyes shut, feeling anger burning inside him. He shrugged Toby's arm away. 'Leave me alone. I can't... I need...' Jake scrambled to his feet and rushed away, no longer hearing Toby call out to him.

*

Amy couldn't believe the state of Jake when he finally returned to her flat; not only was he soaked by the rain, but there seemed to be sick down his top. She took him in immediately and helped him to strip off. He didn't resist, and despite her endless questions, he didn't utter a single word. He merely kept the same vacant look on his face, his eyes haunted by something.

She ran a shower for him and helped him into it. For a moment he stood there, the warm water running over his naked bulk, and then slowly he moved, as if he was just waking up.

He looked at Amy and reached out for her. She attempted to pull back, not too keen about getting in the shower in her pyjamas, but he held her arm tight and within moments she too stood under the hot water.

Jake held her at arm's length, looking her up and down, taking in her own nakedness under her nightclothes.

'Jake, what is going—?'

He put a finger to her lips, so she shushed.

'Do you love me?' he asked, his voice a croak.

A question she never thought he'd ask so soon, but there was something in his eyes, a pleading that needed an answer.

'I think so,' she said, which seemed to satisfy him.

He embraced her with one arm, while his free hand traced a line down her body, working its way under her pyjama top, his fingers gently probing her navel. Amy let out a breath of air, and slipped off her pyjama trousers, feeling Jake's stiff penis against her. All her doubts about him went the way of the water, down the plughole, as he roughly pushed his way inside her.

Within moments her back was against the bathroom wall and he was thrusting away, grunting like some carnal beast, but she didn't mind. He was driven by some need, and Amy was glad it was she that fulfilled his need and not his best mate.

7. Reliving the Past

Lizette still wasn't sure it was such a good idea. Sam had awoken, apparently refreshed for his sleep. This was good news since she wanted to talk about what had happened when she'd got home yesterday. Sam was all for talking, and although he didn't remember anything from his blackout, he did remember their kiss.

'But I'm not sure getting into a relationship with you is a good call,' he'd said.

'Why not?'

'You know why. We don't know the person I might be, the life I used to have. For all I know I might be married with kids.'

'Yes, *might*, but we don't know anything for sure. Except the obvious attraction between us. I'm not a stupid woman, Sam, and I'm certainly not prone to allow my emotions to guide me, but in this case I think it's worth the risk.'

'And if I am married?'

Lizette didn't answer immediately. 'Then we cross that bridge when we come to it.'

'Or fall off it.'

'And if that's what happens, then we'll do what we have to. In the meantime, it'll be incredibly negligent of us to ignore this potential right now.'

The conversation went around the house like that for a little while, as Lizette got herself ready for her long day ahead. But eventually, they both agreed to run the risk. However, Sam insisted they take it slow, which struck Lizette as a very sensible thing to do.

What wasn't as clever, to Lizette's mind, was Sam's game plan for the day.

He was going into Southend to nose around, seek out places that were familiar to him to see what kind of feelings and thoughts they inspired. After two blackouts in one day, Lizette didn't think it was a wise move at all, since no one would be around should he blackout again.

'True, but I can't live a life of mollycoddling, I have to stand on my own two feet and do my own thing. If these blackouts are to become a permanent fixture, better I start to deal with them now than later.'

They were sitting on the train, almost at Southend Central, and Lizette was still unconvinced about the wisdom of his plan, but she did like the new assertiveness that Sam was displaying. Like peeling an onion, she was seeing more of the man Sam used to be in increments, and that suited her just fine.

*

The bruise on her arm was bad enough, but as she dressed in front of the full-length mirror, she noticed bruising by her pelvic bone.

The sex in the shower had got a little desperate, Jake going at it a lot longer than usual; but it was more than desperate, it was almost violent.

She finished getting dressed into her work outfit and stood looking at herself in the mirror. Once again, she looked like the smart businesswoman she really was, the kind of woman who took control and used her mind to solve problems.

Last night she had let herself give in to a side of her she didn't like, a weaker side, the girl who'd listened in silence as her mother received hit after hit from her drunk husband. Although Jake had never hit her or shown any inclination to doing so, and although she had willingly given herself to him in the shower, there was a viciousness in the sex that bothered her. She should have seen it at the time and stopped it.

By the time Jake returned from the bathroom, still wet from his morning shower, towel wrapped about him, Amy was sitting on the edge of the bed, legs firmly together. He stopped and looked at her.

'Ready then?' he asked, even though it was quite obvious that she was.

But she was in no mood to humour him. 'What happened to you yesterday?'

'I had some things to attend, I told you that.'

'No, last I heard the police took longer at Will's than expected. After that, nothing, until you turned up here close to midnight. And you haven't said a single word since then, until now. So...?'

Jake lowered his head and took a deep breath. 'It doesn't matter.'

'Don't you give me that,' Amy said, standing up, and repeated, louder, 'Don't you *dare* give me that shit! You scared me last night. It was like some intruder had walked in.'

'I...' Jake sat down on the bed.

'I feel like I'm losing you, Jake.'

The only response was silence. She looked over her shoulder, but only for an instant. The sight of tears rolling down Jake's cheeks was too much. She had to be strong about this.

'This is about Will, isn't it? You're in love with him.'

Finally, she had said it, and now the words were out she felt like a huge weight had been lifted off her shoulders.

She expected more silence, but instead Jake virtually roared the words, 'I'm not fucking gay!'

Anger was good, Amy could deal with that. She couldn't deal with a hurting Jake, she had far too much of her own hurt to worry about.

'Then what the hell is going on?' she asked, turning back to face him.

Jake shook his head. 'I don't know. I wish I did, but nothing is making sense.'

'No, it's not. I thought you and me... But since Will disappeared.' Amy let out a sigh, trying to work things out before she said them. 'I should have seen it sooner. The way you two are with each other.'

'We're just friends, for fuck's sake. I've never felt for Will in that...' Jake stopped himself. 'That's not true, is it?'

'No, I don't think it is.'

Again, silence sat between them, and then Jake finally stood and walked over to her. 'I'm sorry. I don't want to feel this way, I don't want to hurt you. So... Last night I thought I would do something about it. But being with Toby didn't...' His voice trailed off at the look of disgust on Amy's face.

'You... You had sex with a man last night? Is that what you're saying?'

'No, I'm not saying that, I'm...' Jake took a deep breath, as if somehow *he* needed the courage. Like he was the wronged party here. 'Yes. It's all gone to shit, and so last night I thought if I had sex with a man I could get it out of my system. I don't fancy men, I never have, but how losing Will makes me feel... I'm not gay, I can't be, but I thought maybe I can stop it... You know? I can stop myself from becoming gay, and then I'd be all yours.'

Amy stepped back, away from Jake. It was much worse than she'd thought. Him having feelings for Will, she could deal with. He wasn't the first person to be in love with someone else without realising it. But acting on it, and then trying to justify it like this...?

'Getting it out of your system? What kind of stupid bullshit macho crap is that?' Amy held up a hand. 'No, save it, whatever you've got to say, I don't want to know. Right now, I don't even want to share the same breath as you.'

Anger and pain vied for dominance, but Jake didn't deserve to see the pain he'd caused her.

Amy stormed out of the bedroom, skirting past him, arms held out to prevent him from touching her.

*

He entered The Halfway House, and walked straight up to the bar. A young woman, probably only just eighteen, stood there. He ordered a pint of Peroni and, as she pulled it, he asked after Charlie, certain from his previous research that the man would be working on a Wednesday. The woman pointed towards the raised area left of the bar, and Frederick looked. Charlie was sitting at a tall table, pulling his mobile phone out of his trousers' pocket and handing it to a female police officer.

Frederick quickly exited the pub, ignoring the look of annoyance on the barmaid's face. He walked along the side of the building and stopped by the closest window to Charlie and the police officers. He sat on the bench, and closed his eyes, focusing on the voices within.

'Can you describe the man you saw with Mr Townsend?' the male officer was asking.

'Pretty much, yes. Didn't occur to me at the time, but I served him here that morning. It was only after that I'd realised I'd seen him before, but at the time... Well, those eyes, you see?' Charlie paused, and Frederick smiled at the wavering of his voice. Charlie proceeded to give a pretty good description of Frederick to the police.

This wasn't going to end well; he just knew it. Of course, he'd expected Will to be listed as missing, and Stephen had already confirmed that, but he hadn't expected the police to move so quickly. They should have shooed it away, just another adult running away from his life. But all it took was a sympathetic officer at the initial reporting stage...

His thoughts were interrupted by the buzzing of his phone. He removed it, noticed the caller ID, and flipped it open.

'Reisha,' he said, still watching Charlie and the officers through the window. 'Good morning. This call going to make me happy?'

'Here's hoping,' she replied, her voice very jolly for so early in the day. 'My contact has been in touch, called me early this morning. But I had a birthing class so couldn't contact you until now. Anyway, anyway, thing is she told me that she's been sensing a new vampire presence up in the Chalkwell area the last couple of days.'

Frederick baulked. Checking so close to home would not have occurred to him, after all it was in Southend Central that Will underwent the pontus, so what reason would he have for going to Chalkwell? Frederick smiled. Maybe Will had been drawn there by the connection he shared with Frederick. He knew it was a vain hope, but he couldn't conceive of any other reason.

Frederick stood up quickly, as he noticed the police officers shaking hands with Charlie.

'That's really helpful,' he told Reisha, starting on his way up the esplanade. 'I can feel myself getting closer.' He turned the corner onto Plas Newydd and headed up in the direction of Southend East station. 'Once I've found him, I will introduce you to Ai Ling.'

'Who will explain to me the whole Rebirth thing...?' Reisha chuckled. 'From birthing classes to Rebirth. Seems an obvious step to me. Thank you, Frederick,' she added, her tone now serious, 'I've been waiting my whole life for this.'

Frederick knew she had, which is why she made such a perfect choice for a new upiór. She just didn't realise that, with the Seeker out there, she'd be initiated into a truly glorious era, one of the first generation of upiór to live in the presence of their creator.

He ended the call and continued on his way past Southchurch Park. A quick train ride to Chalkwell and then he'd see if he could sense Will.

Soon, he thought, *soon we'll be together again.*

*

Sam stood outside Starbucks, looking around as people continued about their lives, completely unaware of the darkness around them, the tragedy that lived in their midst.

Whatever had happened to him never made it to the local papers, or the news, but it had started here. He'd been here twice before, and both times with the same person. He closed his eyes.

Yes, the man who had accompanied him here had appeared several times in the memory flashes he'd received since standing before the mirror. The man had been there in Starbucks and at the converted Residence with the twins.

His eyes blinked open, a new image playing over the scenes of everyday life that carried on around him.

It had been a great night; he'd never really been to a gay club before, although he had been out on occasion it was usually to more reserved places. But this was so much different. Dancing with strangers, all joined together by the music that played like an anthem of unity, sweat mingling from body to body. And his date watching him from his place by the bar, where he was purchasing more drinks.

This was truly stepping out of his comfort zone. No one at home would believe him when he told them what he had done in Southend; Jake would baulk at the notion of him dancing with strangers. But he would show them all...

That name again; Jake. There was no face to go with the name, but at least Sam now had one name from his previous life. A friend? Yes, there was a familial sense moving through him at the thought of the name. Someone he had known for a very long time.

But who had been his date? The details were hard to make out, but the indistinct shape fitted the man he had seen in Starbucks and at the Residence. There was also a name, just on the periphery of his memory.

Yes! Charlie.

It was Charlie, Sam felt sure.

Buoyed by this, he set off, letting his instincts guide him.

Walking a path that seemed familiar, with barely associated memories, was a strange experience. Akin to visiting the place you had been born in many years after leaving; you knew you'd been there once, but you were too young to remember the details. Sam hadn't needed to walk too far from the High Street before he was smacked in the face by another dissociative wave of I-know-this-place-but-I-don't.

He stopped and looked past the trees at the old building before him. The words on the blue sign before the church told him it was St John's, which had clearly undergone some kind of reconstruction in recent years.

Something had happened to him in this area, some incident intricately connected to his memory loss.

He crossed the road and set off down the path alongside the church. At the end of the road was a roundabout, the first turning from which was an A-road, the second branched off up a slope. Neither turning really interested him, though; rather it was the immediate right turning that held his interest, a few yards before the roundabout. A massive car park greeted him, mostly empty, with a row of closed nightclubs at the far end. It was in one of these nightclubs he'd been to with his date, the mystery man who was swathed in shadows still.

He tried hard to recall the face of the man, but still nothing came forth. All he knew for sure was he'd got the name wrong; there was a Charlie involved somewhere, but that name did not fit in with the feelings the shadow man produced in him. Charlie brought forth a sense of comfort, but the shadow man only produced a feeling of disquiet.

Sam was drawn to the opposite end of the car park, and within minutes he was actually there. He turned at the end of the street, not towards the clubs as he thought he might, but instead right into an alley that led behind the old church.

It was here that it had happened, whatever it was. The one event that had sent his life out of control, something so wrong that he'd been stripped of his memories and thrown into Lizette's life without preamble. He just wished he knew what *it* was.

In the corner of the alley, which careered off left and around a bend, he spotted a CCTV camera situated high on a wall. Whatever had happened, must have been picked up on the camera. But if that was the case, why had the police done nothing to follow it up? Surely an attack that ferocious would have been enough to spark their interest? Four men attacking two innocent guys had to be classed as a public disturbance at the very...

Sam stopped short.

Four men? Where did that come from?

Before he could ask any more questions of his memory, his mind came under the painful assault of another flashback.

He was barely aware of the activity outside the clubs further along Lucy Road, he was intoxicated and not just on alcohol. This is what stepping beyond your comfort zone was really about. Frederick was pressed against the wall, Will's arm across his chest, while his other hand was helping Frederick continue the steady rhythmic movement over the hardness beneath his trousers.

Will arched his neck, his breathing getting faster and faster, approaching the moment of release. Suddenly Frederick stopped, and Will opened his eyes.

'Why... have you... stopped?' he panted.

No answer was needed. The crunching of glass underfoot was enough. Two men entered the alley from the corner leading behind the old church, and another two blocked the other end, cutting off any possible retreat along Lucy Road.

'You queer fuckers.'

'Oh shit,' Will said softly, the blood quickly moving from his dick and hastening the beat of his heart. He looked at Frederick and almost pulled away at the relish on his face.

A name at least. Frederick... the name of the man he'd been in Starbucks with. Much good the name itself did him.

There was a warm trickling down his neck, just below his jawline. Sam reached for it, and when he pulled his hand away he found blood on his fingers. Once again his ears were bleeding, as if the returning memories were causing some kind of haemorrhage in his brain.

He looked at the blood, squishing it between his fingers, and felt another memory returning.

Lips moist with freshly drank blood edged towards his own dry lips, cracking from the loss of blood that was seeping out from the deep gash in his neck where Frederick had struck out blindly, caught in the moment of his hunger.

'No,' Will tried to whisper, in spite of the promises of his new lover, but the word barely escaped his mouth before Frederick pushed his tongue into Will's. He immediately felt the warm, cloying taste of blood on his own tongue, followed by a sharp sting when Frederick's tongue pierced his own.

He was being pulled down into a darkness... and he knew his life was over. At least the way it had been.

Everything went black for Sam, his entire body stopped, falling against the wall like a marionette with its strings abruptly cut.

At the CCTV Control Centre at Essex Police Headquarters in Chelmsford, Detective Inspector Rochelle Swanson looked from PC Stewart Lumley, who manned the desk, and up at the display showing choice images fed in through CCTV cameras across Essex, signposted for special attention by officers at the CCTV Control Centres throughout the county.

'Tell your associate at the Southend Control Centre well done,' she said to Lumley. 'You were right when you said she could be relied upon, her diligence is commendable. The Three will be most pleased when I tell them.'

'Will this get me my audience?' Lumley asked, his voice hopeful.

'Is the Red Source I provided not enough?' Swanson smiled kindly. 'Assuming you perform the next task with the same diligence, then yes, I should think so.'

Not for the first time in the last few days, the footage on that particular camera would have to be doctored to cover the tracks of her people. Lumley had been right to call her, the man passing out was the one who had been killed during the early hours of Saturday morning, and he was the one the Three were now searching for.

The wiping of the tape would have to be orchestrated by Lumley, for she had to call the Three directly. And right away, before some other came across the unconscious 'man'.

*

Eryn hated to admit it, but she had a very bad feeling about the whole Will situation. Celeste was still resting, but she was looking stronger with every hour. Eryn had done some research, trying to find out what could cause a mind trawler of Celeste's ability to pass out in such a way. Everything led to one immutable fact; only a more psychically adept mind could shut down another. But what troubled Eryn so much was that the mind in question was that of a new upiór.

Now, she didn't know the Book of Sekhmet as well as she liked, and only knew the passage pertaining to the emergence of the Seeker because it was one often quoted by Frederick.

But before he is known pain will rage in him; he shall be rejected by his past and the fires of truth will explode in the hunger.

So much about Will's Rebirth was off-key, according to Frederick, including an amazing hunger while in the pontus, which only served to accelerate the whole process. Eryn considered this and was forced to wonder if perhaps Will was indeed the reincarnated Onuris, as Frederick had first thought. What if Onuris only emerged after the pontus? What if the shroud of humanity only fell once he had a preternatural body?

Eryn was no expert on the brain, but surely it would be a very traumatic experience to have a new identity overwrite a previous one? It was surely possible that they had all misread the way Onuris' emergence would occur.

For the first time in hundreds of years, Eryn found herself in the annoying position of starting to believe Frederick and doubting Julius.

She jumped off her chair and made to leave the meeting chamber so she could make a private call to Julius. They needed to talk. She needed to be convinced that she was doing the right thing, that she *had* been doing the right thing since the revolution of 1788. Eryn barely reached the door when the little-used phone, which sat in one corner of the chamber, began to ring. She stopped and looked at it.

Very few people had the number, being a direct line to the Three, and for it to ring meant something important was happening. Eryn felt her mobile in her pocket, eyeing the phone in the corner.

If the call wasn't connected to Will, she'd have been very surprised. She picked up the phone.

'Hello?'

'Eryn. Oh, it's you.'

Eryn smirked, not put out by the disappointment in Rochelle's voice. 'Yes, it's me. Suppose you were hoping to speak to Celeste, weren't you?'

'I was, actually, yes. Is she about?'

'She's occupied, 'en she? What's the problem?'

Rochelle sighed. 'Okay, very well. We've been keeping watch on the Lucy Road alley, as Celeste suggested, just in case Will returned there. And sure enough, he has. What's more he's just collapsed, so if you get the clean-up crew there quick enough you should be able to pick him up before anyone else spots him.'

Eryn narrowed her eyes. To hell with Callum's clean-up crew, she intended to be on hand herself. Celeste was too weak to move, but Eryn and Theodor could take care of it. Celeste would agree. Eryn said thanks, slammed the phone down, and rushed out of the chamber.

Talking to Julius was one thing, and it might have helped, but talking to Will himself would be much more preferable.

Eryn just hoped that she and Theodor could get to Southend before anyone else found Will.

8. Making the Hard Choice

'You should have called me,' Frederick said, anger coursing through him like a surge of electricity.

'There's a lot of "should" going around, Frederick,' Celeste responded, her voice a lot calmer than Frederick's. Easy for her, she wasn't the one whose future was being controlled. 'One of them, lest I have to remind you,' she continued, 'is that you *should* have told me about Willem. But you did not, and in this instance I thought it best that Willem be brought in before alerting you. Having you around would only confuse the situation.'

'Now I'm not getting that. I'm the one he trusts.'

'It's all academic now,' Celeste pointed out, a sharp sting in her voice, 'since he wasn't there. By the time Eryn and Theodor navigated the traffic, Willem was long gone. We've been in touch with Rochelle, but she was busy removing the taped evidence, and her man stopped viewing the footage after she went off to inform us. So, we have no idea where Willem is now.' Celeste stopped, as if just speaking was tiring her out.

Frederick wanted to reach out to her, but he was still angry, however he realised that her calmness of tone had nothing to do with her usual serenity, but rather her tiredness from the psychic barrage of last night.

'Yes, again,' Frederick said, his voice still carrying the harshness he felt inside. Regardless of how tired Celeste might have been, she should have at least contacted him, if only to keep him updated and ask him to not get involved. Of course, Frederick knew he'd never listen. As soon as he heard Will was in Southend he would have headed back there. If that complicated things, then so be it. He needed to see Will.

He looked around Chalkwell Park. It was late afternoon and the schools were out, resulting in a park slowly filling up with teens who had little else to do than hang around.

'I have to go,' Celeste said. 'Rest some more.'

'Have you remembered anything further?'

She was quiet for a moment before answering. 'Merely shadows of memories, nothing that makes any kind of sense. I will let you know when I do.'

The call ended.

Frederick walked out of the park, his mind a mass of contradictions. On the one hand, he was trying to get a sense of Will, who hopefully had returned to Chalkwell where he was staying, but on the other, he couldn't help but think Celeste was lying to him. She knew much more than she was letting on. That she would keep him out of the loop was unheard of. Sure, over three centuries they had done many things solo, gone their own way from time to time, but they never lied and hid things. But hadn't he done such a thing since Friday night? And now the tables were reversed.

Things were changing. Eryn's involvement with the Brotherhood, whatever it was, and the deceit between Celeste and Frederick... The wind was blowing through their world, shifting things around. Like the Book of Sekhmet had promised, before their creator returned much would change, certainties would become uncertain, loyalties would switch, and the most trusted would betray.

And somehow Will's arrival on Friday had precipitated such events.

When Frederick had gone to meet Will on that train everything had seemed so certain in his world, but now? Nothing seemed to be the same. It was as if Will was the catalyst for the upheaval the Book had promised.

So much was no longer understood. The Book said nothing of an upiór emerging before the Seeker, although there were other texts, also written in Sumerian, which mentioned a rival to the Seeker. A man of power who would play a pivotal role. The author of the text was a mystery, but carbon dating had it as old as the earliest writings of Wamukota, circa AD33.

Frederick never held much stock in the text, but now he wondered. Whatever was happening to Will, and indeed had happened, was powerful enough to cause one of the strongest mind trawlers to melt down.

With a sense of dread, Frederick was forced to consider that Will might well have been the 'man of power' of which the old Sumerian text spoke. Either way, his fate was clearly linked to that of prophecy.

*

Sam wandered around Lizette's house, his mind going over what he'd remembered. It all seemed so unbelievable, and on the way back he'd done his best to convince himself that his mind was making things up. Filling in the blanks with the most outrageous things.

But he knew he was reaching, trying to ignore what was now becoming self-evident.

He looked at himself in the mirror, removing his top and studying his almost perfect physique. His body was changing, and through no effort of his. His muscles becoming more defined. He'd first noticed that morning in the shower, when he'd become almost obsessed with his body. Overcome with the notion that it was wrong, that it *wasn't* his body at all. It was perfect, no blemishes, except a strange scar next to his groin.

He undid his trousers and pulled his shorts down. The scar was more than strange, it had a definite shape. Not some damaged tissue. In fact, it almost looked like a brand of some sort.

That was ridiculous. As ridiculous as the memories he had unlocked.

Frederick had been a vampire, of that he was now certain, as much as he hated to admit it. But if his memory was true, then did that make him a vampire too?

He did his trousers up and leaned in closer to the mirror, studied his transparent eyes. He opened his mouth, checked for fangs. But nothing. Sure, his canines were a little pointy, but no more than other people's.

This was stupid.

He walked out of the bathroom. What he needed was some mundanity, something normal, real world, something completely disconnected from the idea of vampires.

He glanced left, drawn to Lizette's kids' room. For a brief second, he saw the face of a child, brown chubby cheeks, an adoring smile... And then it was gone. He opened the door to the bedroom, and stood there, surprised at what he saw.

Nothing. Literally, the room was empty. No beds, nothing that would suggest teenagers even used it, and not even an ounce of junk. Just a perfectly clean carpeted room with no discernible function.

Sam closed the door and leaned his back against it, baffled by what he'd seen.

*

Frederick spent the evening surfing the net.

There were plenty of websites about vampires, written by both human scholars and upiór alike, most pertaining to sightings over the years, myths and legends. So many accounts that seemed contradictory, detailing the vampire lore from almost every country across the globe. Although most human scholars were unaware of it, what they were detailing was the natural evolution of the vampire to upiór, although most of them missed the events of 1788. Fortunately, there were plenty of scholars who were upiór and their sites, although harder to find, continued the true story of upiór. Talk of the Seeker was rare, though, despite it being known to most upiór. It was one secret the majority of upiór wished to keep away from prying human eyes, but those few sites that did talk of the Seeker myth attempted to correlate the teachings spread by the Brotherhood with those taught by the Three.

It was on one of these sites that Frederick found a very detailed, and accurate, translation of the Lost Pages of the Book of Sekhmet.

Fredrick never considered the ancient Sumerian text to be part of the Book, but the website gave a lot of compelling evidence. The rhythm and rhyme of the writing matched that of the Ancient, everything down to the syntax.

Wamukota had lost several pages in Moldavia, so it had to be possible that other pages had been lost prior to the Book being returned to him.

Indeed, Frederick knew from first-hand experience that some pages had been removed and translated, albeit badly, before the Ancient had retrieved his work. It was such pages that had started Frederick on the journey that had led him here.

He cursed his own sense of importance. Ever since he had been given the Book, ever since he had supped on the blood of the oldest of their kind, he had believed himself chosen above all others. With the exception of Melinda, about whom Wamukota had foretold, Frederick had never sought any other views or opinions on the Book. He was convinced that he was the final authority on the writings of the Ancient. The blood in his veins made him so. Thus, he had never bothered looking into the work and research of other scholars, he never considered that they could offer a fresh, and plausible, view on things.

But now, with so much in flux, he was forced to look into other sources. And, for the first time in 221 years, he realised he had not been right about everything.

For the rest of the night, until his eyes could function no more, he read and read. Digesting everything written about the Lost Pages.

*

Jake was in a void; his feelings no longer understood, and from the moment Amy walked out on him he wandered, seemingly in an aimless direction, going wherever his feet took him.

He had ended up at the Adomako house, and had even gone for a drink with Francis; that he should visit the closest place he had to a home and spend time with the only father figure in his life in what was shaping up to be his darkest day, was not lost on him.

He had treated Amy like a total bastard, and he wasn't sure he could forgive himself for that. He wanted to explain things better, so she would understand that he had not meant to hurt her; indeed, last night's rather stupid actions were supposed to have made things better between them. But it had backfired somewhat.

Of course, the biggest issue was still his evolving feelings for Will, and deep down he knew that they would forever be the one obstacle he and Amy would never be able to scale.

Toby had tried to contact him a few times, but Jake either ignored the texts or pressed dismiss when the calls came through. Toby was another person Jake had treated disgracefully. He was, without doubt, more ashamed of himself than he'd ever been in his life.

Once Jake had finally returned home, unusually just sitting in silence, he sent a text to Toby, saying he would explain what happened later. It was, of course, a lie. Jake would never explain; he couldn't.

There came a knock at the door around six in the evening, and although not really up to receiving visitors, Jake wasn't in such a funk that he was willing to be rude to people. So, he went to the door and opened it. Standing there was the one person he'd never expected to see again.

Amy.

'Knew I'd find you here,' she said, and Jake moved aside so she could step inside.

Here was, of course, Will's house.

Jake stood by the door for a few moments, his heart a mix of confused emotion. But he eventually swallowed his fear of what was to come and followed her into the room.

She stood by the window, her back to him, arms folded. Jake looked around, feeling like a lost boy, about to be scolded by his teacher. He sat on the arm of the nearest chair and waited.

'I've been thinking a lot since this morning,' Amy began, still keeping her back to him. 'About you... us. I even took the afternoon off, cause I needed to come and see you.' Jake smiled, not that Amy could see it, and a glimmer of hope sparked in him. 'And I absolutely believe you are in love with Will. Every fibre of your being screams this fact.'

The air rushed out of him. He was so very tired now.

'But I'm not gay, Amy,' he said, no longer able to sound angry. 'If I was, then last night I would have enjoyed every moment, but I didn't. It made me physically ill. Everything about it, especially the thought of betraying you like that.'

Amy looked over at her shoulder, and offered a slight smile. 'That's something at least.'

This was his chance, to tell her how he really felt. 'I'm sorry,' he said, his voice hoarse with emotion, so he coughed and said it again with a firmer tone. 'I really did not want to hurt you, that was the last thing on my mind. But I've been so confused, and I didn't know what to do, I just—'

'I believe you,' Amy said, interrupting him. 'And I have to apologise for my comments this morning... This is not about what you did last night. Sure, that smarts, and it's a betrayal I may never forgive you for. But I *do* understand why you did what you did, even if it does sicken me.' She looked away again, then after taking a deep breath she turned away from the window and walked over to him.

Jake watched her, struck by the pain in her eyes.

'As I said, I've been thinking. Sometimes you meet a person and they totally spin your head, and you just know they are the one. You don't see it coming, but when it hits you, you can't deny it.' She sat on the chair beside him and reached out for his hand. Jake's breath caught in his throat at the touch of her skin. 'I thought that was us. The last few months have been great... Well, until Will went missing. But I honestly thought we had something.'

'We do.'

'We *did* for a while there, but it's gone.' Amy swallowed and looked down at their joined hands, Jake's thumb gently stroking the back of her hand. 'It's you and Will. I never noticed before, but the source of your closeness is so obvious now. Your love for him is something so raw it destroys you to just think he might be gone forever. And I'm not saying you're gay, Jacob, not even a little bit. But I am saying Will is your "one", and that he's a man makes it harder for you.'

Jake looked down, hating to admit the sense she was talking. But she was right, and he couldn't argue the point.

'But what if I do find Will, and things come together? What am I supposed to do then? No one else will understand. I don't even understand.'

'I don't mean to sound harsh... Well, maybe I do a little, but that's not my problem. It's something you're going to have to deal with.' He looked at her sharply, but he could see no malice in her eyes. She was merely telling him the cold hard facts.

'But...' Jake choked on the words trying to come out of his mouth, his eyes welling up. He had never really broken up with someone before, at least not someone who actually mattered to him. He had heard the phrase 'heartbreak' thrown around a lot, but it wasn't until that moment, looking into Amy's eyes, that he truly understood what it meant to have your heart broken. 'What about us?'

'There is no us. There can't be,' Amy said, the pain of that truth written all over her face. She got to her knees and leaned towards him until their foreheads met. They remained like that for a few moments, the tears of regret and mutual hurt flowing freely.

'Life's so unfair at times,' Amy said, her voice shaking. 'I barely had you for three months...'

'You deserve better than me.'

'Damn straight, mister,' Amy said with forced joviality, pulling her head away from his. Despite her tone, the tears continued to slowly run down her face. 'I deserve someone who thinks I'm the most important person in their life. A man who is all mine.'

'I can be that man,' Jake said, hating the desperation in his voice, but he was beyond the point of trying to hide it. He had made some mistakes in his life, and he didn't want Amy to be one of them.

Amy smiled sadly. 'No, you can't be. Will is in you too much.' She removed a tissue from her pocket. She dabbed her eyes carefully, to ensure minimum damage to her mascara. 'No goodbyes, I'm just going to leave. I... I don't think I can say goodbye,' she added, standing up, sniffing back the new tears already forming.

*

Jake wandered the streets of South West London.

There was little coherence in his mind, just a jumble of thoughts and feelings. He had no idea what to do with himself; he had considered catching up with Mike, perhaps going for a drink, but found he really wasn't in the mood for company.

He received a text from Toby, but Jake had no intention of going there again. If there was one person so interconnected with his split from Amy then Toby was it, and Toby didn't deserve the kind of bile Jake directed his way.

It was only when he looked up from the pavement that he realised his legs had brought him back to Barclay Road, and he had stopped outside Will's house.

No matter what he did, he just kept on returning to Will.

He reached out to the nearest lamppost and took a deep breath.

Will is in you too much. Amy's words resonated in his head, and looking up at the house he knew that she had been absolutely right. Somewhere along the way, Will had become the most important person in Jake's world.

He felt a vibration in his jeans pocket and removed his phone before the ringtone could sound. For a second he hoped it might be Amy, that she was calling to say she'd changed her mind. But he didn't recognise the number.

'Hello?' he said, his throat dry.

'Hi, Jake, it's Becky Medeiros, sorry to call so late in the day, but I've got some new information about the case that I thought you'd want to hear. Officers in Southend have visited and spoken to Charlie Connolly...'

As she told him about what Charlie had told the officers, his last vestige of hope evaporated.

Contacting Charlie was supposed to bring Will closer to home, but instead it pushed the likelihood of his return further away.

9. Placing A Call

Jake had expected that accessing Will's email account would be difficult, but he cracked it with ease. It was only through talking over things with Francis, telling him about Charlie's report, that Jake came to realise he had an opportunity to do something proactive. It was he who had galvanized everyone else into action in the first place, but the last couple of days he'd been so caught up with trying to work out what was going on in his own head that he'd lost track of actually *doing* something to help find Will.

But now, in Charlie, he had a possible source of help. From what Medeiros had told him, it seemed Charlie was just as concerned as they all were. It worried Jake that Will would actually hook up with some random bloke en route to meet a man he'd only known via the net. It wasn't Will at all. Something untoward was most definitely going on. And Jake had to find out what.

To that end, he had got Will's laptop out. He'd discovered from Toby the other day that you didn't need a password to activate the laptop, and it automatically connected to Will's home network. He went straight to Gmail and entered the only word Will would possibly use as a password. Access granted. Jake felt a little proud of himself, knowing Will that well; although if Amy was to be believed it shouldn't have been much of a surprise.

What did surprise him, though, was an email from Charlie dated 29/03/2011. Only yesterday. At first, warning bells alarmed in his head; could it be that Charlie knew exactly where Will was, and he'd lied barefaced to the police? If so, that would have been seriously dumb, since Medeiros had told Jake that they were pulling the CCTV to corroborate Charlie's story. Any such lie would soon be discovered.

Jake quickly opened the email, any guilt over searching Will's private correspondences being flushed away by his concern.

The email was a last-ditch attempt by Charlie to make direct contact with Will. Charlie said how he didn't care why Will had treated him like shit on Friday; he just wanted to know if Will was okay now. Everyone was worried; *he* was worried.

They could have just been words written to throw people off the scent, but Jake didn't think so. Mostly because they echoed his own feelings so well, and so he quickly sent an email to Charlie.

He got back to Jake soon enough, and the two of them spent a few hours talking on MSN. At the end of their time, Jake was left feeling bad; it was quite clear that Charlie cared a lot for Will, almost as much as Jake did himself, but he also knew that if they found Will he would, without compunction, do everything in his power to ensure that Will returned home with him. He hadn't gone through hell with Amy today to let someone else win Will's heart now.

The next morning, after the first almost-normal sleep since last Thursday, Jake went to meet Mikey for some breakfast at the old Greasy Spoon. He sidestepped all the questions about Amy, instead letting Mikey know that he wouldn't be back to work until at least Monday, since he was planning to visit Southend himself. Jake could see that Mikey had something to say, but instead of saying it he just slipped into his usual innuendo and lad-talk. Jake was grateful for the distraction of nonsense and joined in.

Mike returned to work, and Jake returned to Will's laptop. It was only when talking to Mike that he'd made the decision about Southend, although he'd been thinking about it ever since talking to Francis yesterday, but now he needed to broach the subject with Charlie.

This time they spoke on the phone, having exchanged mobile numbers.

'Sounds like a good idea to me, mate,' Charlie said. 'Do you have anywhere to stay in Southend?'

Jake had hoped that Charlie would ask this. 'Nope,' he said, not surprised in the least when Charlie offered him a place to stay. Canvassing Southend would take a lot longer than one day. Plus, by staying at Charlie's, Jake would be able to see just what it was about this man that Will liked so much.

Will never had many boyfriends over the years, and other than Jacen, Jake had no barometer by which to gauge the type of man Will went for. The type of man he needed to be for Will.

'I've been to Southend before, but can't say I really know it well,' Jake said, in an attempt to quiet his thoughts.

'Seaside trip when a kid?' Charlie asked.

'Yeah, that's the one. Will and I went with his parents. Good times.'

'I can imagine. Must be great having known Will all that time; there's so much I still don't know about him. Stuff I want to know. Hopefully, I'll get a chance soon.'

Jake was silent for a second, then mumbled a 'yeah' in agreement. Once again, the guilt stung him. It seemed recently he had accrued an awful lot of guilt over things, and was beginning to realise how it must have been for Will, always carrying around with him a feeling of guilt and responsibility for others. He wasn't sure he liked all these serious feelings; life had been so much easier before Will had decided to leave for Southend. Jake just hoped those easier, more carefree times would return with Will.

'Hang on a sec, Charlie,' Jake said, as the landline started ringing. He rushed into the lounge and lifted the receiver.

'Hello?' He waited, but there was no answer, just the background hum of life. The call was obviously being made from a public phone box, which was a rarity in this day and age.

'Hello?' he said again, and the line went dead. 'Okay, not liking this,' he told Charlie, once he replaced the mobile phone to his ear. 'Someone called, but no one spoke. Who calls from a phone box these days? One moment, gonna check the number.' He punched 1471 into the number pad and listened to the number repeated back to him. He didn't recognize it. '01702... What's that the area code for?'

He didn't really expect Charlie to know; not like he was directory enquiries or anything, but nonetheless Charlie responded immediately.

'That's Southend, mate.'

'Who would call from...?' Jake trailed off, as only one possible name came to him. Charlie reached the same conclusion, and in unison they voiced it.

'Will.'

*

Sam lowered his head against the phone and took a deep breath.

That had been hard, but he didn't understand why. Jake was his best mate for fuck's sake, not some weird stranger. And yet that was exactly how it had felt; Jake's voice was akin to hearing someone from TV speaking to him. A fantasy, not reality.

His blackout yesterday had been most revealing, and thankfully brief, but it had left him with a serious migraine. Lizette thought he was pushing himself too hard, but she didn't know the half of it.

He'd told her only a little; there was too much to take in as it was, without the added difficulty of trying to actualize it to another. Bit by bit his old life, the one before the attack, was returning to him.

Names and places, moments of transition in his life, important decisions made, a lifetime of hard work with little fun, the only moments of relief in the company of Jake and/or his nephew, Curtis. So much that his head felt like it would explode.

He should have been happy with this, after all, as he and Lizette had said countless times, it was what he sought, his past returned. Only now that it was returning, he found he didn't actually want it.

The life of Will was not one he had any desire to return to; a life where he was responsible for so many.

His life with Lizette, although only just starting, held so much more promise. A chance for him to be the person he wanted to be, a new life and a companion with whom he could share it. Of course, he'd have to get to the bottom of the mystery of the spare room, but for now he'd decided not to broach the subject. After all, he couldn't accuse her of lying and keeping things from him when he was still keeping things from her.

Besides which, Sam reasoned, there was still so much to be recalled, not only of this unreal life before the attack but the events that led him to Lizette's garden. Events of great danger that he could not expose his family to.

He picked up the phone receiver. There was one more call he had to make before he carried on with seeking out the truth of his current situation.

A woman's voice, full of attitude, answered. Sam smiled wistfully; nice to see some things hadn't changed – but then, why would they? It had only been a matter of days since he'd spoken to her, even though it felt like a lifetime ago. Her tone made him more determined not to be dragged into that life again.

'Hey, Ren, it's me. Let me speak to my nephew.'

At first, there was silence on the other end of the line, and then the much-anticipated outburst. 'Billy! Where the fuck have you been? Do you have any idea the shit you've left me in?'

'Yeah, missed you, too.' Sam blinked as a new vision overlaid his view of the Thames Estuary.

Tall and brown, the woman was exactly as Will had always thought his sister could be if she had lived to her full potential. She walked past Frederick, whom she had been embracing, and reached out to embrace Will. The twins watched her, the one in the shades impassive as he seemed to always be, the electric blue one casting open hostility Will's way.

The black woman asked him something in French. Will's French had never gone much beyond the standard GCSE fair, but he guessed it was a compliment of some kind, since he at least recognised she called him 'my dear'. She gathered him in her arms and Will was surprised by the strength of her embrace.

'Will,' Frederick said, with a grin Will didn't understand. 'Allow me to introduce Celeste.'

Lawrencia was screaming profanities down the phone at him, but Sam was no longer interested in what she had to say. He slammed the receiver down and left the phone box.

He crossed the road, almost getting run over in the process, and stopped by the small wall running the length of the beach. He looked around wildly. Someone was calling him, or at least calling out to *Will*.

He recognised the voice. Frederick. He screwed his eyes shut, trying to focus, but as soon as he blocked out his view of the water reflecting the perfect blue sky above, the voice dissipated like a mist on the breeze.

'Shit,' he said, opening his eyes and looking towards Canvey Island.

He had been so close then. As great as it was to know of his old life once again, it was his life post-death that interested him. For that he had died in that alley, with Frederick's tongue sucking on his like a leech, was beyond doubt in Sam's mind.

*

Frederick awoke after nine hours of sleep, by which time it was almost two o'clock in the afternoon. Such a long sleep only served to remind him that he was still low on energy, following the telepathic experiment of Tuesday night. It seemed so much had happened in just under a week, and he was drained from it.

It took him longer than usual to get himself together, and en route to Canvey Island he stopped by to see Rhys and purchase some blood. He left the bank refreshed and restored, shameful in the knowledge that he had drank more blood since Friday than he had done in months. He honestly believed that his people were growing beyond their need for blood, but there were times when it was necessary. Frederick contented himself in knowing that, the Sekhite notwithstanding, he had fed off no one in that time.

In all it took him a good three hours from waking to make it to the island. Celeste still looked weak when he found her, resting in her private chamber, an unfinished painting before her. She looked up from her chair and placed the brush and palette on the stool beside her. For a moment neither said a word, both tired and hurt by the deception. Frederick broke the silence, saying they needed to talk, and Celeste readily agreed, although she also needed air. So, with bodyguard in tow, they travelled out to Canvey Heights County Park. The bodyguard stayed back, close enough to keep watch but far enough away that they could speak in secret.

That Celeste needed a bodyguard was a ludicrous notion, really, since she was one of the oldest, and thus infinitely most experienced, upiór still alive. She could more than look after herself if the need arose. Any Sekhite trying to take Celeste out would have been a fool indeed.

However, Frederick reflected, in her weakened state a bodyguard was probably a good idea. Or would have been if Frederick was not there. It would be a cold day in hell before he would allow any harm to come to Celeste.

They reached the topmost peak of the park, the highest spot on the island, and looked out over the creeks and marshes at the Thames as it ran down into the North Sea miles away at Shoeburyness. Some distance behind them was a path that ran through the park, upon which many tourists walked. From their point of view, Frederick and Celeste probably looked like more tourists, wrapped in their warm coats and looking out eastward. The bodyguard perched on the back of a bench near the path, watching his charge, although to the casual observer, he appeared to just be looking out to sea.

'I'm sorry,' Frederick began. Celeste looked surprised, as well she should. Frederick was not known for apologising. 'I should have told you about Will, come to you first. We've shared everything for so very long now...' He smiled slightly. 'I guess I just liked the idea of having something that was only mine.'

Celeste nodded slowly. 'I understand, Frederick. You have had relations with humans in the past, but they never really amounted to much, but this time... It seems, for some reason, Willem has won your heart.'

'No, it's not that simple. Ever since I first saw him, years ago in London, I've felt drawn to him. As if... I don't know.' Frederick let out a hiss of frustration. Expressing such deep feelings was new for him; usually, Celeste just knew how he felt. He struggled for the words. 'What is it Emily Brontë wrote? *Whatever our souls are made of, his and mine are the same.* That's how it feels, right now, in *here.*'

'Emily knew her stuff,' Celeste said softly, reminding Frederick that she had been a friend of the Brontë family. Another brief period of English history which Celeste had been involved in, while Frederick was off visiting the troubled town of Noyeston in New England. 'Humans use this term too often, I feel, and it has lost its meaning, but perhaps you understand it now? Soul mates, Frederick.'

'Like you and I?' Celeste nodded, and Frederick continued. 'That is why you chose me, and why you chose Theodor before me? You believe our souls are made of the same thing.'

'Absolutely. Even as a human, I waited. It didn't matter to whom my father introduced me, if I did not feel a kindling of our souls I was not interested. And so it is with you. You have waited so long and now you have found *your* soul mate.'

'Then you are not angry with me?'

'No. Disappointed in the lies, but I understand why you chose to not speak. Confusion abounded in you; you had convinced yourself that Willem was the Seeker, not realising the truth of your connection with him.' Celeste turned to look him directly in the eyes. 'Seeing him on the ground, dying, must have been the point when you realised.'

As ever, with those words, Celeste proved she knew him so well. He smiled and looked out towards Chalkwell.

'He's out there somewhere; probably living near to me.'

'You have felt him?'

'To be honest I haven't tried. Not since Tuesday night.'

Celeste took his hand in hers. 'Then let's try,' she said, squeezing his hand gently.

'Are you sure?'

Her eyes said no, but she said, 'It was two days ago, I'm sure I've got enough strength to spare. Just.'

Frederick offered no further argument. Celeste didn't look strong enough, but she knew her own mind. He closed his eyes and reached his mind out tentatively.

Will, he called, and for a brief moment he thought he felt something. But then it was gone.

'He *is* there,' Celeste said, as Frederick opened his eyes. 'But the barrier is strong, and until I have worked out what happened on Tuesday I'm not going to push too hard.'

'I still don't understand what would make Will go to Chalkwell. The only thing I can think of is that he was led there by our blood bond.' For a moment Frederick lapsed into silence. Celeste waited. 'What do you know of the Lost Pages?'

'Very little.'

Frederick told her all he had learned last night, and of his suspicions. Now it was Celeste's turn to be silent.

'If you had told me this another time, I would have immediately thought of Julius; he's a man of power, running his own little empire. And his stance would certainly be a threat. But now... In his own way, in London, Willem is also a man of power.' Celeste closed her eyes and swallowed. 'But his psychic protection. That is real power.'

'You think I might be right?'

'I think we cannot afford to take the chance. The nature of his Rebirth is unprecedented, everyone with whom I have talked has confirmed that nothing like that has ever happened before.' Abruptly Celeste turned and staggered. Frederick caught her by the arm. She gave him a weak grin. 'You see, this is what his power has done to me.'

Frederick did not share her humour. In silence he walked with her, his arm linked in hers. They reached the path and began the long walk back to the Residence. The bodyguard got off his perch and started following them.

'What shall we do?' Frederick asked.

'If he is staying in Chalkwell we will scour Chalkwell until we find him. If he is the threat the Lost Pages tell us about, we must get to him first.'

'Before the police do.'

'What?'

'He has been reported missing. Even now the police are making enquiries in Southend.' Now Frederick did grin, but there was no humour behind it. 'His family is persistent.'

'Then we must contact Rochelle. Put an end to their search.'

*

After the silent call, both Jake and Charlie decided that there was no more time to waste. Clearly, Will had made an attempt to call home, an attempt halted for some reason. Jake didn't want to think too hard about what it could be, but he did know that he needed to speak to PC Medeiros.

It was difficult getting through to her, and when he did he was met with some curious news. There had been a development which she could not disclose yet, but it did mean that the investigation was being taken out of the hands of the regular police and passed over to the Criminal Investigation Department at New Scotland Yard, led by one Detective Inspector Alyson Rowe.

Jake didn't like this development. If CID were getting involved, then that could only mean bad news. CID were notorious for their involvement in more serious far-reaching investigations, and for the life of him Jake could not comprehend how Will's disappearance would fall under their purview.

He tried to push for more information, but Medeiros would not, indeed *could* not, tell him any more than she already had. Even when he told her all about the phone call, she would say no more, except that this was the second report of such a phone call today.

It turned out that shortly after his own aborted call, Lawrencia had also been called, although she had spoken briefly to Will before the line went dead. Medeiros wouldn't confirm anything, or deny anything, but she did point out that CID were aware of the situation and would be in touch shortly.

Once the call had ended, Jake dialled Lawrencia's number, not surprised that she hadn't called to let him know.

'Hey, the police tell me that Will's been in touch with you today. Why didn't you call me?'

'Didn't know I was supposed to,' Lawrencia responded blithely. 'Anyway, got my own shit going on. You were bound to find out eventually.'

Jake bit his tongue, holding back the response he wanted to give. Instead, he said, 'And I have. Listen, Ren, CID are now getting involved, and for those not paying attention at home it means some serious shit has hit a fucking large fan.'

'CID? Why would they be getting involved?'

'I actually have no—'

'I can't speak to them,' Lawrencia said over him. 'Jimmy will freak.'

Jake was about to interrupt, just to let her know that her brother's safety was a little bit more important than screwing up Jimmy's shady deals, but her next words silenced him.

'I only called the police because Amy insisted.'

For a fraction of a second Jake's heart stopped. He stumbled over his words, cleared his throat, and tried again. 'Amy? You've spoken to her? Is she okay?'

'Of course she's okay, why wouldn't she be?'

'Yeah, of course she is,' Jake responded quickly, realising that Amy hadn't confided her troubles to Lawrencia. Why would she? She had agreed to help Lawrencia, not become confidantes with her. Jake smiled, glad to know that Amy was still around and, at least peripherally, still in his life.

*

Sam popped two pills into his mouth and washed them down with water, not that he really expected aspirin to make a huge difference to his ongoing migraine, but he could at least try.

He turned to the oven bowl and carefully placed it in the pre-heated oven. He stepped back and grinned. Yes, Lizette would be pleasantly surprised when she returned home from work.

He'd been having a nose through her books earlier and came across a Gordon Ramsey cookbook, and hit upon the idea of making dinner for Lizette. He had hosted a few dinner parties for his old university chums in the past, and thanks to his restored memories he knew he was a dab hand around the kitchen. Lizette had done so much for him it seemed only fair to return the favour. Granted, all the ingredients were from her kitchen, but it was the act that counted in this instance.

Making a classic *Lasagna Al Forno* was messy work, and he had about half an hour to clean up the kitchen. It took him only fifteen minutes, so he removed all the salad he needed from the fridge and placed it on the side. There was little point in preparing the salad until she was home, so he walked the book into the passageway and returned it to the shelf.

He went to stand up again, but another book grabbed his attention. *Discovering Ancient Egypt*.

He was never massively into Egyptology, although considering the careers of Lizette's birth parents it was not surprising that she should have some books on Egyptology, but the spine of the book had caught his eye, and he still had the best part of an hour to kill before Lizette returned.

He removed the book and headed into the kitchen to check on the lasagne, before placing the book on the sideboard and opening it directly to the section about the Hem-Netjer, the servant of god.

*

Jake was in a good mood, despite his growing concerns about Will. The sun was shining, and he was all set to head to Southend. Once there he and Charlie would work out a strategy for their canvassing, which would start with the nightclubs later in the night.

He knocked at the door of the Adomako house, determined to not even let Eon ruin his optimistic mood. Yes, he was still tired, but he was thinking positive thoughts. Whatever had happened to Will, the fact that he'd attempted to call them had to count for something.

The door opened and once again Jake was surprised by the person who greeted him.

'Well, hello, son. You would never believe who called here earlier,' Francis said, with a grim smile.

'Francis. Hi, erm... Eon not about?'

Francis stepped back so that Jake could enter. He closed the door and followed Jake into the living room. 'No, he's gone walkabouts. Having a bit of a hissy fit because Sandra's sticking by her kids.'

'Well, sod him then. So, progress for you and Sandra?'

Francis shook his head, smiling. 'No, son, I'm just here to offer support. A united front, in the hope that it brings my boy back home sooner.'

'Right.' Jake wouldn't swear by it, but he was sure he recognised that glint in Francis' eyes. Either way, it was great to see him back in his old home again. Things were looking up finally.

Sandra entered the lounge, carrying a plate of biscuits. She sent Francis out to get the tea tray, and the three of them sat around the tea-table in the middle of the lounge. Jake didn't fail to notice how close Will's parents sat by each other on the sofa. He hid a grin behind his cup.

After a little small talk, Jake went on to outline his basic plan. At first, they were both a little opposed to the idea, still not trusting Charlie, but Jake explained how much the two of them had talked and he believed Charlie was the innocent party in all this. At least they knew Will was alive now, whether he was well or not was another thing entirely, but at least he'd been in contact. Will's folks already knew this, since Lawrencia had popped in earlier with Curtis to let them know, as Jake had suggested she do.

He was surprised to hear that she had followed up on his suggestion. Since when did Lawrencia listen to anyone, let alone Jake? He could only assume that Amy was having a good effect on her.

'Did Lawrencia tell you about the CID involvement?'

Francis and Sandra exchanged concerned looks, and Jake could see that they did indeed know. He tried to assuage their worries, a task not made simple since it concerned him greatly too. They all agreed there was little they could do about it until someone from CID contacted them, and it was then that Jake informed them that he'd given PC Medeiros Sandra's number. It seemed pointless for him to be the first port of call if he was out and about, and it made much more sense for Will's parents to be the first informed of any future developments. Now that Eon was gone, Sandra agreed.

'You just be careful out there, Jake,' she said.

'Yes,' Francis added, giving Jake a knowing look. 'Bring our boy back to us, and do what you need to do.'

Jake wondered at his blindness. Was he really the only person who had not seen his love for Will? It seemed obvious to so many others. Amy, Mikey... even Francis. Jake still didn't quite know what this new awareness would mean for his life when he returned home with Will, but he'd soon find out.

In truth it worried him more than not having Will about.

New territory that he was so not prepared for.

*

Tomorrow was the First of the Month festival and as such Onuris, a lowly Wa'eb in the Temple of Sekhmet, had his work cut out for him. It was several hours after dusk, and the supper ritual was long past. Onuris worked mostly in the dark, his chamber lit only by the flickering of a candle flame. Before him, laid out carefully, were the vestments of Sekhmet, which he was cleaning with great care. Everything had to be perfect for tomorrow's festival; the people of Memphis would all be out, looking to pay tribute to the Goddess Sekhmet. One day Onuris would be among the Hem-Netjer, but until that time he would serve in his own way, just as his father had before him.

His chamber was bathed in a flash of blinding light, and for a moment Onuris staggered back. He shielded his eyes until the light dimmed to a manageable level, and then peered around. The source of the light was coming from outside. It was many hours until sun-up, and a fear gripped his heart.

What force was strong enough to turn night into day?

He stepped out of his chamber carefully and looked around the outskirts of the temple. His chamber was located on the perimeter; as a Wa'eb he was not permitted to approach the sanctuary of the temple without a Hem-Netjer by his side, but most of Memphis slept and there were no other priests about. He chanced a look around, just in case the light had awoken others, but there was no indication of such a change.

He walked softly through the temple, up the slight incline and past the forest of columns, glancing up at the constellations crafted into the roof above. He stopped just outside the Shrine, blinking all the while. The light was still brightly pouring through the cracks of the door, but not so much that it was blinding anymore. He reached out for the door seal and paused.

It was drummed into him that he had to perform the cleansing rituals before entering the inner sanctuary, but his need to discover the source of light outweighed his sense of duty, so he broke the seal and stepped into the Shrine.

Once across the threshold, Onuris fell to his knees in awe. His head lowered, not daring to look at the woman standing before the statue of Sekhmet.

He had seen her only briefly, bathed in the bright light, and in that moment he saw the perfect image of the statue behind her. A tall woman, bronze of skin, naked in her glory, with the head of a lion, her green eyes glaring at him. A snake coiled on her head, hissing in warning at the intruder.

'My loyal Hem-Netjer Tepey, you have come to serve your god,' came a voice of such depth that Onuris trembled on his knees. 'Look at me.'

'I cannot, Your Highness. I am only a pure one, and not worthy to look on the face of a god.'

'How can you serve me if you do not look upon my countenance?' Naked feet came into his line of sight, and he felt tender fingers, cold to the touch, lift him by the chin.

He raised his head, looking into a face of unrefined beauty. Long red hair flowed down her shoulders, covering her breasts.

'You will become my high priest; I will need no other.'

The image faded from his sight, and Sam was left wondering just what his death had done to him. It was no memory of his, of that he was certain.

Frederick and his friends, including the beautiful Celeste, had clearly organised the events that led to his dying in the alley, and somehow he came back. Only as what? Sam didn't know, but he was absolutely certain the events that had played out before his eyes were true, something that happened centuries ago in Ancient Egypt.

Not only this new scene of Onuris meeting his goddess but before he had witnessed an older man, also bronze of skin like Onuris, running through a burning monastery in Moldavia, long after Ancient Egypt had fallen. Perhaps Celeste and his one-time date had turned him into some kind of... what? An oracle, a person able to see into the past...?

He didn't know, neither did he have the answer to the bigger question; why?

10. Scales Falling

'Yes, I'll keep an eye on things. But I'm telling you, Jake, things are not looking good there.'

Jake closed his eyes, focusing on the sound of Amy's voice. He didn't think she'd answer her phone, but she had. He told her that he was heading to Southend, indeed he was at Fenchurch Street now waiting for the train, mirroring the journey Will had taken almost a week ago. Amy wasn't much interested in his plans, but she did agree that Lawrencia needed keeping an eye on.

'Truth is, I'm not sure I am getting through to her.'

'But you are,' Jake pointed out. 'She even listened to me earlier when I asked her to pop over to her mum's. And she never listens to me. You can get through to anyone.'

'Hmm,' was the only response to that compliment.

Jake cringed. He didn't want to come on strong, but he couldn't help himself. Talking to Amy was hard, and he felt impelled to try and make her feel better. He still harboured much guilt and wasn't sure how to handle it.

'You better bring Will home soon, Jake, because I've seen what's going on. Lawrencia's got a broken finger, a black eye, and you can bet she never got that falling over Curtis' toys.'

'Shit.'

'Exactly. Jimmy's got himself into something big, and he's not playing ball very well. Which probably explains his broken arm. How long before Curtis gets dragged into this?'

Amy was spot on; it was just the same thing he'd warned Will of before he'd headed off to Southend himself.

Jake sighed. 'I'll be back soon.'

'Whatever, just make sure it's with Will.'

Without even a goodbye Amy ended the call, and Jake stood there on the platform, stung by her coldness. He knew he deserved it, but it still cut him to the core.

*

'This is all crazy talk,' Lizette said, as together she and Sam cleaned up the plates. Sam stood beside her, leaning his back against the draining board, cloth in hand and drying the crockery as she handed it to him. 'An oracle of the past?'

Sam shrugged. 'Why not? I'm only guessing, of course, but isn't it possible? I know what I'm seeing, and I know what happened to me in that alley.'

'Maybe you did escape some mental hospital?' Lizette asked playfully. 'Seriously, though, I don't know. Sure, there is a lot of historical fact that backs up a lot of the mythology, but usually such facts are only as good as the context. And we understand things a lot more these days, science gives rational thought to such supernatural occurrences.'

Sam looked at her closely. 'I'm not one of your students, Liz, you don't need to give me the party line. I *know* you don't believe that.'

Lizette was beat, and she knew it. 'Okay, fair enough, I'll admit there is something very odd going on, and your description of Ancient Memphis is scarily accurate, based on my studies.'

'Exactly, and I've never even been to Egypt, all I know of it is the little bits I've seen on the Discovery Channel and what I learned at school. Which wasn't a lot.'

Lizette handed him a plate, a curious look on her face. 'You're remembering more of your past?'

'A little bit,' Sam said quickly, in what he hoped was a convincing manner. She looked at him oddly for a moment, then turned back to the sink. Sam rolled his eyes. Got out of that one, just about. 'The past will keep, it's the present that interests me more.'

Lizette pulled the plug out of the sink and watched the water drain away. 'I can't deny the oddness that is you.'

'Well, no. We didn't meet in the conventional way, and then there's my eyes. And,' he added, placing the cloth on the side and turning away, 'have you seen me working out at all?'

'No,' Lizette said and looked over at him. He stood there, topless, his tee in one hand, and Lizette blinked in surprise. She stepped over to him and reached out for his six-pack. 'Wow. You weren't skin and bones when I found you outside, but...'

'Exactly.' Sam tensed himself, displaying his new definition. 'Even now I can feel my body just... *changing* somehow.' He shivered as Lizette's cold and wet palm pressed against his new abs.

She looked up at him and smiled. 'You know how I agreed we should take it slow?' she said, still looking him in the eyes, even as her free hand started gently pulling at his belt. 'Well, I'm tired of that idea. It seems very unfair that I spend all day working, knowing you're here, and not being able to test-drive you when I get home. Especially now. Not sure what these people have done to you, but it's amazingly hot.'

Sam raised an eyebrow, unable to keep himself from blushing. It was very clear from the life of Will that he'd been a man without even the remotest interest in women but, as Lizette pulled him closer to her once again, he felt that life belonged to a different person.

He held her hands steady, stopping her from unbuckling the belt. She looked up at him, her green eyes searching his face suggestively.

'Your hands are shaking,' she said, gently.

'Maybe I've never done this before,' Sam said just as gently.

This idea clearly appealed to Lizette, and she held his hand in hers and led him out of the kitchen. 'Don't worry, I'll guide you around the curves.'

Sam allowed himself to be led up the stairs, calmed by her words and assurance. He'd had sex before, of course, but this was a whole new world to him. And he found, as they entered her bedroom, that it was one he was looking forward to.

They stopped at the foot of the bed. She sat down and removed his belt, and then, slowly, began to unbutton his jeans. All the while he watched her, his breathing slow. He let out a gasp as her hands traced the outline of his boner pressing against his boxer briefs.

'There he is,' Lizette said, running her fingers around the band of his boxers, and carefully pulling them down. He stepped forward, leaving his discarded jeans and boxers on the floor behind him. 'Ooh, what's this then?'

Sam didn't need to look down to know that she had found the brand just above the pubic bone. 'Yeah, I noticed that myself.'

She ran her fingers over it, and Sam shuddered, the thinner layer of skin more sensitive than the rest. He smiled at Lizette and leaned over her. She lay back on the bed, lifting her arms above her. She smiled at him, and he reached out to remove her blouse.

*

Lizette rode him gently, building up a steady rhythm. He closed his eyes, enjoying the feel of her surrounding him. This was so unlike being with another man; gentler, the moistness of her lips puckering around his dick like a perfectly fitting glove. He let out a gasp of pleasure, feeling a sudden jerk down below.

Sam opened his eyes, looking up at Lizette, who was looking down at him with a smile, her hands running over his sweaty chest, fingers playing with the slight hair there. He reached up and caressed her breasts.

'Slowly,' she said, releasing him from her hold.

She rolled over, and he manoeuvred himself so he was kneeling between her legs. He brought his mouth down over a pert nipple, sucking softly, and with his free hand he guided himself back inside her.

'Yes, Onuris, give yourself to your god,' she said.

Sam let out a gasp...

... and Sekhmet arched her back as Onuris ran his tongue around her brown nipple. Her bronze body was moist with sweat, looking not a day older than when he had first seen her in the temple five years previously.

He, however, had aged. His body leaner, more toned. As she had promised he was now her high priest, her Hem-Netjer Tepey, and so much more than any other priest had been. He was the lover of a goddess, her chosen one.

He pressed himself deeper, gratified at the look of pleasure on Sekhmet's face.

She lifted her head, and as their lips touched Sam closed his eyes, quite delirious in the knowledge that, somehow, he was making love to two women at the same time.

*

'Anything in particular?' Sam called in from the living room.

Lizette grinned, still glowing, and called back. 'Oh, I don't know, something nice and post-coital.'

She listened to Sam laugh, then turned back to the coffees she was making.

116

They had crossed a new bridge, and for a while she had wondered if it would affect them in a bad way, but lying there beside each other afterwards had just been nice. Comfortable.

And the sex had been great. It was both tender and passionate at the same time, convincing her that Sam had never been with a woman before. He didn't strike her as a virgin, but the way he gently entered her told of his inexperience in such things.

She closed her eyes, and could still see him looking down at her, smiling, as his red eyes burned with his desire to make her happy.

His stamina was also amazing, holding back until she was ready to climax with him. They had truly crossed the bridge now and found themselves on green pastures.

Even more, she was certain that the future for them was going to be great, and she didn't mind that he was lying about recovering his memories. She could tell by the look in his eyes that he knew more than he was letting on, and that was okay. He had been through a lot, and even more was happening to him; there was only so much a person could process at once.

Lizette doubled over in pain, the spoon falling from her hand as she reached for her chest. She stumbled backwards but was just able to balance herself before falling against the washing machine.

For a moment she stood there, looking around, and a look brushed across her face. It was hard, mean, accompanied by a smile that spoke of perverse pleasure.

A knock came at the door, and her face returned to its usual gentle composure. She picked up the spoon and replaced it on the side. She was expecting no one, and it was unlikely to be someone for Sam.

'It's okay,' she said. 'I've got it.'

*

Frederick felt much better for his talk with Celeste, feeling like they were back on even footing again. He stuck around for a couple of hours, helping her where he could and talking more. Most of their conversation seemed to be about the old days, their long life together, as if they both knew on some unspoken level that those times were drawing to a close. He left her at the Residence to rest some more, after she had got in touch with Rochelle who had agreed to make some inquiries.

It was almost half eight, his train nearing Chalkwell, when it happened. Like a cannon ball smashing through the wall that stood between them, Frederick was hit by a clear sense of Will. He almost slid off his seat, knocked into near unconsciousness by the sudden contact.

An old woman reached out for him, but he had enough awareness to steady himself in time. The woman offered some advice about young people, and enjoying the drink while they could, then returned to her crossword.

The feelings Frederick was picking up from Will were intensely erotic. He frowned, wondering just what Will had been doing since Sunday night. The train stopped at Chalkwell and Frederick rushed out, clearing the steps up to the ticket office in three bounds. He came outside and paused, reaching out with his mind. He set off.

The house he found himself outside was familiar, facing out towards the seafront, just a few doors from the corner that turned into Ridgeway Gardens, leading to his own street. There was a blue Yaris parked in the driveway. Liz's house.

He reached the door and knocked. He waited a few moments before the door opened, and even though he'd been expecting Liz, his mouth still fell open in an 'O' of surprise at the sight of her in her pyjamas.

The reason for Will's erotic feelings was suddenly clear.

*

It was Fred.

Maybe he was calling to explain why he had almost ignored her outside the pub on Monday eve? He seemed the kind that needed to explain himself, although it did make her wonder how he knew where she lived. She didn't actually know him, but they'd often exchanged polite smiles and helloes. He looked to be about six feet, wearing a faded brown leather flight jacket and looked at her with brown eyes, his mouth an 'O' of surprise.

She wanted to get this call over as quickly as possible; all she really wanted to do was return to Sam, but in front of Fred she had a role to play, and politeness was expected.

'Can I help you?' she asked demurely.

Fred's face hardened, and he shook his head, looking at her coldly. She blinked, and then it came to her.

She knew exactly what Fred was, feeling the pull of the blood flowing in his veins. She held herself in check; it was too soon to give herself away.

A role was a role, and she suspected that she ought to be intimidated, but she knew that in truth Fred was as nothing before her. She forced herself to shudder.

Fred smiled thinly. 'I doubt it. I need to see Will.'

*

For a moment Liz seemed confused. 'There's no one of that name here.'

'Yes, there is. I can smell him all over you.' Frederick made to step into the house, but Liz held her ground, although she did take a step back.

'I've told you, there is no one of that name here, now please leave.'

'Oh, he's here, I can finally feel him.' He pushed past Liz. 'I've searched too long to be denied now.'

Out of the corner of his eye, he noticed Liz stagger into the kitchen, no doubt going to grab her phone and call the police. That didn't matter now. He had Will, who was standing at the edge of the room before him.

*

Sam sat on the sofa, fully dressed once again except for his socks and trainers, which were still in Lizette's room, mindlessly flicking through the channels, still pondering how it had felt to be with a woman. There was a time when such an idea would have made him shudder. Will could no more sleep with a woman than Jake could with a man. And yet, Sam could.

The changes his death had brought him seemed to include his sexuality. Certainly, the thought of relations with men still held an appeal for him, but he wasn't interested in getting with men anymore. He was only interested in Lizette now.

Sam was pulled out of his reverie by the voice at the front door. He froze for a second, then slowly stood.

Like a shard of metal pulled towards a magnet, he found himself drawing closer to the open living room door. The voice he knew well; he had heard it enough in his flashbacks. It was the same voice he had felt calling him earlier today.

Sam stopped at the doorway. Frederick was exactly as Sam remembered;

the brown leather jacket, the stubble on his handsome face, the short dark hair, and those deep brown eyes.

A feeling of dread welled up inside Sam. This was the man responsible for his death, who had the audacity to say that he'd done Sam a favour.

Everything came rushing back into his mind, every second of every moment, from inching his way out of the alley all the way to his meeting Lizette in the garden. He knew exactly what had happened to him, and more, what he could do to Frederick, who now stood at the door arguing with Lizette.

'I've told you, there is no one of that name here, now please leave.'

'Oh, he's here, I can finally feel him,' Frederick said, barging past Lizette. 'I've searched too long to be denied now.'

Over Frederick's shoulder, Sam saw Lizette turn and walk into the kitchen; he expected she was going to pick up the phone and call the police. Not that they could help now. Frederick stopped abruptly, his brown eyes alighting on Sam.

He smiled, but it was not a smile returned.

'You should have left me on the train,' Sam said. 'It's a mistake you're going to regret.'

*

Frederick smiled. Will was looking good, healthy, dressed in the same kind of clothes he had been wearing when they'd met on the train on Friday. He opened his mouth to speak, but Will's lack of smile chilled him.

'You should have left me on the train,' Will said. 'It's a mistake you're going to regret.'

'What? I...'

'What have you done to me?'

Frederick stepped closer. 'I saved you from death.'

Will reversed into the room, never taking his eyes off Frederick. 'Saved me? You killed me.'

'No, that was an accident, I...'

'An accident is falling over something you don't see, not ripping someone's throat out with...' Will paused and looked down at his hands as the skin around the tips of his fingers ripped open. 'With these!' He raised his hands, looking at the nail-like talons with a mixture of horror and wonder.

Frederick opened his arms out. 'Will, come with me, I can explain everything. You've entered a big world now, you need to...'

'No,' Will said, shaking his head. 'I will never come with you.' His eyes were burning red, the blood behind them bubbling away. 'You've made me a monster!'

Before he had a chance to react, Frederick was on the floor, one hand supporting his weight, the other cradling the gaping wound in his gut. Will had acted so fast, lashing out with the talons, ripping through Frederick's jumper, shirt and skin. Frederick took a deep breath and winced in pain. He looked up.

Will was standing there, looking at the blood on his talons in horror. Without a second's pause, he spun on his bare feet and ran.

For a moment Frederick remained as he was, trying to gather his strength. He was thankful for the blood he had procured from Rhys earlier that day, without it he would have been too weak to give pursuit. He stood up and licked his free hand. As he staggered out of the house he wiped his saliva over the wound and set off in the direction Will had fled.

Tracking Will, now the barrier between them was gone, would be child's play.

*

Time passed, and the house was empty but for Lizette who lay unconscious on the kitchen floor. She came to with a start, looked around confused, then nodded her head slowly. Of course, she remembered now.

She picked herself up. The front door was still ajar, so she walked over and closed it. She sniffed, smelling the blood in the air, and looked down at the spots of red that ran from the living room to the front door.

For the first time in years, she was truly awake again. Sleeping with Sam had been the catalyst, stripping away the life that had been Lizette. The fiction was gone, no more invented ex, no more kids...

She glanced up at the stairs, towards the bedroom her teen children used. Only now she knew, now she remembered, they never existed. All fake memories, created by her when she had returned to the world. A story to hide herself behind. Curiously, despite this knowledge, she still felt the tug at her heart, the sudden absence of the children who had been so real to her.

She shook it away. They had been a fiction... her real children were still out there.

She smiled and walked to the lounge.

The rug was stained with blood. She sniffed again, her lips pulling back in a grin, enjoying the coppery scent. She let out a yawn, tired all of a sudden, as if she'd just woken from a very long sleep. Which, she knew, in a way she had, and it was a sleep that carried with it a dream of decades.

She knelt on the carpet and placed her palm on the still-wet blood. She looked at her palm and brought it to her mouth.

It had been so long since she'd had the taste of fresh blood on her lips, not since she was known as Sekhmet, but how she remembered the taste of it. Only this was different. There was no purity in the blood, a hybrid of mixed cells. Human and something more.

She got a head full of Fred's face, his expression going cold. She smiled. It had been a long time since she had seen any of *her* children, and she had forgotten the impurity they carried with them. It was a necessary taint, a small price to pay, but still they carried a part of Sekhmet's ka with them.

She rose to her feet and looked around. Both Fred and her love were gone. But Sam would return. He always would, just as he had in Egypt when she was Sekhmet; as they promised centuries before. And when he did, he would find his wife waiting for him once again.

11. ABOUT CHARLIE

Marseille, 2006. It seemed so long ago. Celeste had taken a walk through the Residence, on her way to speak with Theodor and Eryn, when she found herself stopping in front of the painting that showed her and Frederick outside her home in France; *Château de Maupassant* looking out towards *Notre-Dame de la Garde*. She had been old back then, her body nearing the end, and even though the artist had captured her hidden strength, Celeste saw the truth. Another body used up, and the end of another member of the Maupassant 'family'. She had been fortunate to find Jasmine, a black beauty of thirty-four years, drifting through life, travelling the world, with little or no contact with her family and friends. A perfect choice to bring into the 'family'.

When the picture was painted, Frederick had just returned from one of his frequent trips to London, and now Celeste knew the nature of those visits. Keeping tabs on Willem. He had prepared things for almost a decade, believing the human to be the Seeker, not even realising that he was becoming more and more infatuated with Willem. She, too, had not seen it. Almost a decade, and not once did she pick up on the signs.

Celeste placed a hand against the wall and took a deep breath. She was still so very tired from the psychic assault, but she could no longer just sit about her chambers and rest. She was Celeste, of the Three, and had to be seen to be doing something. *Especially* now.

Rochelle was making waves, attempting to find out what she could about the investigation into Willem's disappearance; Frederick was off looking for Willem himself, while Theodor and Eryn were working the problem from other angles. Willem would be found and once he was, they would discover his true role in prophecy. Was he the Seeker, or the 'man of power' of whom the Lost Pages spoke? Or could he really be just an innocent caught up in this because of Frederick's attraction? The last option seemed increasingly unlikely in light of the psychic protection Willem's mind had, which left one of the two other options.

Frederick knew the Book inside out, and if he doubted Willem as the reincarnation of Onuris then she had to accept that as a very real possibility. But she knew little of the Lost Pages. Research was needed.

A prickling at the edge of her mind caused her to pause in her ruminations, and with a smile she realised it was Frederick. This was the first time in a week that he'd initiated a mind-link.

Celeste closed her eyes and saw what Frederick was seeing. He was walking into the same living room they had previously seen through Willem's eyes, and there was Willem himself. At last, they would get to the bottom of the mystery.

Celeste knew that her sense of joy was not totally her own, but rather she was feeling what Frederick was feeling. She could not hear the words being passed between them, Frederick was keeping that from her, but she could feel what Frederick felt. And more. Frederick was letting his happiness at finding Willem blindside him; he was not seeing the truth of things.

There was anger in Willem's eyes, the blood behind boiling in righteous fury.

'Frederick!' she hissed, a stab of pain forcing its way through her gut. She staggered against the wall and slid to her knees.

Frederick had been attacked. And with the pain of the attack, their link was severed.

'My lady!'

Celeste craned her neck up and spotted Nate on one of the upper gantries overlooking the long passage that ran the length of the Residence. She lifted a hand out to him, and frowned. She looked at her hand curiously, as if she had never seen it before.

She opened her mouth to speak, but before words could form darkness claimed her.

*

What Amy had said still troubled Jake. Was he doing the right thing in coming to Southend to find Will, leaving Curtis in a rapidly worsening situation? He had promised Will that he'd keep an eye on Curtis, but then that promise was made when they both thought Will would return after two nights... Jake tried to console himself with the thought that he and Will would come back to London together, and then they could take care of the fall of Jimmy.

It was almost eight by the time his train pulled in at Leigh-on-Sea Station, and he emerged onto a platform that was alien to him. He looked around for the exit, espied the stairs and set off, hefting his knapsack over his shoulder. He had his ticket ready, but found the gates already open, so he just passed through them and stepped outside the small ticket office into the cold and darkening night. He stood there for a moment, feeling a little bit lightheaded from the sea breeze. Having spent most of his life in the heart of a city, he was not used to such a ready supply of fresh air.

Directly in front of him, across the road from the station, was a grassy hill, steps leading to the top, passing through a dense clump of trees and foliage. Way more steps than Jake wished to manage. He wasn't unfit, working on a building site saw to that, but they were an awful *lot* of steps. A much more manageable road wound its way around the hill to the right. The area seemed to be mostly deserted, but for a few vehicles driving up and down the road, and someone slowly working their way down the long flight of steps.

Charlie had told him to wait by the taxi rank outside the station, so Jake crossed to the small island where two young men were waiting for a cab, both leaning against the railings, their hands linked together. They were only teenagers, and clearly had no issue with displaying their affection for each other in public. Jake frowned, wondering why it was that young people had no problems, and yet he, supposedly an older and wiser man, was still fighting it.

He turned away from the teens and looked out at the estuary beyond the station.

'Sweet, ain't it?'

He looked at Charlie, who had approached him from behind. 'Will would probably think so,' Jake offered.

Charlie nodded briefly at the teens. 'All right, lads?' They smiled at him. 'Cute couple,' he said, turning back to Jake.

Not sure what to say, Jake reached out a hand. Charlie took it and hugged Jake.

'Nice to meet you in the flesh, as it were,' Charlie said.

Jake pulled away, noticing the smile from the lads at the two men hugging. *Great*, he thought, *they think I'm one of them now*.

'Can I get your bag?'

'It's cool, I'm good,' Jake said, repositioning his knapsack onto his other shoulder, thinking that Charlie didn't look like he could lift a feather, let alone his densely packed knapsack.

For some reason, Jake had been expecting Charlie to be shorter than him, like most people he knew, but Charlie matched him for height, give or take an inch. But bulk-wise, Jake had him beat. Charlie was what people in fashion would probably call model slim, but Jake just saw it as skinny. Although Jake had to confess, the man did have a great smile.

'Okeydoke, then.' Charlie set off towards the road that wound its way up Belton Hills.

*

Will was definitely out there, that much Eryn *had* been told. Beyond that, she knew nothing of Celeste's and Frederick's meeting out at Canvey Heights. She didn't need to know anything else. It was enough to know that Will was still in Southend somewhere, and Eryn knew she could rely on Frederick to ensure he stayed there for a long while yet. Long enough, certainly, for Eryn to do what she needed to do.

For centuries she had played it carefully, keeping her arrogance and cantankerous nature on full display, hiding the truth behind such a rough exterior. Ever since she had returned to Theodor's side in 1739, no one had come close to guessing what she had committed herself to in Rome a couple of years before. She had still been young, and those close to Theodor accepted Eryn's ways for Theodor's sake, none had questioned why she had needed to travel. Since then, she had been careful, watching things, learning things, patiently waiting for the time Julius and she knew was coming. She had believed every word Julius had said, every word written in the Sekhmet Codex, but now...

Now she knew what she had to do. For the first time, doubts clouded her mind, and she was at a crisis of belief. Despite all she had learned, the facts surrounding Will's Rebirth needed further investigation. And to do that, Eryn needed the Book of Sekhmet itself. She knew enough of what it said, but this was only through what Frederick had shared with her. She needed to see it, to *read* it, herself.

To that end, she waited. For hours she waited until Frederick finally left the Residence. She followed Frederick, careful as ever to not be seen. All the way off Canvey, a few carriages away on the train from Benfleet. When Frederick alighted at Chalkwell, Eryn feared the worst. That he would return home. But instead, Eryn watched from the opposite side of the road as Frederick approached a house facing the seafront. There was some kind of altercation at the front door, a redheaded woman who didn't seem too happy to see Frederick. Eryn didn't care, once Frederick was inside the house she carried on her way. Turning at the next corner and walking up Ridgeway Gardens and onto Hill Way until she stood outside the house that contained Frederick's own little flat.

Frederick lived on the top floor, a converted loft. Eryn scanned the street, some homes were occupied, but she didn't mind. She was used to stealth. All that mattered was the rest of the house before her was unoccupied, no cars in the driveway and no lights on in any rooms.

She approached the door and put one hand to the Yale lock as if she were holding a key. With the least bit of pressure, she busted the lock clean off the door and stepped inside. So as not to arouse any suspicion, she punched on the hall light before heading up the stairs.

Frederick always remained coy about the location of the Book, but Eryn knew him enough that she was sure the Book would be hidden in some secret place in his flat. A place of residence kept secret from the upiór world at large. Anyone foolish enough to try and procure the Book would aim for the Residence.

Luckily Eryn was no fool. It might take her some time, but she would find the Book.

*

Charlie's house was big; too big for one person. Charlie explained that the house actually belonged to his great aunt, but she was very ill and now lived in a care home, and had asked that Charlie move in and take care of the old house. It had been in his family for eighty years and Great Aunt Mable couldn't bear the thought of selling it or renting it out to some stranger. This worked out quite well for Charlie since it was close to Old Leigh, a place he often liked to visit to chill out with the fishermen, surrounded by the smells of salty water and freshly caught fish. Jake turned his nose up at this, and Charlie had laughed. His dad had been a fisherman in Old Leigh, and so Charlie had been brought up with the smell.

Jake stopped when he entered the lounge, located at the front of the house, and looked at the glass-framed picture that took pride and place above the antique fireplace. It was a play on the old Obsession from Calvin Klein ad from ten years ago; a Travis Fimmel look-a-like glancing down, his fingers lifting the band of his boxers, with the legend above his head now reading 'OBSESSION FOR MEN'. Jake smirked.

Charlie noticed Jake's smile. 'Not wrong though, eh? Never met a man that it didn't apply to.'

'Some men more than others,' Jake said glibly, thinking of Mike, and wandered further into the room.

It was a strange place, a mix of old and modern as if Charlie was fighting a never-ending battle to put his own stamp on a house that had lived many lives that it did not wish to give up.

Much of the furniture was old but well kept, no doubt owing more to Great Aunt Mable than Charlie, with occasional pieces of ornamentation scattered around the room. A shelving unit in one corner of the room housed DVDs, with the top shelf reserved for a collection of toys. Jake walked over and smiled at the memories the old toys brought back. *Transformers, He-Man and the Masters of the Universe*, and a couple of very rare action figures of Admiral Kirk and Spock from *Star Trek: The Motion Picture*. It was funny; on several outings with Curtis, he had taken the kid to many toyshops that were full of modern versions of the toys set out carefully before him. In some ways the contemporary toys were better sculpted, much more detail and scale, but there was a lot to be said for the clunkiness of the older toys.

A row of DVDs on the next shelf down caught his eye. Suppressing an unexpected shudder, Jake noticed that Charlie had the full series' of both the British and American versions of *Queer as Folk*, not to mention several discs of *Will & Grace*. Next to them was something called *Dante's Cove*, which Jake did not recognise, but judging by the almost naked man in the thumbnail picture on the spine, he could work out what it was about. He was reminded of Will's own collection, and he was sure it didn't contain half as many gay DVDs as Charlie owned.

Jake hated the feeling, but he suddenly felt uncomfortable. Being around Will was one thing; they had known each other since they were kids, but with Charlie it was different. He felt awful for feeling like he did, but he couldn't help it.

He looked over at the small clock sitting on the mantle above the fire. It was almost a quarter to nine, which meant it was nearing time to hit the nightclubs. His eyes came to rest on a pair of tickets beside the clock, and for a moment forgetting how nosey he was being, he walked over and looked closer. They were for a show at Cliff's Pavilion. He looked up and saw a sadness in Charlie's eyes that made him want to offer some kind of comfort. Jake looked back at the tickets and noticed the date.

He offered Charlie a smile. 'Hey, when we find him, you guys can probably take in another show, yeah?'

Charlie smiled back, but Jake was not sold on the sincerity of it. 'That'd be nice.'

The smile got broader as Charlie considered the idea further, and Jake felt a brief stab of jealousy. That Charlie cared deeply for Will was obvious, and he still held on to the hope that soon they'd get the chance to be together. The jealousy was washed away by guilt; Jake knowing for sure that he'd be the one obstacle that Charlie would not be able to climb.

Once found, it was clear in Jake's mind who Will would choose.

Jake shifted his weight from one foot to another. 'Hey, can I borrow your toilet? Not had a pee since I left London. Not keen on those train toilets.'

'Can't blame you on that score,' Charlie said and led Jake out of the lounge. 'You could use the loo in the back yard, but it's cold out there and can't see how that'd help your case.'

Jake consciously glanced down, wondering if perhaps his jeans were too tight. He glanced back at the picture over the mantle.

Obsession ain't the word, he thought.

As he mounted the staircase, Charlie was still talking. 'I'll show you where you're crashing, too.'

Jake followed. He had visions of Charlie leading him to his bedroom, explaining how the big house got cold so they'd have to snuggle up, but instead Charlie took him to what was obviously a little-used spare room. Everything was so clean and in its right place.

'There you go, make yourself comfortable. Place has been prepared for a while now, ever since I knew that...' Charlie shrugged. 'Well, you know.'

'You mean...?' Jake was puzzled. 'You were gonna let Will use the spare room? But I thought you and him...'

'I know, but playing over Skype isn't the same as expecting someone to share your bed. Besides,' Charlie added with a smile, 'I like to think I'm a gentleman where it counts.'

Clearly he had misjudged Charlie on an epic scale. He was suddenly reminded of something he'd said to Francis and Sandra, about how Charlie was the innocent one in all this.

Jake offered a smile, and Charlie returned it.

I've misjudged a lot of things lately...

12. An Outpouring of Hate

Lawrencia was glad Curtis was in his bedroom and more that he was keeping quiet. He was still fully dressed; all set for a visit to see his nana, unfortunately Jimmy had arrived home before she could leave with her son. And, once again, he was not in a good mood.

She stood in the corner of the pokey kitchen, the sink just to the side of her below the window, with the cooker on the other side of her. Jimmy stood in the doorway, raging about the deal that had fallen around him.

Lawrencia let him carry on. There was nothing she could say that would make it better. Already he was on his favourite subject, apportioning the blame. In this case, it was lying squarely on Billy's shoulders; if he had returned when he said he would then they would not be in the trouble they were now. Owed money would have been paid, leaving the door open for Jimmy to get more gear, which he could have peddled out for a nice tidy profit. Instead, her brother had decided to dump them in the shit, and look what had happened. At this point Jimmy had begun to wave his broken arm around, which, Lawrencia noted with a touch of satisfaction, was still covered in a clean fibreglass cast, free of any messages or jokes from friends. For that Jimmy would need actual friends.

Lawrencia glanced down and made an effort to stop rubbing her own broken finger. Thanks to the metal splint the finger would heal fine, it would remain weak for a long while, but it would be fine. In the meantime, it was a constant reminder of how things had escalated since Billy had gone missing.

Her own anger towards him had gone, replaced by common sense. She had to thank Amy for that; Jake was a lucky man to have found someone like Amy. She had talked much sense to Lawrencia, told her about her own upbringing. How her mother had been in an abusive relationship, and how she never managed to get out of it. Amy had explained what it was like growing up in such an environment; she had been lucky to have her brother around, but Curtis had no such peer support. At first, Lawrencia hadn't wanted to hear it, but she saw the truth in Amy's eyes, and she knew the woman was right.

As she stood there, not really listening to Jimmy, she knew she had to get out. For both her sake and Curtis'. But she needed help; she needed her big brother.

'No.'

Jimmy stopped abruptly, looking like he'd been slapped.

Lawrencia shook her head and repeated herself more firmly. 'No. You're always blaming everyone else, but it's you. You did all this to us, because you're weak.' Now she had said it, Lawrencia felt stronger, buoyed by the truth of her words. Jimmy *was* weak, he was an addict, and he didn't have the balls to try and get help. She opened her mouth to speak more, careful not to allow her nerves to get the better of her. 'You did this,' she said, raising her finger, 'no one else! It's you who's making my son into a gibbering wreck. He's barely three, he shouldn't have to put up with this shit.'

Lawrencia stood up straight, enjoying the look of surprise on Jimmy's face. She knew it wouldn't last, so she had to make the best of it. Keeping her head held high, hiding the fear, she made to leave the kitchen, keeping her eyes on Jimmy. All she had to do was get passed him, grab Curtis and leave. It was so simple; she could do it.

'You bitch,' Jimmy said in a voice so low that Lawrencia thought she had only imagined him speaking. But then he turned his head and looked directly at her. Lawrencia froze. 'Who the fuck do you think you are?' he asked, his voice rising slightly.

Lawrencia gathered her wits and was ready to tell him exactly who she was when he lashed out, and she found herself back in the corner, a trickle of blood running from the cut just above her eye.

'You think you know me? You don't know shit,' Jimmy said, advancing on her. 'You're mine. Curtis is mine.'

Lawrencia watched him approach, his free hand unbuckling his belt. He wasn't going to hit her with it, that much she knew. He was going to show her how much she was his to do with as he pleased. Her hand went to her belly, forever barren because of a previous demonstration of his control. Lawrencia closed her eyes, hating herself.

Amy was wrong, she thought as she heard Jimmy popping the buttons on his jeans. There was no fighting, there was no escape.

She could only give in to the inevitable.

She felt his fingers lift her skirt, violently pulling down her knickers. And then, with a force that made her gasp, his disgusting dick, that weapon he had used against her so many times, was inside her. Her back was pressed against the sink, and Jimmy thrust deeper into her, his anger spilling out.

Still Lawrencia kept her eyes screwed shut, hoping against hope that Curtis would not venture out of his room.

There was no escape. She knew that now.

Will, she thought, as a single tear rolled down her cheek.

*

It was as she had expected. She had her ways, and it didn't matter how many lives she lived they would always remain the same. Once the new identity was set up, she would retreat into herself, yet still maintain a periphery of awareness, subtly preparing for the time when she would awake again. Keeping an eye on her children, while all the time waiting for her love to recognise her, to see her for who she was, and to truly realise who he was.

She hoped this was the time. Her husband had returned, only he didn't know it yet, but he was so close this time. *So* close.

Sekhmet reached into the back of the wardrobe and there she found it. She remembered buying it, forking out much more money than her mortal self would ever have normally spent on a dress. But nonetheless, she still bought it, brought it home and stored it in the back of her wardrobe, and there it remained, forgotten about until her true self surfaced again.

And now she laid the dress on the bed and looked it over. It was of the finest white silk, straight and tailored perfectly for her body. There was little about it that would draw the eye, no silly frills, it was merely plain. But then Sekhmet knew that her allure would not be a result of frills and spectacle, it came from a deeper well. She had always had a way with men, able to lure even the most ambivalent to her, and from her life as Lizette she knew the world into which she had awoken. Men were driven by their lusts more than ever. All would fall before her.

She turned from the dress and walked across the landing to the shower. It was time to freshen up. To take in the world with her own eyes, no more encumbered by the morality of the human identity she had built. She needed to prepare, for Sam would return to her, and when he did she would be ready for him.

*

Tracking Will had been child's play, just as Frederick had expected. Will had turned off into Ridgeway Gardens, heading past the green and up Hill Way. Frederick followed, passing by his own home, so focused on Will that he failed to notice his kitchen light on at the top of the house. Instead, he carried on, up the tree-lined street, knowing full well that Will was heading towards Chalkwell Park.

Frederick stopped outside the entrance on Old Leigh Road and looked around. It was almost nine o'clock now, and on a Thursday night the road was mostly deserted, apart from the odd car heading to or from London Road at the far end of the park. As he jumped the fence, he was reminded of a similar event in another park barely a week earlier. He suspected this encounter would go better.

He landed on the path and looked about the park. The park itself was in darkness but for the lights of the surrounding buildings and streets. In front of him, just past the field was a small wooden fence circling a little pond, to the left of which sat a play area for children. Frederick could sense Will in that direction, and for a moment he wasn't too sure where exactly, but then he saw him.

Back to Frederick, Will was sitting on the wooden fence, his head lowered, body visibly shaking. Frederick smiled. It was time.

'Will.'

Frederick stopped a few feet away, the pain from his healing stomach a reminder of the strength now wielded by Will. The fledgling showed no sign of hearing Frederick whisper his name, but Frederick knew he heard. Will was now an upiór, and even though he had spent the best part of a week without the guidance of his maker, he still had their preternatural gifts, and that included enhanced hearing. Frederick put a hand on his stomach, testing the wound through the tear in his shirt, and stepped closer to the wooden fence.

'I've been looking for you.'

'Now you've found me,' Will pointed out, his voice also soft.

Frederick smiled, glad to hear the anger gone. Will still looked away, though, his head lowered.

'What did you do to me?'

Frederick took a deep breath. There was much to explain. He could barely begin to understand how it must have been for Will the past four days, living as an upiór but with no understanding of how or why, or indeed *what*, it meant for his life. Not wanting to risk damaging his healing stomach, Frederick walked around the fence.

'I saved you,' he said, once he was near Will.

'From what?'

Still Will looked to the grass, and Frederick wondered if he was as clueless as he seemed. It was possible. His whole Rebirth was off-key, and it was very possible that he had lost his memory as a result of the whole strangeness of it. It would explain why Will had done nothing to find Frederick.

'You were dying, don't you remember?'

Will swallowed and looked up. 'We were mugged, right?'

'Yes, in the alley near Zinc.' Frederick offered a weak smile. 'We went into the alley to...' He raised an eyebrow. 'Well, you know.'

Will smiled briefly and looked away. 'Yeah, I remember that. There were four of them. You took them on, and I...' He shook his head. 'Well, one moment I was almost there, and the next I was on the ground with some bastard cracking me in the ribs with his boots.'

'I took care of him,' Frederick said and reached out for Will.

Will flinched, and Frederick pretended to not be bothered. But the rejection stung.

'It was supposed to be a perfect night, the start of something amazing, but then I saw you on the ground and...'

'And you took care of them.' Will was silent for a moment, before adding, 'Then took care of *me*.'

The accusation was clear. 'No, it wasn't like that. I didn't mean to...'

'Yeah, an accident. You said.' Will looked up again and fixed Frederick with his transparent eyes. 'These are not normal, are they? I had brown eyes, but now...' He held his hands up, showing the drying blood on his fingertips from where his talons had ripped Frederick's skin open. 'And these? What the fuck have you done to me, Fred?'

'I saved you. You have to understand, Will, you were dying. Things escalated and before I knew it you were there, and I...' Frederick lowered his head.

There really was no excuse; he had been caught in the hunger, in a blood frenzy. And he had struck out blindly. But he had honestly never meant to hurt Will. That was never his intention.

'I'm sorry,' he said, beginning to hear a familiar ring to his tone. Not only were they the same words he had used with Celeste, but the truth behind them was just as real. 'I'm sorry for how it happened, and for not finding you.'

'Did you really try and find me?'

'I did, tried everything, engaged all the contacts I knew that might be of help. I...' Frederick looked away, towards Chalkwell. 'All this time you were so close, but I still couldn't feel you. I should have sensed you somehow. Should have tried harder. I'm sorry.'

'Are you? I mean, really? Do you even understand the meaning of the word, Fred? Cause, you know, I've got to wonder.' Will climbed off the fence and walked over to the pond. 'Did I see what I thought I saw? You were lapping up the blood of those bastards, weren't you? Like some animal.'

Frederick watched him, but he didn't move himself. 'Yes,' he replied. 'You did see that. But we're not animals, what you witnessed was a rare instance. The blood hunger got the better of me, yes, but we're not animals.'

Will glanced back, and the disgust on his face was clear. 'We?' he repeated quietly, almost to himself. 'Yes, I guess I'm one of you now. A vampire.'

'We're not vampires. We are upiór. Vampires are monsters of myth, of supernatural fiction. We're real, and we are not monsters. As I said, you saw an extreme case. Sometimes we can get caught up in feeding, and the hunger overwhelms us. This is why we don't usually drink from people; it's too dangerous for us.'

'Right, and not exactly a picnic for them, either.' Will rubbed his throat. 'You fed off me, too. I remember, after you ripped into my throat...' He stopped at the pond and looked over towards Frederick, but Will was not looking *at* him. 'You held me in your arms, and you kissed me, and then you drank... No, you sucked the blood out of my mouth. *Through* my tongue. Why?'

'Because you had lost much blood, you were dying,' Frederick replied, and began walking over to Will.

'Trained doctor now, are you? You could have called an ambulance. I might have been okay.'

Frederick shook his head. 'No, I couldn't. The human world mustn't intrude on ours. We have our own way of dealing with things, our own people to call in.'

'Your *own* people? What the hell is that supposed to mean?' Before Frederick could answer, Will waved it away. 'It doesn't matter.' His eyes narrowed as a new thought came to him. 'Why didn't you call these people? Instead of—'

'I panicked,' Frederick said, cutting in. His voice almost sounded desperate and he hated it. He began to draw closer to Will, his steps small and measured. 'I saw all the blood coming out of your throat from where I...'

'Ripped it open with those talons?' The sarcasm was laced with bitterness. Frederick couldn't blame him.

'Yes. I couldn't lose you, Will; I had only just found you. I thought you were someone else, but I was wrong, the connection I felt with you, it was... Real.' He was barely a foot away from Will now. Frederick reached out. 'From the moment I saw you I wanted you, and that night was going to be so special for us. I could not let you go.'

Will said nothing; he just looked into Frederick's eyes. The anger seemed to be fading, replaced by a confusion Frederick understood all too well. He'd felt it himself enough over the last few days. He knew a way to prove what he said, to remove the confusion.

He leaned forward and kissed Will full on the lips. At first, Will tensed, but then he took Frederick's head in his hands and parted Frederick's lips with his tongue.

Frederick knew this would happen. Others may have doubted him and his motives, but his reasons for following Will's life, for waiting until he finally headed towards Southend as the Book had said he would, making sure Will had been on that train, had been pure. He had truly believed Will to be the Seeker. But when he'd seen him dying in the alley, Frederick had known the truth. And from the moment he had passed his own blood into Will's he had known this moment would come to pass.

That Will and he would be together, just as Celeste had known the same of Frederick centuries ago when she had first laid eyes on him in Posen.

Will pushed him away.

'What?' Frederick asked, barely a second before Will's fist caught him clean on the jaw, the sudden impact knocking him off the ground.

Frederick flew backwards and landed with a splash in the small pond. He lay there for a moment, overcome with both pain and surprise. His head felt like it had been knocked clear off his neck, but it hurt too much to be so. He looked over at Will, who stood at the edge of the pond, his fists clenched, face contorted in disgust.

'What the hell do you think you're doing?' Will growled.

Frederick struggled to his feet, keeping his eyes on Will all the while, a task not made easy by the dizziness that was threatening to drop him back on his arse. 'I was trying to...' He stopped, his own anger suddenly springing forth. 'You kissed me back! What the hell is wrong with—?'

He was on his back again, winded by Will's shoulder as the younger man cannonballed into him. Frederick struggled beneath Will's weight, as he claimed a position of control. Fortunately, the pond was so shallow that the water barely reached Frederick's ears, and so there was no fear of him drowning. Not that such a thing would kill him, of course, but now was not the time to slip into unconsciousness. So, he stopped struggling and allowed Will to sit astride him, pinning him by the arms.

'Isn't this what you wanted?' Will whispered, his voice a rumble of hate. He leaned down until his face was barely inches away. 'You want to be inside me, right?' He squirmed on Frederick, pressing against Frederick's rapidly hardening dick.

For a brief second he closed his eyes, and let out a whisper. 'Yes.'

Will smiled, and moments later his tongue was in Frederick's mouth again. He shook his head, pulling away from Will's face as much as he could.

'No,' he said, 'not here. Not now.'

Will smiled again, but it was a smile of darkness, promising much in twisted pleasure. Frederick liked it. 'Then where?'

'My place,' Frederick said. 'It's not too far away.'

13. The Fact of Fiction

He sat on the arm of the chair, looking out of the window, down at the darkened street below. From his vantage point in the converted attic flat, he was higher than the trees that lined Hill Way, their dense leaves and branches concealing much of the street. It was early, and there was nothing to really see anyway. Cars parked up, the distant sounds of cats fighting and foxes wailing.

Will.

It was a name that Frederick had used a lot since he'd stormed into Lizette's home, a name Frederick had practically screamed when he had shot his load deep inside him. It was the name of the man who owned the two bags sitting on the carpeted floor next to the chair, the contents of which were like a snapshot of Will's life. But they, like the name, belonged to a different man.

Will would never have done the things Sam had done since Frederick had found him in the park. Sam knew Will better than anyone, and he knew Will would be disgusted by Sam's actions. Will was too vanilla; he played things too safe. For Will, dangerous was going to meet someone he had only previously known online.

Sam stood up. He could hear the wind outside; see the rain pounding against the glass. There was no heating on in the flat, but despite all that, he wasn't even remotely cold, even though he walked the flat in all his naked glory. Clearly a benefit of being what Frederick had called an upiór.

Of course, strictly speaking, he had lived in this state for four days, although he hadn't known it. He had known something odd was going on with his body, but he had never truly bought Lizette's line about his eyes being some genetic defect. And then there was the way his musculature was developing without even the slightest workout. So much he needed to know.

Two things he knew for sure; he didn't crave blood at all (which was a relief since just the memory of seeing Frederick lap up that blood in the alley turned his stomach), and his transparent eyes were a natural thing for an upiór, as he had found out when Frederick had removed his contacts. Seeing the eyes on another person made Sam realise that they weren't see-through as such; you could still *see* the eyeball, it was just clear, all the pigmentation of the pupil and cornea gone, putting the vitreous chamber on full view, allowing all the blood flowing through the optic nerve to be seen.

That he had been turned into a vampire, or an upiór or whatever you wanted to call it, did not explain much. It didn't offer Sam any insights into the memories he had of Ancient Egypt, of being in a burning monastery in Moldavia, or why he had been seeing so many other scenes played over the real-world events around him. Events and people; lives that could not possibly belong to one single person.

Since laying eyes on Frederick at Lizette's, those scenes had faded away, as if his focus on Frederick had pushed them aside. He felt sure they would return soon enough.

There hadn't been much conversation between him and Frederick, though, since leaving the park, mostly small talk, innuendo and the like. Words pretty much went out of the window as soon as they had entered Frederick's top-floor flat. Clothes were practically torn off as Frederick gave in to the passion, completely oblivious that Sam was merely going through the motions. Sex was a tool to use against someone like Frederick. He was so caught up in Will, believing they were destined to be together, that Sam barely needed to lead him on.

But when they got to the bedroom, it was Frederick who took the lead, taking Sam to places of sexual pleasures that Will had never known existed. The end result had been messy, leaving the bed covers stained with blood, semen and wax, the 'toys' discarded on the floor. He had to admit, to himself at least, he had a feeling he might have enjoyed it more than Frederick, especially when he discovered how easily his body healed. He wasn't sure if it was down to the changes brought on by being turned into an upiór, but his sexual prowess and stamina was something else, and the two of them had come to climax many times over.

Eventually, now spent, Frederick had fallen asleep, his naked body wrapped around Sam's. He had lain there for a while before he disentangled himself from Frederick and crept out of the room. He needed time alone, away from the man who had altered his life so. He didn't know what Frederick had in mind for the two of them, but Sam was certain that whatever it was it would never come about.

He had a shower before entering the lounge, cleaning himself both of the dried mud from walking barefoot in the streets and park, and of Frederick's body.

Frederick was a source of information, and Sam would keep him around for as long as he needed him, no more. He had no loyalty to Frederick, and no desire to be with him. Once done, Sam would return to Lizette.

He looked towards where he knew her house was. It was almost four in the morning, and she would be up soon to get herself ready for another day at work.

He hoped she wasn't worrying too much. She was a very level-minded woman and seemed able to deal with most things. She had adapted very well to the stranger who had entered her life. Sam wondered, if worst came to worst, would she adapt with equal ease to the stranger leaving her life just as quickly? He hoped they would not have to find out.

But, then, he no longer knew what kind of world he was now a part of. Frederick had found him, how many other upiór would eventually follow? And what would that mean for Lizette? For sure Sam was convinced that those people he'd met at the Residence on Canvey were more of the same. Even back then, a week ago today now Sam came to think of it, Will had been a little wary of those people. Business contacts who were more like family to Frederick, something that he'd promised to explain to Will later that night. It was an explanation that had never come.

Sam looked towards the living room door and the passageway beyond. Out there, sleeping like a babe, Frederick held the answers Sam needed.

A week late, Sam was going to get them. Now that he had 'given into' Frederick he felt sure he could get the information he needed, without the emotional crap getting in the way.

He crouched down and pulled the bags towards him, and began to rummage through them. So many things, but, he noted, no sign of his mobile phone. Did that matter, though? What use would that phone be now, with all the contacts contained therein another link to a life barely his?

Still, he remembered everything; the clothes, the toiletries, even the Paul Magrs novel. He turned the paperback over in his hands and read the blurb; *The Bride that Time Forgot*, 'an outrageous adventure with the most terrifying villain Brenda has ever faced – her best friend, Effie...' It felt like it was a book he should like, but like most other things in the bags, it was as if they belonged to someone else.

He had to force himself to remember that he *was* Will. That the past thirty-five years were his, all the memories, the relationships, the family. It was as real, maybe even more so than all those memories and events he had experienced since coming to in Lizette's garden. Everything left in London was still his, and it was all there waiting for him to return. But even if he wanted to, and with Lizette here he wasn't sure he did want to, how could he return to that life, knowing what he now knew, having become a creature of the night?

Laughter erupted uncontrollably from his mouth. He tried to hold it back, but couldn't. The absurdity of everything had finally caught up with him.

A week ago he had been a successful businessman in London, with a very dependent sister, a nephew he adored, and a best mate he loved like a brother. And now he was... what? A being of supernatural ability, a drinker of blood, and possibly immortal? On top of that he was convinced that somehow, because of what Frederick had done to him, he had become an oracle into the past.

As the morning darkness turned into light with the rising sun, Sam remained sitting on the chair, naked as the day he was re-born, chuckling away to himself, routing through the stuff that was technically his property.

Waiting for Frederick to awake, so that he could finally get the answers he needed.

*

Frederick awoke to the smell of cooked meat. The unmistakable salty aroma of fried bacon. Which puzzled him a little, since he knew he did not have any bacon in his fridge. He got out of bed, smiling at the memories brought back by the sight of the bed sheets – it was everything he'd expected it to be – and slipped on his boxers as he walked into the living room. Stuff was strewn across the floor, the contents of Will's rucksack and holdall.

He found Will in the kitchen, dressed as he was yesterday, curiously not having availed himself of the change of clothes that his bags afforded him (although he now wore the Vans shoes once more), flipping bacon over in the frying pan. A bag from the nearby Londis at Ridgeway Gardens was on the side, its contents in as much disarray on the sideboard as Will's stuff was on the living room floor.

Funny. Frederick always assumed Will was a tidy person. Not that he minded, after all, he was more than happy for Will to make himself at home. As long as they were together.

Frederick noticed, also, that Will's mobile was no longer sitting on the kitchen counter where he had left it when Celeste came to call the other day.

'Morning,' he said.

Will looked over his shoulder and smiled. 'Good morning, sleepy head. Thought you'd have more stamina,' he added with a wink.

Frederick raised his eyebrows in mock defeat. 'Well, I did, but you...' He grinned. 'You're something else entirely.'

'I know,' Will said and leaned over to kiss Frederick. He closed his eyes to savour the taste of Will's lips on his. 'Now, you go and get cleaned up while I finish breakfast. Then you can tell me everything.'

'Deal,' Frederick said and turned back to the living room. He didn't care if he had the stupidest grin on his face, either.

*

Sam watched Frederick walk away, and as soon as the other man was out of sight his smile faded. Damn fool. Sam figured he should probably feel bad, after all, what he was doing to Frederick wasn't so far removed from the emotional manipulation that Lawrencia often used on their mother, a fact Will had often got pissed off about. But guilt was far from his mind.

If pretence was needed to get the information he required, then so be it. Frederick had led him on a week ago, brought him into a world so different from his own, and had he felt guilty? Sam didn't think so. Frederick wanted

Will and so he had done what he had to do to get him, including alienating him from Charlie.

So much Frederick had to answer for. But first, it was a matter of answers *needed*.

*

'Shouldn't we be burning up about now?' Will asked.

'Why?' Frederick wanted to know, as he followed Will out of the kitchen, holding his cooked breakfast before him.

Such a domestic routine as eating breakfast with a loved one was not something Frederick had really partaken of in hundreds of years. That said, he didn't think he'd taken part in such an occasion when he was human, either. It was so long ago; sometimes he could barely remember what it was like to be human, never mind the smaller moments of his human existence.

Even when around Celeste he never partook in such a convention, preferring to leave such a quaint custom to the humans. He found he was enjoying the unexpected domestication that being around Will was bringing, but of course, he knew it wouldn't last. Much about human ways would slip by the wayside the more Will embraced his new heritage.

He looked back at Will, who indicated the sun poking through the clouds.

'I'm no expert on vampire lore, but I've seen enough films to know that vampires and sunlight don't mix.'

'Right,' Frederick said, thinking it was going to be a long day if he had to dispel every erroneous 'fact' of vampire lore. But still, he was glad of Will's interest.

After last night's initial reunion, Frederick feared for their future, but he now chalked it up as confusion on Will's part. Frederick had been lucky, he had the guidance of Celeste to help him through that first week, Will had no one. Until now.

'Death by sunlight was a dramatic invention of Murnau for *Nosferatu*, and that was only in '22. Of course as you've kindly demonstrated, has become a convention of almost all vampire fiction.' He sat down, with his back to the sofa and placed the plate on the carpet before him.

'Okay, so how much vampire lore is crap, and how much is true? Obviously, I'm gonna have to accept some things now, since I saw what I saw, and... well, can't deny what's happened to me.'

Frederick waited for Will to sit himself on the rug before the mock fireplace, cross his legs, and rest his plate on his lap.

'For a lie to work it needs to be shrouded in truth,' Frederick began, 'and myth is much the same.'

'Right. So, I'm not a full vampire until I drink blood, right?'

'What?'

'I'm sure I've read that somewhere, or seen it in a film.' Will furrowed his brow as he tried to recall the information. His eyes lit up. '*The Lost Boys*, I think it was. Or is that a werewolf myth?'

'Werewolf?' Frederick shook his head. 'I think you need to slow down, there's much to process, and all this subsidiary stuff will only confuse you more.' He reached out and placed a hand on Will's knee. 'Okay? Let's focus, leave all other supernaturals things to one side.'

'Other? You mean there are more than vampires out there?'

Frederick sighed, but he couldn't help but smile. 'Yes,' he said slowly, 'otherworldly *things* have pre-dated man by... Well, millions of years probably. Humanity has only been on this world, really, for a blink of an eye when considering how old the universe is. All you need to remember is that every myth has some bearing in fact. There are many things that go bump in the night, *and*,' he nodded at the sunlight coming through the window, 'in the day, come to that.'

Will ran a hand over his face. 'Right, okay. Still processing.' He looked down at his plate and cut himself a piece of bacon. 'Tell me about where the vampires came from.'

'Very well, best place to start is at the beginning.' Frederick paused dramatically, and then began, for the moment glad of Will's attention. 'First of all, we call ourselves upiór. The legends of our origins are sparse, but there is a little in the Book...'

'The Book?' Will asked around a mouthful of egg.

'Later,' Frederick said with a sigh. Will threw him an apologetic look, and Frederick continued. 'Now, Wamukota tells us that the first vampires were truly demonic creatures. Beasts whose only purpose was to drink the blood of the living; human, animal, it didn't matter. Their appetite was insatiable. Any form of intelligence, of higher reasoning, was lost to them. Wamukota does allude to such facilities once, but something happened, turned them into monsters driven by their base nature. He also tells us that there was a woman, or possibly many women... the texts are unclear... who lifted them above the craven monsters they were. Through the millennia she would come to them, guide them, nudge them up the evolutionary ladder.

'And hence vampire lore and myth spread across the globe; each country had different tales of creatures that feasted on blood. Some stories contained similar themes, the creatures bore the same traits, but others differed strongly. Which brings me to Ancient Egypt.'

All the time Will had been listening, looking down at his food with a thoughtful look, but now his head snapped up, his red eyes piercing straight into Frederick.

Something crawled across his skin, and he wasn't sure why.

*

There was something very familiar about all of this, although at the same time, Sam knew he had never heard or read anything about the history of vampires as Frederick told it. But he could not escape the feeling that he somehow knew it already. The idea of this woman – or women – rang very true to him, as for there being supernatural creatures that pre-dated man...? Yes, deep down he just knew this was all... familiar, if not absolutely true. And then there was the name Wamukota meant something to him, too. He closed his eyes, drifting on the words Frederick spoke, but his mind returned to that monastery in Moldavia, the one he had seen so many times before.

The old man, dodging falling masonry, careful to not let the flames touch his frail skin. The book he carried in his arms. Wamukota was his name.

Sam snapped his eyes open and looked up at Frederick. 'What of Ancient Egypt?'

Frederick looked at him, and for a split second he seemed suspicious. Sam flashed his best smile and laughed.

'Sorry, always had a kind of interest in Egypt, ever since I first saw that *Doctor Who* episode with the mummies in. Every year Jake and I would dress as mummies at Hallowe'en; got kind of old eventually, though.'

The look on Frederick's face softened for a moment, until Sam mentioned Jake, then the look turned to one of jealousy. Sam didn't react, merely remembering the same look in Frederick's eyes outside Zinc during

147

the early hours of Saturday morning. Jealousy could prove to be a useful weapon. Later.

'What do you think of the bacon?' he asked.

'It's good,' Frederick said, forking some into his mouth. 'What do you know of "The Revenge of Ra"?'

'An episode of *SG1*?' The words escaped Sam's mouth before he had even thought of an answer, and he grinned, knowing full well from where such a pithy response came.

'Ah, no,' Frederick said, smiling in return. 'It's an old Egyptian myth.'

*

Frederick indulged Will with a smile. Still Will was so human, but Frederick would remain patient. He was no teacher, otherwise he would have joined the Rebirth Council, and he knew he was out of his depth when it came to teaching their laws to a fledgling, but Will's entering into their world was Frederick's responsibility, and he had to see it through.

'Ah, no,' he said, 'it's an old Egyptian myth.' Frederick paused, remembering the words he had learned so long ago. 'According to the story, Ra the Sun God was angry with his people for failing to worship and fear him as they should. After consulting with the lesser gods, he agreed to send his daughter, Hathor, made from his flaming eye, out to kill those who attacked him. Ra was, after all, still the greatest of the gods and his throne was secure, and so it was right that humanity fear his anger.

'Hathor was sent out in the form of Sekhmet, a mighty lioness. Like the lion, she took delight in the slaughter and discovered much pleasure in the bloodshed. Observing her work, Ra was pleased, and once satisfied that his vengeance was complete, he called her back. But Sekhmet cried out; "By your life, O' Ra, I work my will on the human race and my heart rejoices." And so, she continued, and because of her divine power, none could force her to cease killing, which left Ra only two courses of action. Persuasion or trickery.'

'And I'm guessing persuasion didn't really work?' Will asked, placing his plate on the rug and crawling over to Frederick's side.

'No, Sekhmet was not one to be persuaded from doing that which she enjoyed so much.' Frederick lifted his arm so Will could place his head in

Frederick's lap. A smile passed between them, and Frederick let his arm rest across Will's chest.

'Ra sent out his messengers to get mandrake from Elephantine Island, because not only was its juice scarlet, but the plant was known to cause great sleepiness. Women were called upon to crush barley into beer, and this was mixed with the mandrake, giving the beer the appearance of blood. They made seven hundred measures and spread it over the earth while Sekhmet slept. She awoke ready to continue her joyous work but found no more people on whom she could satisfy her need, and she saw that the earth was already deep in blood. She stooped to drink of it, and she fell into a peaceful slumber, and while sleeping Ra came to her and took her home. And there ended her slaughter.'

Frederick waited for the inevitable question, and after a moment of silence Will asked, 'Sekhmet was a vampire?'

'Yes and no. The myth was a work of fiction to hide the truth. Sekhmet did indeed walk the land of Ancient Egypt, the Book tells us, and created the first of what would one day become the modern upiór.'

'So, no sun god and mixing of mandrake?'

Frederick looked down at Will, who was smiling up at him. He shook his head, glad that Will was taking this all so well.

'Not exactly no. By 2079BCE Memphis was already known for its worship of the Goddess Sekhmet, and it was around that year that she actually appeared in person. Not the Sekhmet of myth, but the woman around whom the legend of Ra's Revenge was built.

'Although the Book doesn't say so, it does seem very likely that she was either one of the women who had appeared throughout the pre-history of the vampire, or maybe even the same woman reincarnated. Depending on which story you believe. Either way, this time around she appeared in human form – and her body suffered from a blood illness.'

'Unfortunate coincidence.'

'Is it?' Frederick shrugged. 'I'm not so sure. Based on my studies over the last couple of hundred years, I'm inclined to believe this was by design. If she was the same woman that guided the evolution of the vampire, I think with each appearance, each incarnation, she becomes closer to her original form. The Mother of all vampires... and upiór.'

'By design. So, this blood disease... It was there to keep her in check?'

'Maybe.'

Will frowned. 'Which implies a higher power at work...?'

'Very possible.'

'Right, okay. Anyway, she arrived in Ancient Egypt...'

'Yes, and she took the name Sekhmet and called to the young priest Onuris, and took him as hers. For decades she worked behind the scenes, setting up Memphis as her main place of worship while war broke out between Upper and Lower Egypt.

'Now the High Priest of the Cult of Sekhmet, and her lover, Onuris brought the Pharaoh Mentuhotep the Second before the goddess. Mentuhotep knew that with the power of Sekhmet behind him, uniting Egypt against the Herakleopolis rule would be child's play. Mentuhotep pledged his allegiance to Sekhmet.

'The Intefs of Thebes made short work of removing the rulers of Herakleopolis and a period of economic and cultural renaissance came upon Egypt. For fifteen years the Pharaoh and his goddess enjoyed a close relationship, her blessing securing the good fortune of his people. But it was a relationship due to sour since the Pharaoh Mentuhotep could only share his position for a finite amount of time; it was an eventuality that Sekhmet believed she was prepared for and had already warned Onuris about.

'By this time, though, Onuris was an old man and did not believe that a mere pharaoh could endanger a goddess.'

'Love blinds, right?'

Frederick nodded softly, rubbing his hand gently across Will's chest. 'It does at times,' he said, thinking of how it had blinded him for so long. But not anymore, now he understood the truth of him and Will.

'While gaining the confidence of Onuris,' Frederick continued, enjoying the sensation of Will's skin on his, as Will stroked his hand gently, 'Mentuhotep discovered that Sekhmet had a blood condition that made copious amounts of alcohol deadly to her. He filled many jars with water, poisoned with beer, and used pomegranate juice to turn the water red, convincing her that her followers had given up their blood for her. Sekhmet was blindsided, since it was Onuris who brought the jars to her. Of course, he did not know of Mentuhotep's betrayal.

'Sekhmet went to gorge herself on the life fluid in the hope that it would cure her body's ailment. Instead, the poison quickly did its work, and Sekhmet found her body dying. She managed to reach the sanctuary of her temple, practically decimating the army of Thebes along the way, feasting on their blood.'

'Not a woman you'd want to cross,' Will pointed out. 'My sister could do with a little of that fire.'

'There Onuris found his former lover dying, still looking as young as the day they had first met. Onuris was horrified by his part in this, but Sekhmet knew that everything came to pass as it was meant to, and so forgave him his human foibles. Before dying she performed one final act, she shared with him her blood, and thus turned Onuris into the first ever human-vampire hybrid, granting him an almost eternal life.

'She knew that one day he would indeed die, since all things had their time, but by then he would spread her blood throughout the known world, creating a new army of her children to continue on.'

Will let out a whistle. 'That's quite a tale,' he said. 'But what's to say that what's written in your book is any more true than the myths spread by the Ancient Egyptians?'

'Because I met the one who wrote the Book, and he passed it on to me, charged me to continue what he had begun.' Frederick removed his arm so that Will could reposition himself onto one elbow. 'The thing is, Will, I...'

'Hold on, that Egyptian tapestry in the factory. A representation of Sekhmet?'

'Yes, you see...'

Will held up a hand and Frederick stopped. 'So, those people *are* upiór, like us?'

'They are the Three, the ruling body of the upiór world.' Now it was Frederick's turn to raise a hand and stop Will from speaking further. He smiled at Will, glad that his fledgling was thirsty for knowledge of his new life. 'We'll get back to them, but there's more to tell about where we came from first, some very important things you need to know. To, erm...'

For the first time since falling into the mode of storyteller Frederick faltered. This was a subject he didn't really wish to broach, but it was essential. 'It will explain why you and I met.'

*

'There's more to tell about where we came from first,' Frederick said.

Sam didn't bother to respond, but he doubted Frederick could tell him where he came from. He had been made by Frederick, but that was not where he came from. Something else was going on, something he didn't understand. But the tale Frederick told, although Will had dismissed it a little, rang very true for Sam.

He had seen Onuris meet Sekhmet in the temple; indeed, it was *he* who had slept with Sekhmet.

Sam didn't understand what it all meant. He had seen much of what Frederick told, but when it came to the actual physical sensation of entering Sekhmet, Sam had felt it. As surely as he had felt himself enter Lizette.

'It will explain why you and I met,' Frederick was saying.

Sam had no idea what Frederick was talking about; he had zoned out and missed it. But it didn't matter; he had Frederick where he wanted him.

He sat up and stretched. 'How about you tell me over a cuppa?'

*

'You thought I was the reincarnation of an Egyptian high priest?' Will asked, the incredulity very clear in his voice.

They were now standing in the kitchen, each holding a cup of Lapsang Souchong aromatic tea in their hands. Will had been a bit dubious, but Frederick didn't stock normal tea, having never developed a taste for it. And Will, it seemed, wasn't too keen on Lapsang Souchong – finding it too smoky a taste. 'Like drinking an ashtray,' as he put it.

Still, all things considered Will took the news well. Of course, Frederick had neglected to mention how he, with the assistance of Stephen, had pretty much manipulated Will into taking a train to Southend. But he had explained about how, when on the train, he had felt something in Will, and how he had thought it was the reincarnated ka of Onuris.

'Mate, I'm not the reincarnated anything. I mean, I'd know, right?'

'Well,' Frederick said, 'that's the thing. Onuris was, according to the Book, supposed to awake during the fires of the hunger. But, well...' He spread his free hand out. 'Clearly that didn't happen. Instead, you nearly died.'

Will nodded slowly. Frederick tried to read the look in his translucent eyes, but whatever was going on inside was being kept secret. Frederick didn't mind. Will had heard much so far, and still they'd barely gone into what being an upiór meant now. He was just happy that Will was taking it all so well.

'So, that mugging... You set it up? To see if I was this Seeker?'

Or not.

'Yes,' Frederick said, knowing at this point truth was best. 'You have to understand, Will, I was *convinced* you were Onuris, that the prophecy was right. I never intended to cause you harm.'

Will turned away and carefully placed his cup on the side. Without a word, he walked out of the kitchen. Frederick watched him go, his heart sinking. He quickly followed. After the progress they made, he couldn't let Will go now.

'Will, wait, please. I'm not explaining this well.'

Will stopped at the doorway leading to the passage beyond the living room. His whole body was tense, his fists clenched.

'I think you're explaining it fine.' He turned slowly. 'Show me this Book that you're putting so much stock in.'

For a second Frederick hesitated, and wondered why Will would wish to see the Book of Sekhmet. It was not as if anyone, bar himself and Celeste, had ever seen the actual Book; not even Theodor or Eryn got to see the original. But then, Frederick reasoned, neither of them had been pegged as the reincarnation of Onuris. Perhaps by seeing the pages of the Book, Will would realise that Frederick's intentions had been noble. Either way, if there was any other upiór alive in the world that deserved to see the Book themselves, Frederick could not think of one.

'All right,' he said, and crossed the room. He could feel the tension oozing off Will as he stepped aside to let Frederick pass. He was understandably pissed off. Frederick supposed he would have been too, if it was he who had died in an intentional ambush. Regardless of the reasoning behind it.

He led Will into his bedroom. 'The Book is kept secure, protected in a box designed by Ryuuzaki, a technical genius from Japan. Only I am able to open it,' he said, crouching down and made to pull aside the chest of drawers.

He stopped, noticing that the chest was no longer flush with the wall. He looked up at Will, but the fledgling wasn't smiling. Instead, he stood there, his arms folded, watching Frederick carefully.

Frederick offered a reassuring smile, but he wasn't sure who he was trying to reassure. Something was definitely off.

He pulled the chest of drawers away and his breath caught. The wooden panel that usually covered the secret compartment lay in shreds on the carpet, previously hidden by the chest.

He reached in to retrieve the box, knowing full well that whoever had found the hiding place would never be able to remove the actual box. He stopped abruptly, feeling his blood go cold.

'No,' he said, his voice barely audible.

The box was in pieces.

The Book was gone, and in its place was a severed arm.

14. Truths and Lies

Eryn never truly understood people, probably because she had never really been one of them. And even then, she had been a kid living in a very secluded farming village, so the natural understanding that came with maturity was lost to her. She had seen much since she'd first met Theodor in Cwm Ogwr in 1733, back when she had been a boy called Iestyn, experienced much more besides, but she had left the 'real' world at fifteen and so her understanding of people was somewhat limited. Upiór she understood, but humans...?

Now that she had only one good arm most of them seemed so much more considerate than usual, offering an unexpected level of sympathy and support. It was a side of humans Eryn rarely saw, but the occasional sly look of morbid curiosity she did understand. She was, however, too tired to really care at that point.

It had been a long night, and finally her train had arrived. She made sure the Book was still secure inside her coat, the useless left arm pressed against it, and set off across the concourse of Liverpool Street Station to the train that would take her on the final leg of her journey.

She approached the barrier and reached for the ticket in the back pocket of her jeans, and let out a growl of anger. She had always been left-handed, and for an upiór *always* meant a hell of a long time, and her instinct was still to reach out with her left hand. It was crazy, but she still felt her fingers, clenching and unclenching in frustration, even though the lower half of her left arm remained where it had been severed in Freddy's flat. The nurse at the hospital had warned her that she'd still feel like she had a whole arm, because the tendons and nerves would continue to send signals to the brain; phantom limb syndrome. Eventually, they would adapt; in the meantime, the ghost of her arm would linger.

*

It was a foregone conclusion that Freddy would have the Book protected, but Eryn had underestimated him. As determined as she was, Eryn wasn't careless and had no intention of giving Frederick any reason to suspect her too soon, and so she had checked the flat with care. Putting things back where she found them. Judging by the initial source of conflict between Freddy and the woman at the door, Eryn didn't expect him to be returning home any time soon. And if, for some reason, he did end up coming back earlier than anticipated, then Eryn would deal with it. No doubt violently.

As it turned out Frederick did not return, and Eryn had discovered the secret compartment hidden behind the chest of drawers in the bedroom. Shredding the wooden panel was simple enough, but as she knelt there, looking at the box inside, Eryn paused and wondered.

Did she really want to do this? For 275 years she'd followed one belief, let it guide her actions; it enabled her to work against the Three from within their ranks. She knew she had been young when she'd first met Julius in 1736; only eighteen years old. She was, therefore, probably more impressionable than most, but over the following centuries, she came to truly believe his teachings.

Want didn't really come into it, she knew. She had to do it. There was something very odd going on and she had to know what it was. For years she'd been kept away from the Book, never being able to see what it actually said, only ever hearing it quoted by Frederick. She hadn't minded so much, though, since she believed what was written in the Sekhmet Codex. But since Will had turned up at the Residence things had happened that smacked Julius' teachings to the ground. And now Eryn had to know for sure. Which meant seeing the Book for herself.

That she was betraying the Three by doing so did not bother her, after all, she had been betraying the idea of the Three since its conception, but she knew Theodor would take this personally. And it was that which did not sit well on Eryn's shoulders.

Nonetheless, she had to do what she had to do.

She reached out for the box, but stopped, her hand inches away. Heat emanated from the box as if it were generating some kind of energy. Eryn pushed on, gently letting her fingers brush against the box. It was warm, the surface smooth and sleek. It appeared to be wood, but there was no grain to it, no tell-tale grooves. She felt on top of the box, and checked both sides, the space of the compartment big enough for her to place both

156

her arms either side of the box. Feeling no hidden catches or super thin wires, she gently pulled the box towards her. It came out easy enough.

Holding the box gently in both hands, Eryn stepped backwards carefully, and sat down on the bed.

She smiled, hardly able to believe she was so close. Of course, she knew that getting the Book was just one step to finding the answers, but it was an important one which she had almost completed.

She placed the box on the mattress beside her and ran a hand around the brim, looking for the seal between lid and box. Finally, she found it, and she carefully lifted the lid, holding her breath all the while. She put the lid on the duvet, and for a moment just looked at the Book. It had a battered and seemingly burned leather cover, with some kind of old script embossed into the bottom right corner. The papers were such a disorganised mess, in differing shapes and sizes, hardly any of them flush with the cover. It was like they'd all been shoved in, made to fit. Which, Eryn guessed, was probably true, after all, she had heard it said that the Book as it was now contained much in the way of unfinished notes, as well as full passages written by the Ancient.

She let her breath go and reached into the box. No sooner had her left hand touched the leather-bound volume, than she felt an intense pain just above her elbow. Eryn's eyes widened as a thin beam of pure radiant energy moved from one end of the box to the other, cutting clean through her arm on the way. She pulled away sharply, but by then it was too late. The laser had done its work.

Unbelievingly she lifted her left arm and looked curiously at the bloodied stump. No blood dripped, the heat of the laser having cauterised the wound. She opened her mouth to shout, but thought better of it, lest she alert those who lived in the other parts of the converted house. Instead, her rage and pain exploded violently and, with her good right arm, she flung the box back into the compartment.

The box shattered under the impact, releasing her dismembered arm. For a few moments more Eryn did not move.

She knew the box would have been protected, but she hadn't expected such an advanced defence.

'Ffycin cont!' she hissed, and stood.

She walked back over to the compartment and knelt down. The laser was now running blindly, no longer bound by the box itself, burning its way into the walls of the compartment. Careful not to get her other arm burned, Eryn reached in and pulled the Book out. She thought about grabbing her severed arm, too, but decided not to bother; instead, she merely grabbed the sleeve of her jumper that had been burned off with the *arm. When Frederick found the arm, it would throw him for a while, but the jumper would lead him and the others to Eryn too soon. She needed time to get away, and the discovery of a mysterious arm would give her just that.*

*

Even now, as she boarded the train, Eryn remembered the pain well. Instead of giving into it, she embraced it, used it to propel her on.

Once she had left Freddy's, she had dumped her jumper in a bin, deciding that her coat and t-shirt would be enough for now. The cold didn't really affect her so much. Stashing the Book inside her coat, Eryn made her way to Southend Hospital. Fortunately, it was very early Friday morning, and the hospital was yet to be hit by the usual rush that a weekend in Southend brought its way, so she had easily managed to nab a nurse who was out having a quick fag.

The nurse had tried to resist, but once he saw the damaged arm his Hippocratic Oath took over and he helped Eryn to clean up and dress the wound. He had asked plenty of questions, curious as to why the wound wasn't bleeding profusely. Eryn didn't answer, after all, how would the human understand that the saliva Eryn had placed onto the wound acted as a healing salve, and within a couple of hours the skin would grow back over the elbow stump? The particulars of upiór existence were not something for which the nurse was ready. For his troubles, Eryn stashed the nurse in a cupboard before leaving the hospital, and caught a cab to Westcliff Station, from where she began the first leg of her journey to understanding.

And so now, at ten to six in the morning, she was boarding a train out of London. Within four hours she would be in Cambridge and she would know what she wanted to know. And if that knowledge damned her, then so be it.

Eryn knew that, sometimes, consequences could not be escaped.

*

Jake was woken by his mobile vibrating next to his ear. He reached up and pressed a button, glancing at the screen. It was only seven in the morning. Four hours sleep really was not enough. He rubbed his eyes and threw his legs over the edge of the bed, looking more closely at the screen of his phone. It was a text message from Toby.

He placed the phone back on the pillow and rubbed his head. For a moment he remained as he was, staring at the floor, his brain not really focusing on anything.

He hoped it had been a productive night, but he had a pretty crap sleep and felt somewhat unmotivated. They had spent plenty of time in Zinc, handing out flyers and talking to people. Going to clubs was nothing new to Jake, although he did prefer pubs, but it was the first time he'd been in a gay club. He was surprised to see so many straight couples there, gyrating on the dance floor, smooching up, before he realised that not every night at Zinc was 'polysexual night'.

Charlie had suggested they try a few of the other clubs along the Lucy Road strip, just in case. After all, it couldn't hurt. So they blitzed the other clubs, including the rather snazzy Bar Blu, which Jake did like. If he wasn't looking for Will he would have been happy to spend the rest of the evening there.

By the time they'd left Talk, the weather had taken a turn for the worse, and as it was almost half two, Charlie suggested they call it a night. Plenty of other places to canvass tomorrow night, plus they had places to visit during the day. Jake agreed, and so they grabbed a cab back to Charlie's.

Jake had fallen asleep in the cab. He hadn't realised how tired he was. But it had been a long twenty-four hours. Charlie woke him as soon as the cab arrived at his house, and after a brief natter, Jake had retired to the guestroom.

He had sat on the bed for a short while, checking his phone just in case he'd missed any messages from Will, but there were none, and so he found himself re-reading past texts passed between the two of them. He vaguely recalled lying back as he did so, but he didn't remember actually falling asleep, or getting undressed, but now he was sitting in only his boxers, so at some point he must have got into the bed.

He looked up, and briefly wondered if perhaps Charlie had come in and got him changed after he had fallen asleep? He hoped not. The idea of Charlie seeing him almost naked did not appeal. Jake shook the thought out of his head and picked up his phone to read the text from Toby.

It was pretty much the same as the text yesterday, asking if Jake was okay and if he needed to talk, he knew where Toby was. Jake should have been grateful, he supposed, that Toby was concerned.

Jake stood up suddenly. He had used Toby, plain and simple, yet still Toby was offering a shoulder despite the lack of response from Jake. He didn't understand it. He threw the phone on the bed. He needed a pee.

He crossed the landing to the bathroom and stopped, the door of Charlie's room opposite slightly ajar. He listened carefully to the sounds of exertion coming from Charlie's room and screwed his face. *Shit, guy, it's only seven in the morning!*

He entered the bathroom, and tried to convince himself that the slight stiffening of his dick was a result of morning glory and the desperate need to take a leak; it had nothing to do with his mental image of what Charlie was doing.

As he passed the full-length mirror, his eye caught something in his reflection. He stopped to look closer. He tilted his shoulder, arching his neck as much as possible to get a better look. It hadn't really bothered him since Monday, and he'd almost forgotten about it, not even bothered looking. But now he saw it.

The scar on his shoulder. It was a definite shape, not the result of him bumping his shoulder somewhere...

He frowned. He'd need to get his phone to take a better picture of it, but there was something very familiar about it. He had seen it before, and not on his shoulder, but somewhere else, on *someone* else... But where?

*

It wasn't her dream, if indeed it was a dream at all.

She had followed him to the small tavern, and waited in silence, until Frederick had turned up. Now she stood watching from afar, the words passing between Frederick and the Ancient as clear to her as if she was standing right next to them. They sat outside the tavern in the small village of Tuzara. How Celeste knew the name of the settlement was a mystery, but know she did. It was as if, because Frederick and the Ancient knew, then it was right she should know too. Tuzara was in Moldavia, and with the arrival of Frederick she understood clearly what the Ancient had been preparing for. It was 1790, and this was the meeting that was due to change the course of history for upiór.

'Why did you send for me?' Frederick asked once he had sat down. Frederick looked old, his body nearing the end of its days. But still he appeared as strong and beautiful as he had when she'd first met him, only now his skin was lined and his hair white. Next to the Ancient, though, he looked young.

Celeste had never been granted an audience with the Ancient, but she knew enough of him to not be surprised by his appearance. Despite his long flowing white hair and his waxen features, still he had the bearing of his heritage, his dark Egyptian skin making Frederick's look like milk in comparison.

'I have been watching from afar,' the Ancient said, his old voice cracked, 'and saw the horror of that "revolution" two years ago. Such a waste of time, and not what she...' He stopped and coughed, waving away what he was going to say. 'That does not matter, what matters is I have seen the way the Three have changed my people, brought them on to the path of civilisation. Things need to be known if the Three are to lead upiór to salvation.'

Frederick smiled. 'You have been watching, if you know of the new name for our people.'

'Yes, a symbolic act I approve of. Although I may not have chosen a Slavic term myself, for we are the children of something much older.' He waved away any questions Frederick was about to ask. 'Now we must talk of the Book of Origin, as it has become known. Or the Book of Sekhmet, as you will now call it, for it is for Her that it is written.'

Celeste listened intently as they talked about the Book, which the Ancient was to pass on to Frederick. Frederick didn't understand why he was being tasked with finishing the Ancient's work, but the Ancient assured Frederick that his blood would help him to understand. The conversation continued on, and she realised for the first time that it was because he had the Ancient's blood in him that Frederick would be able to find the Seeker. She had not known this; a fact Frederick had kept from her.

The two men talked some more, and she followed them as they travelled from Tuzara and up the hills to the monastery of Căpriana. The three stopped a short distance away, she further back than the men, and they watched as a mob, riled up by the war waging about them, set fire to the monastery, driving the monks out. The mob set about beating the monks, and words such as 'traitors' were thrown with the punches.

Celeste had never bothered to learn Romanian, but then since becoming an upiór she had found herself able to understand any language she was exposed to; a curious upiór trait that to this day she did not understand, but as a result she understood the mob clearly.

Once they had moved on, leaving the monks dying where they had been beaten, the Ancient took Frederick to the monastery.

The wind blew heavily over the hill, and Frederick had to support the Ancient, who was being buffeted by the elements. For her own part, Celeste was unaffected by the winds; she was as insubstantial as any ghost.

They entered the old building, the wooden door still open from where the angry mob had dragged the monks out, and a heated discussion followed, while the fires around them continued to grow.

Celeste stood at the doorway, listening as Frederick insisted he go to the crypt and fetch the Book. The Ancient refused the help, saying that it was his time.

Celeste felt a pulling and the scene dissolved around her. She was now in the crypt, watching the Ancient retrieve the Book from its hiding place. At this point, it was barely a collection of paper and papyrus, bound together by string, a result of its tumultuous two-hundred-year journey from person to person after it had been stolen from the Ancient. Many other small pieces of paper were in piles beside where the book lay, notes the Ancient had made in the time the Book had been lost to him. He reached for them and gasped with the effort.

Celeste moved to help, but her words were not heard. She passed right through him, a reminder that she was not really part of the events. She could only watch as the old Egyptian vampire tried to hold all the papers to himself while balancing the Book atop of them.

He stumbled from the crypt, crying out in anguish as papers fell out of his hands. His quick reflexes saved the Book and many sheets, but most of them fell into the flames about him.

Together they watched in despair as the notes burned. So much knowledge was lost there, details of the prophecy destined to remain unknown until Onuris returned. Celeste blinked, unsure of how she knew this.

'My lady?'

A voice she recognised. She looked about her as the scene dissolved once again, and for a moment she was standing back at the doorway of the monastery, watching the Ancient stagger towards Frederick, the remainder of the Book and notes held tightly in his arms.

'My lady, please awake.'

The voice was insistent. She tried to wave it aside, but the scene around her was fading into darkness as if swallowed by shadows. 'Wait, I have yet to finish...'

'Please, it is important.'

She blinked open her eyes only to find herself lying in her bed, the ever-gentle visage of Nate looking down at her. For a moment she just stared, as she allowed her mind to catch up.

She remembered looking at the painting of herself and Frederick from five years ago, and then connecting with Frederick's mind...

She sat up abruptly, causing Nate to jump back. She offered a smile. 'How long?'

'You have been asleep for almost twelve hours, my lady.'

She shook her head. No, that wasn't right. She hadn't been sleeping at all. She had fallen back into the images she had seen in Willem's mind when she and Frederick had linked with him. Only what she had seen... They were not dreams, but memories!

She had felt what the Ancient had felt, knew what he knew. Only the knowledge was slipping from her, and she was left with a sense of great sadness over work unfinished.

The memory of the events, however, stayed with her. And now she understood why Frederick was able to track down the Seeker. Celeste smiled to herself. She had been right to trust him after all. What with recent events, and bad decisions over Willem, Celeste hadn't been so sure of him. Once again, she was certain of Frederick, as certain as the Ancient himself had been.

One thing still puzzled her, though; why was Willem remembering this? He was clearly not the reincarnation of Onuris, but he was more than a normal upiór. Somehow, he was linked to the Ancient. Perhaps that is what led Frederick to him, a blood bond beyond even that which she shared with Frederick?

'My lady,' Nate said, interrupting her musings. 'DI Swanson has been in touch. She left a message for you to contact her as soon as possible. I told her you were non-contactable, but she insisted.' He smiled apologetically, clearly not wishing to impart the news he had been given. 'It would seem that Detective Inspector Rowe has contacted the parents of Mr Townsend.'

This news shook Celeste into action. 'Please tell Theodor and Eryn that we're having an emergency meeting...'

'I'm afraid that Ms Gwyther has not returned since last night.'

Celeste blinked. It was not unknown for Eryn to go off on her own; she had always liked her own time, despite Theodor's best attempts to rein her in. It was a concern, especially now, but Celeste pushed it aside. Eryn would return at some point during the day, and then they would be able to bring her up to speed on events.

'Very well, tell *Theodor* that I wish to meet with him, and then contact Frederick. We need to see him now, before anyone else spots him.' She shook her head. 'Why now? We're so close to prophecy.' She blinked, surprised to see that Nate had yet to leave. 'What is it?' she asked, knowing he would not linger unless he had something important to say.

'Mr Holtzrichter has already been in touch, and he's on his way here now.'

Celeste smiled and took a deep breath. 'Good, then things might yet be okay.'

*

At first Jake had felt a little uncomfortable walking around such a strange house on his own, like he was intruding. But Charlie had insisted he make himself at home, and so after a bit of rummaging about he'd found the frying pan and vegetable oil. While he cooked, he found himself opening the copy of *Attitude* that was sitting on the kitchen side, and on and off, as he prepared the food, he became engrossed in the interview with another celebrity who beat the press in outing him. As well as talking about his view on sexuality, Matthew Phillips partook in a photo shoot, modelling new and interesting fashions, and for the first time Jake actually saw he was good-looking. Phillips never looked all that on *Corrie* where he played a bit of a roughneck builder.

Jake was laughing by the end of it, thinking that Phillips had scored a point against the so-called 'freedom of the press'. Jake didn't understand why the press felt the need to involve themselves in something that was obviously intensely personal.

Charlie joined him in the kitchen just as he was dishing out the fried breakfast, pulling a t-shirt over his well-toned torso. He looked at the plate of food and turned his nose up.

'Erm, thanks, mate, but I try not to have so much cholesterol first thing in the morning. Plays havoc with my morning workout, you know?'

'Oh, is that what you were doing?' Jake asked before he realised what he was saying. 'Shit, I mean...'

Charlie laughed. 'Listening in, eh? Yeah, every morning first thing I do some exercise. Crunches, stretches, sit-ups, some weights. Nothing like getting hot and sweaty in the morning,' he added, with a wink.

Jake felt himself going red. 'Sorry, guy, I didn't mean to imply...'

'Ah, don't worry about it.' Charlie lifted his shirt. 'What do you think, not bad for thirty-seven, eh?'

'Not bad at all,' Jake replied, feeling a bit more comfortable. He patted his own gut. 'Guess I need some work.'

'Well, you know, if you want we can do a little work on that later between canvassing sessions.' Charlie turned to the cupboard and reached for a box of Alpen. 'Will told me you work on a building site, which is probably great for the arms and legs, but a diet of beer kind of defeats all that hard work, yeah?'

Jake found himself smiling, both at the humour in Charlie's voice and the fact that Will had told Charlie about him. 'Not untrue,' he said, and started work on his breakfast. 'Putting away two plates of fry up is certainly going to need a bit of working out later.'

Charlie put the muesli away and poked Jake's stomach. 'Yep, but it can be done.'

*

'Lomax and Maia have disappeared. I know, it is most unfortunate, but no one knows where they are. No doubt they will surface when they're ready.'

Eryn wasn't that fussed anymore. Finding out about the Maia situation was a smokescreen. She had bigger things to concern herself with than setting Maia on her father now. Of course, if she had gone missing it could be that she was nearer than anyone suspected.

'Then what about the fulfilment of prophecy?' Eryn asked. 'We don't want Frederick and the Three getting in our way.'

'Eryn, you worry too much, I always tell you that. Things will come to pass when they do. We are on schedule, and soon we shall find our creator.'

For the first time ever, Eryn couldn't stand the laid-back tone of Julius' voice.

'You mean *you* will find him?'

'Of course, but you will help like you always help me, yes?'

Eryn narrowed her eyes. 'Yes, of course,' she said, no longer meaning a single word. 'Okay, I need to go; if you hear anything about Maia let me know, yeah?'

Julius said he would, and the line went dead. Eryn pocketed her phone and looked out of the window.

She was less than an hour away from Cambridge.

15. AN ORACLE

Sam smiled at Frederick, but the smile was not returned.

Ever since he had discovered the arm and the missing Book, Frederick had fallen into a funk. His mood wasn't helped when he discovered the busted lock on the street door, and he cursed himself for being so caught in the passion that he'd failed to notice it the night before. Sam *had* noticed, but said nothing about it; after all, as far as he was concerned the 'passion' served its purpose. Frederick said little else unless asked a question directly, which suited Sam just fine. He had his own thoughts to occupy him for now.

They were sitting on the train, nearing Benfleet. Soon they would be at Canvey and Sam would meet the Three. Of course, he had met them before, but that was before he understood the truth of them. Now he would be watching them more carefully, observing how they interacted, gauging their threat through their interactions with each other.

With a few pointed questions he had learned a little more from Frederick about being a vampire (Sam refused to accept the term they used for themselves – they were *vampires*, no matter how much they wished to dress it up!). Unlike the vampires of old they were not, apparently, subject to the fatalities of garlic, wooden stakes, or sunlight. Neither did they have a problem with reflection. He had asked Frederick about how one became a vampire, but the response was garbled, so intent was Frederick on finding a suitable container for the severed arm.

Frederick stood up as soon as the automated voice informed them that they were approaching Benfleet. He picked up the holdall that had once belonged to Will, now containing a box which in turn housed the severed arm. Sam stood and followed him to the door.

He placed a hand on Frederick's shoulder. 'It's going to be okay, we'll find your Book,' he said gently.

Frederick smiled, but there was little hope behind it. 'We better. Last time it was lost our world was almost torn apart.'

Another story for another time, Sam guessed. Although, now that Frederick mentioned it, a bell rang in his head.

It had been lost in 1588. Sam frowned. Like those memories of the burning monastery of Cāpriana, and the arrival of Sekhmet in the temple, he just knew he was right.

Once again, he pondered what he had become.

Could it be that as an oracle into the past he had a role to play in helping the vampires find the Seeker? That made sense to him. Although he wasn't entirely sure he wanted to help them. He would wait until he had a chance to study the Three, see what he could learn from them, before he decided on what he wished to do.

*

It was a familiar journey to Sam, more so than he had expected. But this time he didn't feel any sense of trepidation approaching the Residence, he simply followed Frederick in. They passed through the great passageway that split the Residence in two; all the while he could *feel* the vampires around him. The place was oozing with presence, and for a moment it felt like Sam had come home. Among his own people.

In almost thirty-five years he had never felt such a sense of belonging, and he didn't like it. This new life had been fostered on to him by Frederick; it was not one he had wanted.

He had been happy. Okay, so not ecstatic, but content with his life. Sure, there were things in his life that irritated, but it was all part of who he was. But now, now he had no idea who he was. Or what.

Without knocking, Frederick opened the door and entered the antechamber of the Three. Sam followed him in and stopped abruptly once his eyes came to rest on the tapestry. He had seen it before, of course, a week ago, but now he was really *seeing* it.

Frederick turned to speak to him, but Sam ignored him and walked straight over to the tapestry. He ran his hand along the surface.

'Sekhmet,' he whispered.

*

Frederick eyed Will suspiciously. The man had been very quiet since they had found the severed hand, apart from when he asked his annoying questions about being an upiór. Frederick was never designed to be a teacher, and he had allowed his attraction to Will to blind him, lose his focus. As a result, the Book was missing.

He blamed no one but himself. Celeste had tried to warn him, but he hadn't listened.

The inner door opened and Nate stepped out. He bowed before Frederick. 'Mr Holtzrichter, the, erm, Three await you.'

'Fine,' Frederick said. 'Can you entertain Will here?'

'Of course, sir, I can...'

Will threw Frederick a look. 'Right, after all this you think I'm taking a back seat and being fobbed off with Jeeves here again? Sorry, Fred, but don't think so.'

Frederick opened his mouth to explain the rules concerning the Three, but before he could say anything Will walked on through the door. Frederick stormed in behind him.

'Look, Will, you can't just...'

Celeste held a hand up. 'Everything is fine, Frederick, Willem is always welcome here.'

'He is?' Now Frederick was confused. Celeste never welcomed anyone into the meeting chamber so freely. He shrugged and dropped the holdall. 'We have a problem,' he said, opening the bag and removing the box.

'You are quite correct,' Celeste agreed, walking over to Will. 'What are you?'

Will narrowed his eyes. 'I don't know. Thought you'd be able to tell me.'

'A few days ago, Frederick and I tried to contact you, to open the connection that usually exists between a maker and his fledgling, but a barrier protected you. Knocked me unconscious,' Celeste added with a smile. 'Unheard of, really. But last night I went back into the mindscape I had witnessed before, and I experienced twelve hours in the life of the Ancient.' She placed an ebony hand against Will's pale face. 'Events that you saw in your own mind, from preparing to meet Frederick in Tuzara, all the way up to the burning monastery at Cāpriana.'

The surprise on Will's face must have matched Frederick's own expression. He still had one hand on the box, ready to open it, but Celeste's words had stopped him in his tracks. 'How is that possible?' he asked.

Will looked over at Frederick, and for a moment there was doubt in his eyes, but then he took a deep breath and spoke.

'Ever since I came to after Frederick "saved" me, I have been seeing all kinds of strange things, events that I could not possibly remember. Including the events at that monastery. I think I'm some kind of oracle into the past.'

The room was silent for a moment, and all eyes remained on Will. The new upiór was clearly uncomfortable with the attention, but he bore it well.

Celeste turned to Frederick. 'Is it permissible?'

'Everything is permissible, but the Book says nothing of an oracle.'

'No, but much was lost in the monastery fire, much more than even you know, Frederick.' Celeste lowered her head. 'I saw it, felt the Ancient's sadness at the loss.' She shook her head. 'So much we do not know. Including, perhaps, tale of an oracle?'

Frederick thought about it for a moment. 'If it is true, then Will's help could be invaluable. He could see into the past, when Sekhmet made the promise to Onuris.' He walked over to Will and reached out for his hand. 'That's why I was drawn to you; you're here to help me find the Seeker.'

Will allowed Frederick to hold his hand. 'I was thinking that, but...' He swallowed. 'I thought you were drawn to me because...'

Frederick squeezed Will's hand, sorry that he had got annoyed at Will earlier. 'That, too. We were meant to be together, and together we can find the Seeker, and he will lead us to Sekhmet.'

'Sekhmet?'

'Yes.' Frederick nodded and was about to explain further when he felt a mental tug. He turned to find Theodor looking into the box. 'Ah, yes, as I was saying. We have a problem.'

Frederick walked over to the chair and opened the box. 'The Book has been stolen. And, as you can see by the hand, it was clearly—'

Celeste let out a gasp, and Frederick nodded. Even Theodor seemed perturbed by this revelation. Frederick removed the severed arm.

Theodor snatched the arm off Frederick and sniffed it. His face paled and he dropped the arm back into the box. Waves of confusion hit both

Frederick and Celeste at the same time. Celeste moved forward, but Theodor stepped back and exited the chamber swiftly.

If anyone could find Eryn it was Theodor. Frederick wanted to go with him, but Celeste held him back.

'Frederick, we have other problems that need to be discussed.' She shook her head. 'The timing of this is all wrong. To be offered an olive branch like Willem, and then all this. Come with me.' She led Frederick out of the chamber and looked back at Will. 'Please remain here, Nate will be on hand should you need anything. We shall return shortly.'

*

'Erm, okay,' Sam said, putting that little bit of extra confusion in his voice. He watched the two of them cross the antechamber, and once they were gone he stepped out of the main chamber himself. He walked over to the tapestry.

'The Seeker will find Sekhmet,' he said, reaching out for the tapestry. 'Is that so?'

*

Francis waited. From the moment DI Rowe had entered the house, he could tell she was someone who liked to command attention. She was a big woman, in all ways.

She looked at them with her steely eyes; stretching the drama of the moment was her chosen method of extracting information. Prolonged silences, designed to make people sweat and feel obligated to fill them with words. Any words. But Francis wasn't going to be pulled in so easily. He cast a quick look at Sandra, and it was clear she was near breaking.

So far, DI Rowe had asked some odd questions about Will's spirituality, his religious beliefs, if he was a follower or a leader... They were all very pointed questions, and Francis didn't like where they were heading. Not that he actually knew, but he had a nasty suspicion he wasn't going to like it.

'I have reason to believe that your son has become caught up in a cult,' Rowe finally said, once she realised neither Francis nor Sandra were going to break.

At this Sandra looked close to panic, so Francis offered her a hand of support. They had tried to get Lawrencia to attend, but she had told them

171

that Curtis had playschool at half eight, so she would never be able to make it. Francis was glad of that now, since he knew she'd react in a much more vocal, and completely unhelpful, way than Sandra.

'Will and religion?' Francis shook his head. 'No, he doesn't follow his father in that way. But... a cult? And what reason is this?'

'Almost nine years ago, actually on October 28th 2002 to be exact,' Rowe said, not bothering to check any kind of notepad, Francis noticed, 'a nineteen-year-old boy, Robin Turner, went missing in Ashington. He was on his way to see his girlfriend after work, and as usual, he would pop in to see his mother on the way, even called his girlfriend to let her know he was ten minutes away, but never materialised.'

'As sad as that is, it's a long time to keep an investigation going.'

'Yes, and the official investigation was shut down several years ago, once there were no further leads. Robin was reportedly seen in London in early 2003, but after that nothing, just unsubstantiated sightings. I have kept it open as my own personal project.' At this point, Rowe leaned forward, and her voice became softer, no doubt affecting her maternal tact. Francis didn't buy it for a second. 'I got to know the Turner family well, and I saw the devastation Robin's disappearance caused their lives. I'm sure you can understand,' she added, looking directly at Sandra.

'Yes,' Sandra said, her lower lip quivering. Francis squeezed her knee.

'My investigations led me to a vampire cult, and I have reason to believe one of their more esteemed members is now Robin Turner.'

'Vampires? That's ridiculous,' Francis blurted out. 'What has this got to do with my son?'

'Glad you asked. After painstakingly searching through the CCTV of Southend High Street to verify the story Charlie Connolly told officers in Southend, we discovered that your son has been seen, in quite intimate detail, with Robin Turner.'

'This is insane. Will called his sister yesterday morning, and tried to call Jake, too...'

'Which means there may be hope for him.' Rowe offered them a sad smile. 'Unfortunately, Robin is so brainwashed that it's almost impossible to extract him now, and his family have to live with that, but you don't. With your help, we may yet be able to rescue your son.'

Her children were everywhere.

Sekhmet had spent much time walking around Southend, taking it all in now that she was seeing and feeling clearly once again. She had missed chunks of time in the past, sleeping until she was needed again, but her latest absence from the world had been the longest yet, and so much had changed since the time of Egypt and Memphis, well over four thousand years had passed and humanity had advanced very far.

From her time as Lizette, Sekhmet knew plenty of the world, and the way humanity had tamed it, but she knew little of what her children had been up to in her absence. What she really needed was someone who could tell her everything.

She had passed many of her children, but none of them seemed to be aware of Sekhmet's presence. The gifts her blood had imbued them with had faded from lack of use, and now they were much like the humans among whom they lived. Gone was the natural enmity.

Disgusted, she had returned to Lizette's home. She was about to enter when she felt the one presence she wished to share. Crossing the road was Sam, and with him another of her children. The one called Frederick. Although his sense of presence was not as strong as Sam's, Sekhmet could feel her blood in Frederick's veins, much more so than any other of her children.

She followed them all the way to Canvey, careful to shield her presence from Sam. He was still not ready. Just a gentle probing of his mind showed her that; he was barely aware of his true self. But soon he would be, and when the time came, she intended to be nearby.

She watched them enter the converted factory, and for a while she remained outside, reaching out to feel her children within. Most of them were like those she had already seen around Southend, closed to their potential. But there was one, a female presence, who was more.

Content to leave Sam with the rest of her children, Sekhmet left the factory to explore the island of Canvey. She found the residential area, and again many of her children mixing with humans. There was a small holiday camp on East Canvey, and she watched as families played. So much joy, thinking they knew love.

'Hey, you're in my light,' said a small voice from ground level.

Sekhmet looked down at the small girl who was lying on a blanket spread out on the grass. In her hands she held a pink Nintendo DSI, one earphone in, the other dangling on its wire, and looked up with something like contempt in her eyes.

Sekhmet frowned at the affront. Her shadow swept across the girl, blocking the sun's rays from hitting the girl's skin.

'Am I?' Sekhmet asked, not especially bothered by this.

'Yeah, think you can move?'

Sekhmet gave this careful consideration, her eyes never leaving the girl, who couldn't have been much more than twelve. There was something about her, almost as if she was... Sekhmet focused, seeing the blood that ran through the girl's veins. Only the child was not of her blood. Sekhmet pulled back in disgust.

The girl was nothing, some strange hybrid, the offspring of a union between one of hers and a human. The thought of such pollution sickened Sekhmet. She made to move towards the girl, end the misery of her life, when she felt a tug of familiarity.

Sekhmet looked up and narrowed her green eyes. Yes, she had heard right. Even now Sam's mind was on her, his thoughts consumed by her.

She glanced down at the girl, and turned away. 'Today's your lucky day,' she said and walked off, heeding the silent call of her love.

*

Frederick looked out towards Kent, the sun bright against his eyes. Even so, a wind was wiping up along the marshes, which suited his mood just fine. During the walk from the Residence, Celeste had finally admitted her doubts about Eryn; for a long while she had suspected Eryn was up to something, but she did not know what. Her stealing the Book confirmed Celeste's worst fears.

'She's a Sekhite,' Frederick repeated out loud again, hardly able to get his mind around it. But saying it made it seem real somehow. As much as he disliked Eryn, and had suspected her of shady dealings, to think that she would betray the Three to the Brotherhood... 'How long?'

'Have I suspected her?' Celeste asked, closing in on him, after allowing him to walk ahead in silence for a time. 'For a few months, mostly in the lead-up to our visit here. Ever since we started making arrangements she has been more... irritable than normal. If that's possible.'

For a second Frederick did not respond. 'How long do you think she's been a Sekhite?'

'That I do not know.' Celeste shook her head. 'We shall deal with that once we return, by then perhaps Theodor will have a lead on Eryn's whereabouts. But for now, we have another problem.'

'Like we need another problem,' Frederick said with a grim smile.

'Oh, you shall like this one. Alyson Rowe is visiting Will's parents.'

The silence hung over them like a death shroud.

'Robin Turner,' Frederick said.

'Yes. Both you and Will were caught on CCTV in Southend.'

It had been a long time since Frederick had taken Robin Turner's body as the new vessel for his ka, and for a long while he had stayed away from England while the investigation had run its course. But the then-Detective Sergeant Rowe was tenacious, and had continued her own private investigation. For almost nine years she had not let up. He had hoped that while he spent a few years in France she would have given up the ghost.

'What are we going to do about her?' he asked.

'I do not know, but we shall have to take care of it once and for all. But carefully. In the meantime, you need to return to France.'

Frederick turned on Celeste. 'What? Now? No, I am needed here to find the Seeker. We are so close to the fulfilment of prophecy, the return of our creator. Rowe cannot stand in the way of that!'

Celeste took in his anger, and let it slide off her. 'You are not thinking clearly, Frederick. Your presence here endangers everything. With Rowe so close on Willem's trail it is only a matter of time before she starts snooping around Southend. We cannot risk her seeing you.' She looked towards the general location of the Residence. 'Now we shall have to put our new oracle to the test.'

Frederick swallowed his anger, feeling pushed aside. 'You're not serious?'

'Very much so. What you know of the prophecy only scratches the surface. Having experienced the Ancient's final moments, I now know this to be true. But with Willem we can reach further back, maybe into Onuris' experiences in Ancient Egypt. Then we shall find Sekhmet.'

Frederick folded his arms and turned away. 'This is going to end badly,' he said.

*

Eryn leaned against the cabinet, one hand in her pocket, the useless arm just hanging – folding her arms simply did not work anymore – and waited as Professor Malory transcribed the pages Eryn had pointed him to.

Eryn had found Malory on the internet, an expert in dead languages, now retired from academic life. But he still offered his services for the right price. He had a healthy retirement fund, but Eryn guessed that a man like Malory needed to feel useful too. Although, once Eryn had arrived at Malory's home, the old professor confessed that he simply loved pouring over rare texts. He had heard rumour of the Book of Sekhmet, which proved how well connected the professor was, but he believed it to be little more than the rumblings of disenfranchised university professors looking for something to make their lives a bit more interesting.

When Eryn handed him the Book, Malory held it with reverence. For sure he didn't truly understand the significance of it, but the historical importance is what interested him so much. This served Eryn fine. As long as the professor was only engrossed in the Book for its place in history, then he would not ask any awkward questions.

Malory instantly dismissed the translations made by Melinda and Frederick, which were written on separate pages inserted into the relevant places of the Book. He wasn't interested in what others had to say about the text, he wanted to transcribe it himself.

'This is most unusual; I have never seen a book written in so many different languages before. Sumerian, Egyptian... There is some Greek in here also, and... Yes! I do believe this is Kassitic.' Malory looked up, removing his glasses, his old grey eyes filled with excitement. 'Dead languages, extinct languages, this book is a cornucopia of language, a linguistic expert's wet dream, you might say. Quite fascinating. The author, or most likely authors, travelled far and wide.'

'That's great, Prof, but can you tell me what this passage actually says?' Eryn was as interested in languages as the next man, well, as long as the next man wasn't Professor Malory, but she wanted to get this over and done with. For she was certain that Frederick would have alerted Celeste by now, which meant soon upiór would be out looking for her. The influence of the Three stretched far and wide. Leaving the country was a priority.

'Yes, yes, of course. Let me see.' Malory replaced his glasses on the edge of his nose and peered closely at the Book. 'Whoever translated this before did a good job, and got a general sense of the passage right. However, from my understanding of Kassitic, it should read; *Onuris shall appear unto the Children of Sekhmet, shrouded in the shell of a mortal man, and with him shall return hope. But before he is known confusion will rage in him; he shall be rejected by his past and the fires of his truth will explode after another's hunger is sated.*'

'Wait.' Eryn rushed to Malory's side and grabbed the translation made by Frederick and Melinda. 'It says here, *he shall be rejected by his past and the fires of truth will explode* in hunger. There's nothing about *another's* hunger.'

'Yes, the previous translator clearly used Sumerian as a guide, but there is a marked difference between Sumerian and Kassitic. The second half of this passage is written in Kassitic, a very little-known language, it died out in twelfth century BCE following the death of the last Kassite king of Babylon in Susa. I'm not surprised this passage was translated wrong, it is a difficult language to understand.' The irritation was plain in Malory's voice. He let out a sigh. 'My understanding of Kassitic is limited, but the meaning is clear. The fires of truth will explode from one person, but only after someone else is consumed by hunger.'

Eryn remembered Frederick's version of the events in the alley, how he had been consumed by the hunger and struck out at Will. *Before* the oddness of the Rebirth that followed. Eryn slammed her fist on the table. 'I was right!'

Professor Malory jumped. 'Oh, I say. You were?'

'Yes, Onuris awoke after dying as a man. It's Will, his whole Rebirth... Everything that has happened since is a result of Frederick's hunger.' Eryn smiled grimly. 'Which means Julius lied to me. All this time I've been...' She blinked. Malory was looking at her like she was mad, and for all Eryn knew maybe she was. Mad to have believed Julius all these years. The gullible young upiór taken in by the wise upiór who spoke of such wonder, such promise.

She grabbed the book, and stole out of the old man's study before the professor could utter another word.

Such was her haste that she failed to pick up the translated passages Malory had removed from the Book.

*

Sam needed someone who knew. Frederick and Celeste had left him about half an hour ago, and in all that time he had done nothing but stand in the antechamber looking at the tapestry. It was typical of Egyptian hieroglyphs, very much the image of Sekhmet that could be found in any book or on any website about Egyptian gods, yet still it captivated him. It had nothing to do with the obvious care with which the tapestry had been woven, but rather the sense of knowing that Sam felt when he looked at it.

He was reminded of the woman who had appeared before Onuris on that first night in the temple. For a moment he had seen her with the head of a lion, but still her green eyes stood out. And then there was that moment when he'd made love to Lizette; when it felt like he was two people.

On the one hand, he *had* been Will making love to a woman for the first time, and on the other he *had* been Onuris, lover of the living goddess Sekhmet, pressing into her in the way that she liked.

Two sets of green eyes, their emerald sparkle enticing him, drawing him in.

The Seeker will find Sekhmet.

No, he corrected himself. Not two sets of green eyes, but one set belonging to two women.

He *had* been drawn to Lizette's garden. Up until now so much of why they had connected made little sense. It seemed as if Frederick had been...

Someone was standing behind him.

He turned and found Nate watching him from the doorway. Again, the short vampire was dressed in an immaculate suit, and Sam wondered if he ever wore anything else.

'I see you are captivated by the work of our Lady Celeste.'

'Yes,' Sam said, turning back to the tapestry. 'Celeste did this?'

'Yes, sir,' Nate said, sidling up to Sam. 'Art is her way, always has been. Perhaps you are also captivated by the promise our goddess brings us?'

'Something of that ilk.' Sam thought for a moment. Nate had to know the story. If what Frederick said was true, then it was the linchpin of the vampire world. 'Celeste wishes me to help her find the Seeker.'

'Yes, my Lady explained this to me before she left with Mr Holtzrichter. You are an oracle into the past.'

'So it would seem.' Sam smiled. 'But I know very little of the prophecy. What can you tell me?'

Nate was quiet, and looked at Sam, probably deciding if he was allowed to explain. 'Very well, sir, if it will help. The prophecy tells us that the Seeker, the reincarnation of the High Priest Onuris, will come to a small fishing settlement south of Prittlewell a decade plus one after the millennium has turned. The Book mentions the name of this settlement; Stratende.'

Will remembered studying English history when he was in school, including the history of Essex. 'Right, the twelfth-century name for Southend, which is presumably when the Ancient deciphered that piece of prophecy from his dreams.' Sam swallowed. He did not remember seeing that in one of his visions, yet, somehow, he knew it precisely. 'How will this Seeker know Sekhmet?' he asked quickly, before Nate could pick up on his little slip.

'We do not know, sir, we only know that he will find her. Be drawn to her. The Book says; *And the High Priest will seek her out, And he shall come unto her; He shall know her and she shall know her.*'

'*She* shall know her? What does that mean?'

Nate gave a small shrug. 'It has never been clear, even Mr Holtzrichter is uncertain as to the meaning of that.'

Right, because he's so clever. He thought about what Nate had said and smiled to himself. He certainly had come unto Lizette, in more ways than one. Sam turned from the tapestry and walked towards the outer door. He needed to think.

'I have to walk for a bit, is that okay?'

'Of course, sir, please do explore the Residence. If you need anything then by all means call on me.'

Sam nodded. 'Thank you, I'll do just that.' With that he left the antechamber, his mind awash with dots linking together.

*

Celeste passed through the Canvey Wick nature reserve, but she did not pay any attention to the wildlife there, nor the wonderful foliage that brushed against her. She was lost in her own thoughts.

She had left Frederick out on the marsh, still smarting from her commands. He was adamant that he would remain, that he was the key in finding the Seeker. Celeste knew it was true, that he had been chosen by the Ancient to be the one to find Onuris, and his role was vital. But his being there was now a risk they could ill afford. Bringing him to England had been a risk in the first place, but with no other means of locating the Seeker, they had had little option.

Now there was another. Will would assist them, of that she felt sure. He was still out of his depth, she had seen it in his eyes, but he also showed a willingness to help when he had freely offered up the truth of his visions.

Frederick could smart all he liked, ultimately he would do as Celeste wanted. He always did.

And once he was gone, the Three, well, Celeste remembered ruefully, the *Two* would find a way to deal with Alyson Rowe. Celeste wasn't sure how yet, but Rowe had been a thorn in their side for long enough now. Perhaps it was time to call Rochelle in from the sidelines, too. She had served them loyally, played an important part in recent events. It was time such loyalty was rewarded.

With Eryn's defection there was a vacancy in the Three to be dealt with, too. But that would keep for her return to France. Alas, it would never be Frederick. Even after they'd found the Seeker, Frederick's focus would be on Will.

It was time to accept that Frederick's path no longer merged with hers.

*

Once again, the weather was beginning to turn, the previously blue sky now invaded by greying clouds. Sekhmet smiled, thinking of that ignorant half-breed child and how the weather would disrupt her sunbathing.

She stopped a few feet from the factory and looked up.

Sam was still in there, his mind a jumble as he attempted to sift through the detritus of the life he had lived for the last thirty-five years and the life he had lived for almost four thousand years. So much that still didn't make sense in his head. But he was on the way to becoming the one she remembered.

She closed her eyes and linked directly with his mind. Doors were still closed, hiding important memories that would clarify things for him. Some doors had to remain shut for now, to open them would bring so much forth that his mind would shut down. But there was at least one door she could open, to help him understand who he was.

It was the least she could do, after all, it was his union with her that had brought her out of her slumber, as their bodily fluids mixed at the moment of climax.

Sekhmet smiled and cast the door open.

16. THE TRINITY OF WILL

With a scream that was a mixture of pain and elation, Sam fell to his knees.

Frederick had been such a fool, deluded by a physical attraction, blinded by lust. Things made such sense to Sam now. Like a lightning bolt striking him, clarity came with a flash.

For a moment longer he remained on his knees, his eyes closed, drifting back into the past. What he had seen were not visions, as he had convinced himself, but memories just as he had first thought. But not memories of another person, no, they were his memories. Of a life he had once lived...

'You okay, mate?'

Sam opened his eyes and looked up. A youngish-looking man stood before him in the corridor, dressed in a black outfit that reminded Sam of combat wear.

'Yeah, I am now.'

'Cool. Got a little blood there,' the young man said, indicating Sam's nose.

He felt the blood. 'Oh.'

The man offered a hand and helped Sam to his feet. 'I'm Callum, by the way, welcome to the team. Nice to meet you properly, Will.'

'You know me?' Sam asked, wiping his bloody nose on his sleeve.

'Not exactly. I'm in charge of the clean-up crew that disposed of your human body.'

Sam held up a hand. 'A pleasure to... Hang on, my what now?'

Callum smiled. 'Yeah, it's what we do. Can't have evidence of your death for the locals to come across. So, we incinerated your body, and...' He faltered, the smile fading. 'You have no idea what I'm talking about, have you?'

'Not really.' Sam offered his best disarming smile, the same one that worked on Nate so well. 'I'm still a little new to all this, and a few things are unclear.'

'Right, okay, this is how it is,' Callum said, putting an arm across Sam's shoulder like they were old chums sharing a secret. 'Once your human body dies, and your ka leaves the body, my crew dispose of the body. After all, your ka creates itself a new body, an idealised copy of the original.'

'What, like in *The Matrix*?'

Callum laughed. 'Yeah, but without the virtual reality shit. Now obviously it would draw attention if your dead body was found *and* you were seen walking around. Anyway, now you have a new preternatural body, you don't need the old one. And that's why your body looks so much better than it was. Your ka, your essence, shapes the body into the way you always imagined it being. All the little imperfections gone. Not a bad deal, really, yeah?' Once again he flashed his perfect smile.

'Yeah,' Sam agreed with equal joviality. Inside however his mind was racing as it fought to catch up. Not such an ideal recreation, since he still had that brand/scar on his groin area. But that wasn't as important as knowing that Frederick had *killed* Will in that alley, his body incinerated so that the new improved vampire version could live. Which meant...

'You okay? Going a bit pale there,' Callum said, reaching out a hand.

Before it got to touch Sam, though, he lashed out, snapping the arm in two. Callum looked at it in surprise, the pain not quite registering yet. Time, however, was not on Callum's side. Sam grabbed him by the throat and threw him through the nearest wall. Plasterboard and bricks crumbled under the impact, and Callum's bones shattered. His body landed, limp as a ragdoll, in the room beyond. A vampire couple looked up in shock, but before they had a chance to react further, Sam was on them.

Like a feral animal, he tore into them, his talons ripping through the skin of his fingernails.

Will died. You killed him, Frederick! You all did. Burned his body to a crisp, ended his life. What am I now?

*

Outside the Residence, the wind blowing a gale against her white dress, Sekhmet smiled, soaking up Sam's rage.

You know who you are, my love. But there is so much more to come...

*

Nate was concerned. Things used to be so simple before they had returned to England. Back in Marseilles his mistress was of sound mind, going about her business without danger of undergoing psychic attacks. Mr Holtzrichter was at peace with himself, and...

He was pulled sharply away from his thoughts by the sight of plaster and broken bricks on the floor of the corridor. He moved quickly, looking through the hole in the wall, unable to believe what his eyes were seeing.

Callum lay in a heap on a pile of bricks, looking up at the ceiling helplessly. Nearby, amid pools of blood were Connor and Alice. They were still alive, but definitely not at their best. Their skin and clothes in tatters. Nate stepped through the hole and walked over to them. They looked at him wildly, still in shock.

'What happened?' he asked.

Neither answered, instead one word came from Callum.

'Will.'

Nate frowned. The source of all that was wrong since they'd returned to England.

He moved over to Callum. 'Can you move?'

'No,' Callum said, through gritted teeth. 'I think every bone in my body is broken. But I'll heal. Go, tell the Three. Will needs to be stopped.'

Nate nodded and went to leave. There was no Three to tell anymore, but he would surely find Celeste and tell her.

*

It didn't take Sam long to find Frederick. He had never been to Canvey before last Friday and only knew the way to and from the Residence, but he didn't need to know his way around. He could smell Frederick's blood on the wind.

Sam ran, faster than he had run in a long time, and reached the marshes in fifteen minutes. It had been a long time since he'd had a body young enough to run like that, not in thousands of years. And it felt good.

The rage at being killed by Frederick had dissipated after he'd left the Residence, but he could still feel the anger bubbling inside.

Anger was good, he knew that, it could be a righteous tool to use against the unjust, but right now he needed to be level-headed. He couldn't blame all vampires for what had happened to him, but he could blame one man. Frederick Holtzrichter. Nonetheless, taking Callum out left him with a sense of satisfaction, after all, he was the man who had incinerated Will's body. And that sleight could not go unanswered.

Frederick was wandering through the marshes, his boots squelching in the water beneath the reeds, a look of concentration on his face. Sam smiled.

'Hey, Frederick,' he called out. Frederick looked up. A smile appeared on his face at the sight of Sam, and he waved him over.

Sam bit his lip. He wasn't really dressed for walking through a marsh, but considering why he was there he decided he could deal with it. He walked over to join Frederick, glad about his new vampire constitution. The wind was getting bitter, a storm front brewing in the sky, but even without a coat he didn't really feel so cold.

'What are you still doing out here?'

'Thinking,' Frederick said, once Sam was by his side. 'Look, I'm sorry for having a go earlier. It's just that with the Book being stolen by Eryn, and everything else...'

Sam placed a finger on Frederick's lips. 'It's okay, I understand. Everything makes sense to me now.'

'Wish I could say the same.' Frederick kissed Sam's finger and smiled slightly. 'Celeste wants me to return to France, thinks my being here is too much of a risk to the prophecy.'

'How?'

Frederick told him the deal with DI Rowe and Robin Turner. Sam wasn't sure how he felt about that. He seemed to recall knowing something about how the vampires continued their existence, and he was as repelled by it now as he was then. Of course, back then he was not subject to that bizarre imitation of their creator's method of reincarnation, but now his body was vampire. Could he wilfully kill an innocent just to continue on? Sam wasn't so sure.

'What is it?' Frederick asked. 'I don't want to leave,' he continued, totally misreading the look of doubt on Sam's face.

Sam wanted to smack Frederick in the face now, for being so up his own arse.

'Not now that we've found each other, but... Celeste is right, my being here is a risk.'

'But that's the thing,' Sam said, taking Frederick's hands in his. 'We can all leave now. Your mission is complete.'

Frederick pulled his arms away sharply. 'Celeste's already got to you, has she?' he snapped, angrily. 'Convinced you that as an oracle you can do my job, find the Seeker?'

Sam laughed, and shook his head, playing the part of bemusement at his partner's silliness. 'You're not hearing me, Fred.'

'For over two hundred years I have devoted my life to this,' Frederick continued, 'and now you come along and suddenly I'm redundant? The Ancient tasked me with this; he gave me his own blood to find the Seeker.'

Sam took Frederick by the shoulders. 'Calm down and listen,' he said. Once Frederick stopped ranting, Sam said, 'Your mission is complete because I'm not some oracle. I thought I was, but I got it wrong. These are not visions, but memories.'

Now Frederick look confused, the emotions running across his face. He settled on disbelief.

'It took me a while to work out, but I've been talking to people at the Residence, and now it makes sense. I'm the one you've been looking for. I *am* Onuris.'

Frederick opened his mouth, but no words came. He shook his head, and again Sam laughed. This was priceless.

'Fred, think about it. When we met on that train, you felt something in me.'

'Yes, I thought it was the ka of a upiór.'

'And you were right.'

Sam watched him closely. It was clear that Frederick wanted to believe him, but was having a hard time doing so. Sam couldn't blame him; it took him a long while to understand, and he had lived it. There had to be a way to convince him. But what? Sam thought hard.

That was it! Thought.

'Fred,' he said, taking Frederick's hands in his. 'Look at me. A fledgling and his maker share a psychic link, right? Isn't that how you and Celeste tried to find me?'

'Yes, but...'

'Then open your mind to me, look inside my thoughts. There will be no psychic backlash this time, I promise.'

Frederick nodded slowly and closed his eyes. Sam blocked much out, but he left just enough for Frederick to see the truth of what he was saying.

The disbelief slowly faded, replaced by a huge smile.

'Finally,' Frederick said, opening his eyes, and squeezing Sam's hands. 'I've spent so long looking for you. When I first bumped into you in London nine years ago, I just knew... I had to keep an eye on you, guide you to Southend like the Book said. If only Stephen knew what he was helping me with.'

'Stephen?' Sam asked, feeling a darkness growing inside.

'Yes, I enlisted his help. As soon as he told me you were coming to Southend I got him to fix your car so that you would be on that train.' Frederick shook his head, smiling. 'It is so good to be able to tell you this at last. Been a long time coming.'

'Yes, it has,' Sam agreed, his voice going cold. With effort, he softened his voice. 'There's more to tell you,' he said, wanting to pay Frederick back for everything he had done. 'Did you ever wonder what happened to Onuris after Sekhmet turned him into the first vampire?'

'The Book says nothing on that.'

'No, it wouldn't. That's because I wrote the Book.' Sam paused, letting Frederick's mind catch up, much like his had been doing most of the day. 'The name Onuris means "brings back the distant one"; I don't think it was a coincidence that I was given that name. Just as the name I chose when I left Egypt was no random name. Wamukota means "left handed", chosen because I once sat at Sekhmet's left hand as her lover.'

'Then...?'

'Yes, Onuris, Wamukota... The same person. Why do you think he ended up being called the Ancient? Always different from the vampires around him. Because he, I, was the original, created of Sekhmet.'

Frederick struggled to take it all in, and looked away, out to the North Sea. Sam watched, glad of his confusion. It was good that Frederick knew all this now. He turned back to Sam.

'Then in Tuzara, the blood you gave me...'

'Led you to me in London. *That* is the source of the connection we feel.'

'So, you got me to drink your blood so that I would recognise your ka?'

Finally! Realisation dawned in Frederick's mind. Sam nodded slowly as if humouring a particularly slow child.

'Of course, how else would the blood of Wamukota lead you to the Seeker, unless they were the same person?'

Frederick nodded slowly. 'Then... it's all true. But, one thing I don't understand... Why the Seeker? What do you seek? I've a few ideas, but recent events have shown me my ideas were wrong.'

'Because that's who Will was, who I was before I awoke to my true self again. He was always seeking more, a way out of his life, his way to me. He didn't know it, of course, but he sought his true self.' It felt odd to Sam to talk of Will as if he were a separate person, much like it felt odd to think of both Onuris and Wamukota as individuals.

'I'm a trinity,' he said, his thoughts crystalising.

'Come again?'

'Right now I am three in one. Onuris, Will, and me, Sam.'

'Sam...?'

He grinned. 'Yes. It's obviously the short form of something, but I have yet to discover what, but it is who I am. My real name is Sam.'

'Okay, this all makes a kind of sense. I think. Like... a reflection of the divinity? No, that doesn't...'

Sam smiled. He liked the sound of that. It felt... ironic, somehow.

'Will,' Frederick tried again. 'Sam. This is a lot. But. I can help... Let me help you discover the truth.'

'You? How can you possibly help me?'

'I have lived every single day in this world since you've been away, there must be some way I can help.'

'No, you haven't *lived* in this world. For nearly thirty-five years I *have*. I'm the one who's been part of this world, the real world, the one the humans inhabit. I know how to function in it, you don't. You're a vampire.'

'So are you,' Frederick pointed out, his eyes narrowing.

'Am I? For four thousand years I lived in this world, a vampire, the progenitor of a new race, following a mission given to me by my goddess. And then my time was done, I died. For the last thirty-five years I've known who I am, but now?' Sam turned away, clenching his fists, trying to contain his anger. It was not time for anger. Not yet. 'Now I don't know who I am, or what I am. All thanks to you.'

'You set this up!' Frederick shouted, and grabbed Sam by the shoulders, turning him to face him. 'What choice did I have?'

'Like you gave Will a choice,' Sam said, his voice low.

'You are Will.'

'And I am also Onuris, or was once.' Sam shook his head. 'Just who am I really? Oh, I know I am Sam... But who is Sam? And why do I *know* that is my real name? I...' He stopped and closed his eyes. It was there, on the edge of his mind. Something that wanted to reveal itself. 'There was more, before Onuris, before Egypt, only...' He opened his eyes slowly, gratified by the look of doubt and anger on Frederick's face. 'Will died in that alley a week ago, I know this. Callum told me he incinerated Will's body.'

Frederick lowered his head. 'I'm sorry, all this is...'

'It doesn't matter,' Sam said, hiding one arm behind his back while Frederick looked away. He smiled as soon as Frederick turned back to him. 'I just wanted you to know all this, to understand that you found the Seeker... Before...'

With lightning speed Sam lashed out, his talons slicing Frederick's throat clean open. Instinctively Frederick's hand went to his throat, but he was too late to stop the flow of blood which seeped between his fingers. Sam kicked Frederick in the chest, causing him to fly backwards, landing with a splash in the reeds. He writhed in the water as Sam slowly approached him, one hand grasping at the reeds, the other trying to staunch the blood flow. All the while the fear and disbelief shot out of his eyes like hot needles.

Sam knelt over Frederick, and grabbed the hand holding his neck, pulling it away so the blood could gush out freely.

'I should have had a nice weekend with Charlie. Who knows what might have happened there?' he said calmly. 'I deserved a chance to find out, but you took that choice from me.' He gripped Frederick's top and brought his face to his. 'It's important that you also know this. I have found Sekhmet, as she told me I would. You've seen her. But I'm not going to fulfil your precious prophecy.' He lowered his head towards Frederick's neck. 'I make my own destiny. Take that to your grave, you bastard.'

Frederick struggled, but he was too weak to stop Sam as he opened his mouth over the gaping wound and sucked Frederick dry.

Thanks to his restored memories he knew how to kill a vampire, and bleeding them dry was one sure way.

As the blood flowed down his throat, Sam soaked up everything that was Frederick. His entire life flashed before Sam's mind, from his birth in Posen in 1722, through his initial meeting with Celeste just after his twenty-first birthday, and all that had happened in the 289 years since. Including Frederick's horror and confusion as he felt his life ebb away. The darkness came, and Sam pulled away before he was dragged down with it.

He looked up, letting the lifeless body drop into the water one final time.

Now he knew everything that had happened to his people since his first death.

*

Sekhmet stood some distance away, on a slight incline, and watched as Sam finished draining Frederick. She waited as he stood and looked around, his face flush with his first feast. She smiled to herself. There was no going back now. Soon her husband would return to her.

He thought he understood what the Seeker meant. Yes, it could be applied to Will, but there was more... Things to find, to discover, to bring forth.... The Seeker hadn't finished seeking yet.

And to that end she put herself in his mind and opened one of his closed doors slightly.

Just enough for him to get a glimpse of what was to come.

*

Celeste barely made it through the front door of the Residence before she was accosted by Nate. He practically grabbed the sleeve of her dress. She snatched her arm back, shocked at his lack of decorum.

'Nate, I think you are forgetting your place,' she said, scowling at him.

'I'm sorry, my Lady,' he said, his eyes wild. 'But we have a problem.'

Celeste sighed, wishing the day would end. But she knew it had barely begun really. It was only just gone midday and already she felt like she'd been awake a full day. Twelve hours she might have been unconscious for, but rested she was not.

'Another problem? What could possibly be wrong now?'

'It's Willem. He's gone mad, attacked Callum, as well as...'

Celeste let out a sudden gasp of air and grabbed at Nate. She stumbled forward, pulling him with her. He attempted to hold her weight, but she fell to her knees, the pain flowing through her.

'Frederick!' she yelled.

'My Lady, what is it?'

She looked up, but all she saw was Willem's face, bearing down on her. Although his face was calm, his red eyes burned with hatred and revelation, while the wind blew his hair into his face.

'I make my own destiny. Take that to your grave, you bastard,' he said.

She felt it keenly, Frederick's life pulling away, a sensation she had not felt since her own mortal life had ended at the hands of Pierre.

Celeste opened her mouth to speak, but nothing came. There were no words to say, just the feeling of darkness encroaching all around her. No, not her. Frederick.

She released her hold of Nate's blazer and let her hands fall to the floor. For a while she remained as she was, breathing deeply, the sense of loss overpowering.

For almost three hundred years he had been by her side, sharing so much of her life, and now...

'My Lady?'

Nate's voice was like a distant echo in her mind as she closed her eyes.

Gone. Frederick was gone from her.

17. The Hardest Thing to Say

Sam boarded the bus at Benfleet, looking forward to the slower journey back to Chalkwell. He had much to think about before he saw Lizette again, and he needed time to do it. But he also needed to be on the move.

He knew all about the link between maker and fledgling, and thanks to soaking up Frederick's lifetime of experiences he knew that Celeste was aware of her consort's death. That Frederick considered himself the consort of Celeste was news to Sam, and made him wonder why, therefore, had Frederick made such a big deal about falling for Will? It almost seemed a contradiction to Sam that Frederick could feel so deeply for Celeste and still lust so much after Will.

Sam shook his head. He had enough memories to sort out as it was, working out Frederick's life would have to wait.

Right now, he knew it was only a matter of time before Celeste sent people after him, although a part of him welcomed that outcome. It would certainly make a statement. Namely, that he was neither an instrument of prophecy nor a tool to be used by the Three.

But he didn't wish to risk Lizette in this.

He wasn't sure if the Sekhmet side of Lizette had awoken yet. In spite of what the Book said, he had slept with her and he had not felt an awakening, so he assumed she was still living in bliss of who she really was.

That was how he wanted her to remain, he realised.

It was bad enough that his life had been turned upside down by events that Sekhmet and he (when he was still Onuris) had set in motion over four thousand years ago, and he did not see why it should be the same for her. She had taken him in, shown him much kindness. True, now he understood why it was so, but neither of them knew that then and had acted of their own free will.

He wanted to say goodbye to her, though, thank her for everything. And then get the hell out of her life before the Three learned of their connection.

For now, they believed him to be an oracle, but it was only a matter of time before the truth came out.

He had to keep moving. There was something out there calling to him, although he had no idea what it was. But something in his mind, just beyond reach, told him he needed to look. To find... whatever it was.

*

Celeste knew the answer before Derek came over to her. She was looking out towards the North Sea, the shoreline of Essex running down to Shoeburyness, wrapped up in her coat, the rain crashing down on her head. Neither the wind nor the rain bothered her, but still she was cold. And empty. Oh, so empty. She sniffed back a tear and turned to look at Derek.

His face told her all she needed to know. Derek had one of those faces that were so easy to read, deeply lined and very flexible. A canvas of emotion. Beyond him she could see other upiór still searching, but they looked as defeated as Derek.

'He's gone.'

Celeste nodded. She had organised a search party as soon as she had recovered from the initial shock of her loss. Whether she would fully recover she did not know, but nonetheless Frederick needed to be returned to the Residence. She could not have the body of an upiór lying about in the marshland of Canvey.

'Willem,' she mumbled, certain that he had taken Frederick's body.

Head lowered, Celeste turned from Derek and began the long trek back to the Residence. All was lost now. No one had heard from Theodor since he had left to find Eryn, but she no longer cared.

As she walked, she sent out a mental command to Theodor.

Meet me at the Residence. Now!

She paused, and glanced back.

'Frederick.'

*

'I still don't get it,' Jake said, looking over at Charlie who sat in the opposite seat at the front of the bus. They were on the number one, going up London Road towards Leigh. The news from Francis had taken the wind out of their sails, although they continued on canvassing for a little while longer, before both had decided to call it.

'What's not to get?' Charlie wanted to know. 'It explains why Will was with that, what was his name, Robin Turner?' Jake nodded. 'Right, with Robin Turner in Starbucks. Probably met him on the train. Must have been some spiel.'

'But that's the thing.' Jake leaned forward, resting his elbow on the ledge before the front windows. 'You've known Will for a month. I've known him my whole life, and supernatural shit ain't his thing. Hell, that guy doesn't even like horror films. And you should have seen his reaction when his dad turned to religion.'

'Religion is one thing, Jake; we're talking about a cult. They know what they're doing. Can brainwash the best of us.'

'Sure, I get that. But Will was convinced his dad had joined a cult at first, went nuclear about it.' Jake shook his head. 'No, sorry, I just can't believe he'd get caught up in a cult. Especially not a vampire cult,' he added, his face screwed in disgust.

Charlie agreed there. He looked out of the window and jumped to with a start. 'Next stop,' he said, getting up and ringing the bell.

Jake followed him down the steps and together they waited in silence near the driver's cabin as the bus pulled up outside the Chinese take-away. Saying thanks to the driver, they stepped out into the rain.

'Gotta love sunny Southend, right?' Charlie said as they set off down London Road.

'Right,' Jake agreed with a grim smile, feeling the rain run down his stubbly head. An umbrella would have been good, but when he'd come to Southend yesterday he had not expected rain. Then again, he hadn't expected to learn that Will had joined a cult who believed they were vampires, either. He laughed suddenly. 'Vampires! Ha.'

'Yeah, tell me about it,' Charlie said, laughing too, as a single-decker bus came to a halt at the bus stop across the road.

They set off towards Charlie's home, and Jake did his best to ignore the sudden itch coming from his new shoulder scar.

Sam looked at the mobile in his hands. Will's phone.

It represented a direct link to his old life. Well, he reconsidered, not his *old* life, but rather the one he had been ripped from a week ago. The phone had sat in his pocket the entire time he was at Canvey, and he still had yet to turn it back on. Did he even dare to contact his family? How could he possibly tell them what had happened to him?

The only one who might possibly understand was Jake. He liked his horror films and knew his vampire lore, but even so...

Knowing the vampire lore of fiction and being confronted with the truth of it. That was something else entirely.

He returned the phone to his pocket, deciding to dump it once he was off the bus. Will's world was safer without him in it.

The bus shuddered as the driver made a false start. He called out sorry to his passengers and started up again. Sam felt an itch near his groin; it was intense, almost burning. He readjusted his trousers and looked out of the window. Two men were walking through the rain on the other side of the road. As the bus continued on its way he got a good look at their laughing faces. Charlie and Jake.

Before he knew what he was doing, Sam got to his feet and hit the button for the next stop.

*

They sat in the meeting chamber of the Three. Celeste and Theodor, the only two left. Celeste could see in Theodor's eyes that he knew she was right, but he didn't want to accept it. She understood his reticence. For 221 years things had been leading to this point, they had set so much by it, built their world around it. But now, with Frederick and Willem gone, it was over. Already Celeste had sent word out; Willem may have been an oracle into the past, and thus a potentially powerful ally for the Three, but he had killed her consort. An act that she would never forgive.

Willem would understand the power she wielded. He would be hunted down. His stay in their world would be short indeed.

Then there was Eryn. Theodor felt her betrayal the most. That Eryn had blocked her mind off to Theodor made it worse. Celeste suspected that the Book would soon be in the hands of the Brotherhood, and all hope of finding the Seeker went with it.

'Come,' she said, rising and walking over to Theodor. 'It is time to leave this blighted land.'

Theodor took her hand and stood. For a moment they looked into each other's eyes, and their thoughts became one.

It was agreed. They would return to France and try to regroup. Prepare for Julius' next move. It had taken much to bring unity to the upiór after the revolution, and back then they had the Book of Sekhmet to guide them. To bind them together in the hope of salvation. That, too, was lost to them.

Celeste wasn't sure how they would combat the Brotherhood now, but she sure as hell wasn't willing to let her people fall to the false doctrine taught by Julius, supported as he was by a traitor. No, she would be ready.

Together, arm in arm, Celeste and Theodor left the chamber, leaving the idea of the Three behind. Now they were just the Two.

They stopped at the door, and Theodor looked back. Sitting on the side was a small bottle of hair dye. Electric blue.

Theodor lowered his eyes. 'Eryn,' he said, the sadness so strong it brought a tear to Celeste's eye.

She took him in her arms, giving him the strength he had always given her.

*

She looked up from the sink to the clock above the door. It was just gone two o'clock, only twenty minutes until it was time to board the plane to Rome's Fiumicino Airport. All she needed to do was get her ticket.

She splashed some water on her face and turned the tap off. Still she could feel her left hand, and had to remind herself to turn off the tap with her right. She wasn't sure how long she could go on like this. She was an upiór, and such a handicap was not acceptable.

Eryn shook her head; she had liked this body, too.

The door opened and a woman walked in. Eryn watched her in the mirror, as she had watched her since the woman had walked into the terminal at Gatwick. The woman was taller than Eryn, curvier, a strong body under her sharp suit. And at the ticket desk, Eryn had watched her as she purchased a return ticket to Fiumicino, which suited Eryn fine.

The woman opened a cubicle door and stepped inside. The door began to shut, but before the woman had a chance to lock it, Eryn busted in and pushed the woman against the wall. She fell over the toilet, folding into the gap between basin and wall. Eryn closed the door with her boot, and turned slightly to lock it with her hand.

She looked down at the woman, who was struggling to get up, shouting the odds at the bitch over her.

'Oh no,' Eryn said, her talons slowly tearing out of her fingers, 'you're my ticket out of here.'

*

Finding Jake and Charlie took him a bit longer than he would have hoped, since the next stop was further up the road than expected. Sam had got off the bus and ran across the road, before doubling back. He turned the bend in the road lined with thickset trees and came to the row of shops he'd remembered seeing them outside. He stopped at the top of Hadleigh Road and glanced down it, but there was no sign of Jake or Charlie, so he crossed over and approached the bathroom shop. Before he reached it, however, he staggered.

It was becoming a regular occurrence and Sam knew what it meant. He bent double, resting his hands on his knees as the new memory overflowed.

He looked up and, for a second, he didn't see the shops, just a new vision, a memory of something long forgotten. He shook it away, having no time for it now. The image, however, persisted, fading slightly into the background. Once again, a view over a view.

After the amount of overlapping views he had seen in the past week he was getting used to dismissing one and focusing on the other. He looked to the road that reached the pavement he was walking along.

Herschell Road. Some way down the road, walking close together, still laughing about something, were Charlie and Jake.

Sam set off after them, still wondering just why he was doing this.

*

Charlie popped his head around the living room door. 'Nutri Grain bar?' he asked.

Jake looked up from where he was sitting. He made a face. 'Nah, not quite ready for that kind of healthy kick.'

'Okay, just don't forget, we got a workout to do yet.' Charlie winked and returned to the kitchen.

Jake laughed to himself. He wasn't convinced that Charlie was the one to get him in shape; he liked his beer and meat pies too much. He was about to call out and ask if it was okay to spark up when he felt his phone go off. He manoeuvred it out of his pocket and stared at the screen in disbelief.

Message received from Will.

Jake almost dropped the phone, his hands suddenly filling with sweat.

He took a deep breath and opened the message. After reading it, he stood up and walked to the living room doorway. For a moment he stood there, unsure of what to do. If he followed the instructions in the text, then he would be betraying Charlie's hospitality. But he had little choice.

Despite how much he was growing to like Charlie, Jake had always known that it would come down to a choice between them.

He pulled his still-wet coat off the banister and called out to Charlie. 'Just popping outside for a smoke.'

'No problem,' Charlie called back. 'I'll make sure there's a nice healthy sandwich waiting for you.'

Jake smiled and immediately felt guilty. He turned and left the house.

As soon as he stepped outside he lit his cigarette and took a deep drag. He stood on the porch, watching the rain fall while he allowed the nicotine to calm him. His heart was going ten to the dozen, adrenalin coursing through his body at the thought of seeing Will again.

So much had happened in the week since he'd last seen Will. Amy, Toby... and his changing feelings for Will.

Jake stepped off the porch and into the rain.

He looked up the street towards London Road but saw no sign of Will, so he looked down towards Marine Parade and Belton Hills. Standing at the corner was a figure he knew well. Unable to contain his broad smile, Jake made his way down the street.

He slowed down as he approached Will, once again feeling the itch flare up on his shoulder. He resisted reaching for it, instead focusing on Will.

He was standing there in only his jumper, the rain soaking him through, he looked much as he should. His hair was plastered to his head, but rain would do that to a person. Only there was something different about him, a coldness to his eyes, which were regarding Jake narrowly.

'Mate, you're going to catch your death like that,' Jake said.

Will looked down at himself and shrugged. 'I should be so lucky. Anyway, it's only a bit of rain.'

'A bit?' Jake looked up at the thick grey clouds. 'Right, a bit.' He looked back at Will, noting how he was not looking directly at Jake. 'You okay, man?'

'On a scale of one to a hundred? Not even slightly.' Will looked at him for the first time, full-on eye-to-eye contact. Jake pulled back in surprise, then leaned in closer. 'Yeah, things have changed,' Will said.

'Shit. What the hell has happened to your eyes?'

'It doesn't matter, the less you know the better. I just wanted to say thank you.'

Jake didn't like the sound of that. It felt final somehow. 'For what?'

'For coming here, to look for me. It means a lot.'

'Mate, how could I not? After all we've been through. I love you, Will, no way I was going to lose you.' The words came out a lot easier than Jake would have expected, his voice controlled and natural. Maybe he had finally come to terms with it after all.

'You're going to have to.'

Jake took hold of Will by the shoulders. 'No way, not now. I don't care what's happened, what cult you've joined, I'm not going to lose you again.'

'Cult?'

Jake shrugged. 'Yeah,' he said, releasing Will. 'Heard you joined some cult who believe they're vampires.' He offered a weak smile. 'Dumb, eh?'

'Yeah, dumb,' Will agreed, his voice a lot more serious than Jake cared for. 'I'm going now.'

Jake reached out for him again, to stop him turning away. 'Like that? What the hell's wrong with you? We've been worried sick about you; no one had any idea what happened to you. Not even Charlie.'

'Yes,' Will said, nodding slowly. 'I noticed you found Charlie. That's... good.'

'Good? What's that supposed to mean?'

'Just that. It's good you have found each other.'

Jake scowled, his head a mix of notions, his heart tearing through all kinds of emotions. 'Fine, whatever. Point is, you're needed back home. You have no idea what's been going on while you've been away. The things that have been happening. Lawrencia... The shit that's going on in her life. Amy left me.'

Throughout the tirade, Will just watched him impassively.

Jake shook his head. 'You don't care, do you?'

Will frowned. 'Care? I...' He looked down and turned away. 'Of course I care,' he said over his shoulder. 'That's why I have to leave.'

Jake didn't get that. It sounded too much like what Amy had said. Like the twisted logic he had used to convince himself he was doing right by copping off with Toby.

'This is bullshit, Will! So much has happened; you're not the only one who's changed. I *need* you!'

Will turned back to him in surprise. 'Why?'

Jake let the breath escape between his teeth. 'Because I love you, is why. When you were gone... Well, I realised how much I needed you.' He stepped forward to take Will's hand. 'Don't you get it?'

Will looked down at their hands and pulled away sharply. 'I'm sorry, Jake. But I have to leave. Just do me a favour.'

Jake swallowed hard, unable to believe his ears. 'What?' he asked, trying his best to control his emotions.

'Keep an eye on everyone for me. Especially Curtis. Can you do that?'

'Of course I can, but I won't have to. You're not just leaving.'

'I'm not?' Will was silent a moment. And began to turn away. 'I have to. Sorry.'

'No.' It was as if the ground had dropped from beneath Jake. After everything in the past week, after decades of friendship... He couldn't buy the vampire angle, but the cult thing made a lot of sense. He'd seen news reports about cults, heard family members talk about loved ones lost to such organizations.

He grabbed Will's arm. 'I'm not letting you do this. People love you, and you can't just turn your back on them. On your life.'

Will wrenched his arm from Jake. 'It's the only thing I can do.'

Jake rushed around Will, attempting to block his way. 'No way,' he said, feeling the rawness in his voice. 'What sort of friend would I be if I just let you do this?'

Will stopped walking. 'Friend? You mean lover, right? That's what this is all about. You suddenly realised how you feel about me, and now you expect me to just fold into your arms. Well, it's not happening.'

The words and tone were hurtful, and Jake tried to ignore the feeling welling up.

'It's more than that,' he began.

'No. Thank you.' Will leaned forward and kissed Jake on the lips. 'I will be in touch, but please don't try to find me again.'

And with that, he pushed Jake aside with such force, and so little effort, that Jake hit the pavement hard. For a few seconds he was dazed. He went to stand, to try again with Will, but when he looked up Will was gone.

*

Celeste walked side by side with Theodor, arms linked. Nate waited next to the car. She stopped, and Theodor looked at her.

It will all be okay, his mind told her.

She wished that were so. She glanced back at the Residence; perhaps it was time to sell up...? Cut all her ties to Canvey. She had only ever invested in it because of prophecy, because Frederick had convinced her the Seeker would arrive in Southend at the appointed time. And now...?

Everything was lost.

Above the Residence dark clouds were gathering.

Change, she thought, and staggered, almost falling to the ground. It was only Theodor's presence that kept her upright.

He said something to her, but she could barely discern his thoughts. Inside her mind something else was happening, something that was overriding all other senses.

All around her was chaos. Creatures that her mental faculties could barely comprehend were running around screaming. Such agony and torment. And standing above them all, watching with a total and utter disregard stood two beings. It was if they were made of light, and yet somehow Celeste was able to discern some kind of gender. Almost as if they were one male, and the other female... Only it wasn't that simple. They were more, so much more...

Before she could take in anymore, blackness engulfed her, and for the briefest moment she felt something hard beneath her, and she was distantly aware that it was the ground and Theodor's strength had failed her.

*

Seeing Jake had been a bad idea, but it had taught him something. He couldn't return to Lizette, not now. Instead, he had to...

There was a buzzing in his jeans, and he removed the phone. He looked up from the name. Jake, of course.

He ignored the call and considered switching the phone off. He'd need it again sometime, of course, but not right now. For now, the life of Willem Townsend was dead to him. Although Will's bank card would come in useful, he considered, patting the wallet snug in his back pocket.

He glanced over in the general direction of Canvey Island, and the dark clouds that seemed to hang only above that area.

Change, he thought.

He opened the phone and dialled a number. One last call.

'Steve,' he said, as soon as the other end was picked up. 'Hey, yeah, I know you've got lots of questions, but I don't have time to answer them. I'm going to be away for a while, so I need you to keep the business ticking over.'

Of course, Steve agreed quickly enough. After all, he had worked alongside Frederick to remove Will – not for the business, of course, but it was clearly a nice bonus for him. And Sam would let that go for now. Steve's role in things would be dealt with eventually, but for now, he could keep working for 'Will', keeping the money coming in.

Sam ended the call and turned the phone off.

He had much to do. Out there, somewhere in the world, something was calling him. He didn't know what it was, but he knew he had to seek it out.

And to that end Sam set off, leaving Will's world behind.

And the further he moved away from Jake, the less the scar near his groin burned...

EPILOGUE

They met in the catacombs. It always felt like the right kind of setting for Edward Lomax. He stood there in the shadows, waiting, dressed in an immaculate suit, his hands resting on a walking cane, his white hair and beard perfectly groomed. An outward image of geniality. Inside, however...

'Julius,' he said, his voice deep, lacking any real sense of emotion.

The two of them rarely met in person, and every time they did Julius was reminded that Lomax was still in the body he'd been born with. The same body he'd worn when they'd first met in 1729 when Julius himself had turned the then-crazed Lomax into an upiór. There had been no rebirth, no First or Second Death, merely a continuation of his life. But, as an upiór. Julius had always wondered how, but as the years went by, and the more they came to study the so-called Lost Pages of the Book, it became readily apparent that Lomax was the 'man of power' that was to rival the Seeker.

Julius walked up to him. 'Reports are coming in,' he said, ignoring Lomax's attempts at preamble. 'Frederick killing Maia's brother was the catalyst we needed; it put him and Celeste at odds, and deepened the rift between him and Eryn. Disrupted their belief in their chosen purveyor of prophecy. It seems you succeeded.'

'Yes, Maia is the perfect tool.'

'Tool or fool?'

Lomax shrugged. 'She's still holding on, but her edges will be smoothed. Her resistance stamped out.'

Julius smiled softly. 'I've no doubt.'

'Regardless, the Three are now in disarray, their precious prophecy in question. Frederick and Celeste have been torn apart, and if Celeste is in pain, then so is Theodor.'

'Even more so,' Julius said, rubbing his hands in glee, 'since I have also heard that Iestyn has been outed as a traitor. He is now known to be a Sekhite.'

'Still you refuse to acknowledge the choice she made.'

Julius almost spat on the floor. 'It is but a fad. Eryn will be Iestyn again soon enough.'

Lomax shrugged. 'Regardless, it's been a long game, but as I said all those hundreds of years ago, Eryn would be the perfect weapon to destroy Theodor.'

'Why go for the kill, when you can go for the hurt?'

'Just so. Theodor will never recover from this. Make sure it becomes known that Eryn, as she likes to call herself now, was our very first convert. Let Theodor live with the knowledge that he was being betrayed since the very beginning.'

'As you will,' Julius said with a bow. 'One more thing, which may well make Maia redundant to the Brotherhood now. Frederick is dead.'

Lomax raised an eyebrow. 'Oh?'

'Yes. It would appear Frederick's much-revered Seeker has killed him.'

'Ah.' Lomax closed his eyes, for a moment appearing to go inside himself. 'No. He carried in him the Blood of Wamukota, death will not come so easy to him. As for his Seeker...' He reopened his eyes and smiled like a wolf. 'His path is set.'

'Very well,' Julius said, and turned to take his leave of Lomax. He glanced back. 'Is there anything else?'

'One thing.' Lomax stepped out of the shadows and walked up to Julius. 'Put word out. The Seeker is to be left alone.'

'What? But he is a bigger threat to us than the Three were.'

'Nonsense. He doesn't care about the Brotherhood. No more than he cares about talks of prophecy. His concerns lie elsewhere.'

'Like finding Sekhmet...?' Julius almost laughed, but he held back, remembering whose presence he was in. He was about to ask a question, a moment of doubt bringing it forth, but he stopped himself just in time, just before Lomax placed a hand on his shoulder.

An unwelcome shudder came over him, and Julius lowered his head.

'Sekhmet was but a tool, used by our creator,' Lomax said. 'Never forget this.'

'Of course.'

'Good.' Lomax removed his hand. 'Now go, spread the word. Samael is mine.'

To Be Continued in...
AUGURY

?